PENGUIN METRO READS
IF IT'S NOT FOREVER . . .

DURJOY DATTA was born and brought up in New Delhi. He completed a degree in engineering and business management before embarking on a writing career. His first book, *Of Course I Love You . . .*, was published when he was twenty-one years old and was an instant bestseller. His successive novels—*Now That You're Rich . . .*, *She Broke Up, I Didn't!*, *Oh Yes, I'm Single!*, *If It's Not Forever . . .*, *Someone Like You*—have also found prominence on various bestseller lists, making him one of the highest-selling authors in India. Durjoy lives in New Delhi, loves dogs and is an active CrossFitter.

For more updates, you can follow him on Facebook (www.facebook.com/durjoydatta1) or Twitter (@durjoydatta).

NIKITA SINGH was born in Patna and grew up in Indore. She graduated in pharmacy and is the author of six bestselling novels, including *Love @ Facebook*, *Accidentally in Love* and *The Promise*. She has co-authored (with Durjoy Datta) *Someone Like You* and contributed to the books in *The Backbenchers* series.

Nikita received a Live India Young Achievers Award in 2013. She works as an editor at a leading publishing house.

Also by Durjoy Datta

Hold My Hand

*

She Broke Up, I Didn't!
I Just Kissed Someone Else!

*

Till the Last Breath . . .

*

Of Course I Love You
Till I Find Someone Better

(With Maanvi Ahuja)

*

Oh Yes, I'm Single!
And So Is My Girlfriend!

(With Neeti Rustagi)

*

Now That You're Rich
Let's Fall in Love!

(With Maanvi Ahuja)

*

Someone Like You

(With Nikita Singh)

*

You Were My Crush
Till You Said You Love Me!

(With Orvana Ghai)

If It's Not forever

IT'S NOT LOVE

DURJOY DATTA   NIKITA SINGH

Penguin
metro reads

PENGUIN METRO READS

Published by the Penguin Group

Penguin Books India Pvt. Ltd, 11 Community Centre, Panchsheel Park,
New Delhi 110 017, India

Penguin Group (USA) Inc., 375 Hudson Street, New York, New York 10014, USA

Penguin Group (Canada), 90 Eglinton Avenue East, Suite 700, Toronto,
Ontario, M4P 2Y3, Canada (a division of Pearson Penguin Canada Inc.)

Penguin Books Ltd, 80 Strand, London WC2R 0RL, England

Penguin Ireland, 25 St Stephen's Green, Dublin 2, Ireland
(a division of Penguin Books Ltd)

Penguin Group (Australia), 707 Collins Street, Melbourne, Victoria 3008,
Australia (a division of Pearson Australia Group Pty Ltd)

Penguin Group (NZ), 67 Apollo Drive, Rosedale, Auckland 0632,
New Zealand (a division of Pearson New Zealand Ltd)

Penguin Books (South Africa) (Pty) Ltd, Block D, Rosebank Office Park,
181 Jan Smuts Avenue, Parktown North, Johannesburg 2193, South Africa

Penguin Books Ltd, Registered Offices: 80 Strand, London WC2R 0RL, England

First published by Grapevine India Publishers 2012
Published in Penguin Metro Reads by Penguin Books India 2013

Copyright © Durjoy Datta 2013

ISBN 9780143421566

Typeset in Arno Pro by Eleven Arts, Delhi
Printed at Manipal Technologies Ltd, Manipal

To all the lives lost in the Delhi High Court blast
(7 September 2011)

Acknowledgements

We have noticed that the pressure of writing an acknowledgement—funny how it makes authors adorable and popular amongst their friends and family—always gets to us. Plus, it's the first thing that everyone reads, after the blurb on the back cover, which is usually exaggerated and makes the story look like it's the best ever written, so the responsibility to make it interesting is quite unsettling, to say the least.

Since we are failing miserably in being funny or interesting, we will just go ahead and thank the people who have helped us put together what we think is a wonderful book (obviously).

We thank Maanvi Ahuja, for being a guiding light, and Sachin Garg, for being a phenomenal source of inspiration. We would like to take this opportunity to thank two of our friends who were affected by the Delhi High Court blast of 7 September 2011 and we salute them for their courage. This book would not have been possible if it were not for their support. I hope this book does justice to their story, even if in a very small way.

There are a bunch of people whom we would like to thank for a variety of reasons—good, bad and socially unacceptable—and we will just name them because we desperately want to tell them that we love them. We thank Neeti Rustagi, Orvana Ghai, Avantika Mohan, Preeti Shenoy, Arpit Khandelwal, Eeshaan Sharma, Abhishek Sachdeve, Nitin Verma, Komal Rustagi, Roma Thakur, Prashant Bajaj, Naman Kapur, Abhishek Chopra, Priyanka Chatterjee, Gunjan Suyal, Tanu Dey, Siddhi Waingankar, Chandnee Kaurani, Khushboo Balwan Rawal, Pia Balwani, Arushi Sarin, Shraddha Vyas, Sayantini Deb, Ahana Ghai, Uttara Rao, Vaaruni Dhawan, Samaneh Jawad, Pooja Raigandhi, Kruthika Sl, Rini Ghosh, Loveleen Arora, Mehak Srivastava, Ronisha Malhotra, Medha Shree, Aeshna Nigam and many others whom we are sure we have missed.

Also, a big hug goes to all our readers who have been following us on Facebook, Twitter and various other social networking websites. We thank you for all the support you have extended to us.

We would like to thank our extended families and Guruji for his blessings.

And lastly, we would thank ourselves for our limitless compassion and tolerance for the nuisance we create for each other.

Author's Note

Terror struck Delhi again on Wednesday morning, when a deadly bomb went off at a busy gate of the Delhi High Court. It killed 11 people and left 76 others injured. The bomb went off barely 300 metres away from the spot where a minor explosion had taken place on May 25, which was also a Wednesday. Police officials now say that it could have been a test run for this blast . . .

—*Hindustan Times*, 7 September 2011

There are certain incidents in life that shape you as a person, as a citizen and friend, and decide what course you take in life. The Delhi High Court blast in September 2011 is such an incident for me. *If It's Not Forever . . .* is the story loosely inspired by that blast—which left several men, women and children dead or injured—and a search mounted by me and a few of my close friends to find an end to the story of one of the men who lost his life in that unfortunate blast. Names of places, landmarks and people have been changed on the request of those involved in the story in this book.

This book is a tribute to all the innocent lives we have lost to senseless acts of violence and terrorism.

Durjoy Datta

I Was Almost Dead

I have seen dead people before.

I have seen them on television, on the news, on their deathbeds, with their loved ones carrying them to the cemetery. But I have never seen dead people like this. Mutilated, maimed and lying in pools of blood. I have never seen anyone die in front of me, say their last words, cry out for help, look at me with horror in their eyes, choke on their own blood, breathe their last, and die. *Never*.

But right now, they are all around me. Wherever I look, I see them. It's a gory sight. My head buzzes and I cry out for their pain and out of my own. My ears ring from the noise of the blast, my nose bleeds and I have vomited twice. I look around to see chaos all around. The images are blurred. All I can make out is red. *Blood*. Or black, from the ashes of what's burnt now—men, women, children.

There is blood everywhere. On the ground, on the bodies of people, on their lost body parts . . . on me. It's mine and it's theirs. My skin singes and burns from the heat. It is red and slowly turns black and peels off.

I lean against a wall and struggle to maintain coherence. I

can hear sirens blaring in the distance, people running, crying and howling. There is commotion everywhere, cars burn in the background, the fumes of burning tyres fill up the air, and people are running all over. Some of them are carrying people in their arms. I struggle to keep my eyes open but they burn. I am covered in ashes and my head bursts as I look for my car. I cannot spot it. Not in the heap of mangled and charred remains of metal that lie in front of me. It is still hot and I can feel the radiation in my face. My neck hurts. I touch the nape of my neck—it is wet. There is blood on my fingers. I don't know whether it's mine or someone else's. My entire body aches and burns.

'ARE YOU OKAY?' someone shouts in my ear.

I feel like someone has put a hot iron rod in my ear. I stumble across some people—stilled people, people writhing and moaning, dead people, people bleeding on the ground. I see bloodied faces all around, gravely injured, and they are shouting, screaming and pleading for help. I stumble over them and walk away from the site of the blast. I am helpless.

Where is Avantika?

Home, I guess. Where am I? I take out my phone and call her.

'Hello,' she says. 'Deb, where are you? I've been calling you . . . There's been a blast in Chandni Chowk today, where—'

'I am fine,' I say and disconnect the call.

Things blur a little more. I pass out. The world becomes cold and dark. There is no pain. *Am I dead?*

What If

My breathing is ragged and strained. Every breath I take and release hurts a little more. I feel choked and my throat burns. My head hurts. I try to open my eyes but a bandage wrapped around my head obstructs them. I adjust the bandage to open my eyes. My whole body is broken and it pains as if it has been put into a blender and ground.

I take some time to gather where I am. Why does everything hurt so much? Is this a bad dream? I slowly open my eyes partially and look at the ceiling above. It's not familiar. Then it strikes me. *The Chandni Chowk blast.*

It all comes back to me. The noise, the people, the blood, the severed limbs, the mangled remains of people, cars and buildings. It is a lot harder this time. I can think more clearly. I could've been among the dead.

'Deb?' a female voice says. 'Are you okay?'

I look at her and my eyes light up. She is like a shot of morphine that takes every bit of pain away. I feel alive.

'Yes,' I say feebly.

I look at her and I am mortified. She has tears in her eyes and it looks like she has been crying for a long time. Did something

3

happen to me? I force my aching neck to move a little and look at the bed I lie on. I try to move my hands and legs. I am not maimed or paralysed. I have just a few cuts and burns here and there. I have been lucky.

'What happened?' I ask.

'There was a terrible blast in Chandni Chowk,' she says. 'Eighty-nine people are dead so far.'

She sits on the bed, hugs me, and starts crying. I feel a few teardrops percolate through my hospital robe and wet my skin. A few tears find their way into my eyes too. I don't know if it's because she's crying or because of what I saw this morning. People had died, lost their arms, their legs and their loved ones right in front of my eyes. It was like a nightmare. Only, a lot worse. It happened for real. The animal cries of people, the blood and the limbs that had gone flying all around me—it had all happened. All those people are actually dead. Eighty-nine of them. I am not. I am still in one piece and have my girlfriend hugging me.

Why? I ask myself as I see her cry with her head on my chest. I think about all the people who lost their lives this morning or have been crippled. What would their loved ones be doing? If I were dead, what would Avantika be doing? I shudder to think about it. I was almost dead. Or maimed. I feel grateful.

'Do Mom and Dad know?' I ask her. She shakes her head. 'They called you?'

'Yes,' she says, still crying. 'I told them you were in office.'

I smile at her. She knows me and my parents so well. My parents live in Muscat, Oman, and they find it very uneasy to live away from me. They miss me a lot, but Dad has work there. Even though I am a big guy now, they are as protective about me as they were when I was a school-going kid. I still remember the fifteen-minute sermon I used to get from Mom and Dad whenever I would go out. 'Look at both sides when you cross the road,' 'Don't talk to anyone,' 'Don't eat anything that anyone offers.' You get the drift. It continued way into my late teens.

Had they heard about this, they would have come rushing to Delhi and *never* gone back. I don't want that to happen. Avantika and I have been secretly engaged for the past year or so and life is perfect. My parents don't know that. Nor do they know that we live together. They would flip; it is still socially unacceptable. Avantika and I love the thrill of doing something people warn us against. Our judgement and good sense are often clouded by the love in our hearts.

'Thank you,' I say to her. She smiles back at me. 'You should rest,' she says and I see a nurse enter the room.

The nurse plunges a syringe in the tube attached to my hand and I feel a little sleepy almost instantly. Sedatives, I guess. It lessens the pain, in one's body but not in one's head.

'Deb . . .'

'Yes, baby?' I murmur, already half-asleep.

'I love you,' I hear her meek whisper before dozing off. I love her too, more than she will ever know. She is my world. I open my mouth but I drift off before the words can escape my lips. *I love you*. As I say these words, I hope that it's not the last time.

～

When I wake up, I find that the pain has lessened to an extent. I see bloodstained bandages on my head, my arms and my legs. I make my way—with a little help—towards the chambers of the doctor to get a few checks done before they can release me. On my way, I see many people around with far worse injuries than mine, with thicker bandages, smiling and laughing despite all that pain. Some of them are missing a limb or two. It is hard to look at them. Suddenly I feel weak. I always found hospitals very depressing. Given the present scenario, it is even more so. I cannot wait to get out of here and go home. The walk to the doctor's chambers is really long and I try not to look around me.

Inside the chambers, they carry out some final tests on me, ask me if I'm feeling all right, and let me go.

⌒

'Are you okay?' Avantika asks.

It has been an hour since we've been sitting in the car and I haven't said anything. I've been looking out of the window and staring blankly at the Delhi flyovers, the bustling markets, the busy streets. My head still resonates from the noise of the blast, the howls of the women, the painful cries of the men. I look and think—which place is next? The Metro station next to my house, the grocery market, the office Avantika goes to every day? Who will be lying on the bed I was lying on today? It is terrifying. I feel scared and alone. The horror in the eyes of people who died in front of me comes rushing back.

Every time there was a blast in Delhi, Mumbai or Hyderabad, I used to look at the news and think—it cannot happen to me or the people around me. Suddenly, everything changed. I am terrified. What if the car we are in has a bomb? I shift in my place uncomfortably. I suspect everything now. I don't blame those guys in the US who had started hating everything Arab after the 9/11 attack on the World Trade Center. When it happens to you, it is very unsettling.

'Deb?' Avantika says.

'Yes, I am fine. It's just hurting a little,' I say.

I don't want to share my fears with her. I know she's scared too. Had I died yesterday, it would not have been me who would have suffered. It would have been her, my parents and my friends. I am scared for Avantika. We enter our flat and, suddenly, I don't ever want to leave. Neither do I want Avantika to spend a second out of my sight. I have become paranoid. I understand now why my parents used to call me fifty times every ten minutes after ten in the night to make sure I was okay. I understand why they always want me to call them after I reach office. They must have seen a lot of people dying. So, they must be living in constant fear.

Avantika switches on the television for me before going to the kitchen. She starts peeling oranges and I switch to the news channels. I never do that usually, but today is no usual day. A few metres here or there, and I would have been on the news—*dead*.

All channels are brimming with just one topic—*the blast*. There are politicians condemning the attack, angry people, crying people and the junta venting out its anger on the government. Everyone is blaming someone else for what happened. No one has come out to take the blame. I switch off the TV. I cannot watch it. The memories of the dead people and the severed limbs are too much to take. I don't need the flashing images to add to the images already haunting my mind. I can do without the torture.

'Deb? Is something wrong?' she asks again. She must have noticed the pale, worried expression on my face.

'How many people have died?' I ask her.

'Eighty-nine. I told you.'

'I could have been one of them,' I say and she looks at me. Immediately, she has tears in her eyes. I know that she has been thinking about this. She comes to me, looks at me with love in her eyes, and hugs me. I feel wanted.

'Please don't say that,' she whispers.

'Sorry.'

I say the word but I am not. I have said nothing wrong; I *could* have been one of them. Had I not forgotten my wallet in the car, I would have been appallingly close to the scooter in which the bomb had been placed and blown to tiny bits. I had been lucky. I could have been dead or, worse still, maimed. I can feel the tiny goosebumps on my arms as Avantika snuggles up to me. I'm sure she's thinking the same.

I hold her close and try not to think about any of it. However, it's really difficult not to. I shudder to think what would've happened to her had I died. For all her strength and confidence, she is just a baby. *My* baby. Had I died . . .

Time passes and she drifts off to sleep in my arms. I want to wrap my arms around her and never let any harm come to her. The world is a cruel place and I've seen it up-close now.

I switch on the television and flip through the channels. Blood. Gore. Politicians. That's all they show. A little later, there is a special report on the 'spirit of Delhi'. They show how the people of Delhi are affected by the Chandni Chowk blast. The news correspondent tells us that the people of Delhi have come together in this time of need, that they are fighting the tragedy and getting over it together. *Bullshit.*

Getting over it? It's more like forgetting all about it. We, as responsible citizens, are more interested in doctored naked pictures of a wannabe actress than people dying on the streets. We don't care about blood as much as we do about flesh. We don't have time for all that. Who would have cared had something happened to me yesterday? Avantika. Shrey. Benoy. Dad. Mom. Who else?

No one cares about what happens to anyone! It is all just a bloody façade. Every time there is a blast, they talk about the spirit of Mumbai or the spirit of Delhi and how the city never sleeps or stops. They harp about how the city moves on. The truth is that life stops only for the people who had been in the blast. For the others—they just do not care. I don't blame them. I was on their side until yesterday. I was an uncaring Delhiite.

I'm not really sad about that. I'm just irritated. Today is just another day. And I could have been dead? That is so unfair, right? One minute, I have all my limbs, and in the next, I could have lost them? The mere thought makes me sick to the stomach. I look at Avantika, who is now sleeping in my arms. I slowly shift her into a more comfortable position and push the strands of her hair away from her radiant face. Somehow, in the last five years that we've been dating, I am yet to pick a single instant when she doesn't look pretty.

She is breathtakingly beautiful. It's almost unreal. All the things that I used to say just to score with my ex-girlfriends became true when I met Avantika. She is a dream. Even better; you can't even dream of something so perfect. Plastic surgeons still can't rival God. She is so hard to describe. Those limpid, constantly wet black eyes scream to be loved. There is nothing better than her melancholic beautiful face. She has the eyes of a one-month-old child—large and screaming for attention. A perfectly formed nose, flawless bright-pink lips and a milky-white complexion that can put Photoshop to shame. Oh hell, she is way out of my league. She is a goddamn goddess. The first time I met her, I just couldn't look beyond her face. It was strange, as it had never happened that way. Usually, it was always the cup size that had mattered.

I turn the volume low and switch back to the news channels. The news shows have censored the images by now. There are just bloodied clothes and wailing relatives. There are no severed limbs, people crying out in pain or bleeding to death, and no one is shown collecting the burnt IDs of people. I am sure people would have spent a lot more time away from their daily soaps and looked at the news if they showed all the pain that people went through.

But I don't blame them. I was no different. Mumbai blasts, Delhi blasts—they were all the same to me.

RIP, blast victims—a status update on a social networking site, a little prayer in my heart for those who'd lost their loved ones and I would get back to whatever I was doing. This time, it is different. I never thought it would happen to me. I was never in crowded places. Crowded places where people are blown to bits by irrational, stupid terrorists.

ISI, Lashkar-e-Taiba and other terrorist groups cloud my head. I ask the question which many have asked before me and would keep asking after me—*Why?* There is no answer to it. I turn off the TV in frustration and rest Avantika's head on the pillow. I am lucky to be alive, to be in her arms again . . . to be in love again. I kiss her softly on her cheek and get up.

I call Ma. I don't remember the last time I called her. These days, the only time I talk to her or Dad is when Avantika gives me the phone. Mom and Avantika talk a lot and I feel good about it. I never tell my parents how much they mean to me. No guy does. We are men. We do not know how to express love. That's why we buy jewellery. We do not hug our dads. Instead, we talk about cricket.

'*Ki korchho?*' I ask her. (What are you doing?)

'Nothing. What happened? Is everything okay, Deb?' I can sense the surprise in her voice. I usually never ask that. I never call my mom. But that doesn't mean I don't love her. Two women make my world go round—one is Avantika, the other's my mom. The third will be Avantika Jr, I guess. But there is still a decade to go for that. I am obsessed with Avantika and our relationship. It's been like that ever since I was in college.

'Yes,' I say. I have tears in my eyes. I don't know why and I almost feel like a girl for being so emotional about it. I want to tell her that I love her. If tomorrow something happens to me, she should know that I love her.

'Umm . . .'

There is an awkward silence. This is why I never call my mom. We usually have nothing to talk about other than my eating habits, and whether I am gaining any weight.

'Are you eating properly, Deb?' she asks. 'Avantika has been telling me that you skip lunches. This won't work, Tini.'

Yeah, Tini. Like everyone, I too was given an embarrassing nickname by my mom—Tini. And somehow, she manages to use it the most whenever she is around my friends.

'I have been eating, Ma. She is just paranoid! And you have given her this disease,' I say. I know from experience that I should never let Mom start about food. She is obsessed with feeding me. She has happily passed that trait on to Avantika.

'You need to eat, Tini,' she says.

'Whatever.'

I can hear Dad in the background. It has been almost six months since I have met them. I miss them. It's cool to live alone, but not all the time. I miss being irresponsible. I miss being stuffed by my mom, although Avantika is doing a good job of it. Mom knows Avantika spends a lot of time at my place.

I hang up after a while and try to sleep. As soon as I close my eyes, it all comes back to me. I try to push those gory images out of my head. I desperately need a distraction. Maybe thinking about Avantika would help; it always does, but not this time. People died. And it was just yesterday. Right in front of my eyes. Dreams crushed. Lives ended. Children lost.

How can I sleep?

I Am Still Awake

I can feel Avantika's soft hands running over my chest. She is sleeping, tired from what we finished about an hour ago. Avantika has always been good in bed. Over the last five years, she has only gotten better. Even tonight, when she crept up on the bed, her eyes dripping with passion and her hands going to all the places they should have, I felt like a man bereft of love since eternity. It took me just a few seconds to rip every shred of cloth off her and subject her to pain and ecstasy.

She was incredible with her hands, her tongue and her body tonight. I know the reason. She wanted to tire me out and make me sleep. She had her reasons. She was getting worried about me. *I* was getting worried about me. I have not slept for the last fifteen days. Neither have I been to my office or the gym. She was afraid I might fall sick.

Last night she asked me to see a psychologist or a therapist. I was totally averse to the idea.

'Are you sure you don't want to see a therapist?' she had asked.

'No! I have not gone mad yet.'

'But, Deb, you need help,' she said. 'You have not slept since the blast.'

'I am trying, Avantika. It's just that I can't manage to push those images out of my head.'

'What images? You want to talk about it?'

'So you will be my therapist?' I smirked.

'I can try,' she said and gave me one of her trademark cute smiles.

I paused for a while and then started to talk.

'Umm . . . there . . . there . . . were people who were looking at me. With no hands or legs, or whose stomachs had been blown apart . . . they were begging for help. And all I could do was stare. I wish I could've saved them . . . At least one of them . . .'

'It's not your fault, Deb.'

'I know. But those faces, those eyes that looked at me with sheer horror in them, they wanted me to help them. I . . . I . . . just can't forget that. There was a small kid who tried getting up thrice, but his legs had been blown off from below his knees. He . . . he was bleeding. He looked at me. He was crying, screaming . . . and then went silent . . . his eyes went vacant as he lay there in a pool of his own blood. I couldn't do anything. There were scores of people like that kid . . . they wanted me to help them . . .' My voice trailed off.

'They did not want *you* to help, Deb. They wanted *anyone* to help them, and you were there. But it wasn't your fault that you could not be of help. No one could have been . . . It is not your fault. You're only human . . .' Avantika said.

She came close and hugged me. I closed my eyes and those images flashed before me again. 'I wish I had saved just one of them.'

Maybe I do need to see a therapist. It is not that I have not tried sleeping. Sex. Sleeping pills. A Tusshar Kapoor movie. Nothing has worked. Ever since that day, the images have been haunting me. I don't understand why it is taking me so long to recover. I'd never thought I could be so weak. Why should I care about unknown dead people and their families? I mean—*who does that*, right? I should go on with my life and forget what happened. After all, I am alive. Why should I care about the others? I know I should move on. But that's exactly what I have *not* been doing.

I switch on the television. The news of the blast barely finds a mention now. A gay party raid finds more airtime. It is sick and creepy, but I feel like watching the news of the blast repeatedly. It is that place, that moment, that chaos that changed everything. The more I am repulsed by it, the more I am drawn to the same place. I want to be there again. There is a part of me there now.

Finally, I find a channel that is running a report on the blast. I increase the volume a little and listen. There is nothing new. No one has come up and taken the responsibility. I want someone to do that. At least then, I will be able to direct my anger towards somebody.

I turn it off and slowly remove Avantika's arm from my chest. I get up from the bed, make myself a cup of warm milk and stand in the balcony. I stare into the wide empty space and feel nothing. What happened fifteen days ago killed a part of me. I have recurring images of ashes flying around me. In those images, I am bleeding, helpless, staggering and looking around for somebody to help me. I am taken to a dingy hospital on a bloodied stretcher and I wake up without a leg or an arm.

My head is filled with images such as these. They change a little every time. Some of the times I die, at other times I lose an arm or a leg. It happened to someone else. It could have been me. This keeps repeating in my head. I keep telling myself how lucky I have been.

Avantika is happy today. I am smiling today, although it's forced. She thinks it is the sex from last night. Yes, it was good, but that is not the reason. It is just that I don't want to end up crazy. It was just a blast, right? It happens every month somewhere or the other. People die. Some more painfully than others. Big deal! I *have* to forget that day. I have to get over it. Many people have. It should not be too hard for me either.

'Are you feeling better, baby?' Avantika asks. She is wearing a skimpy silver night suit with white lacy embroidery on it. I'm sure she expects me to skip breakfast and make love to her. At least a shower together. I can sense it in her eyes, in her lingering touches and her quiet whispers. However, I must disappoint her today. I have to leave for office and *not* think about the blast.

'Yes, I am,' I say. 'Can you pack the breakfast? I will have it on the way?'

'You are going to office? Are you sure?' she asks.

'Yes,' I say and get up. I can see Avantika's face droop. Obviously! I should have been making sweet love to her and not be thinking about what happened sixteen days earlier, but I cannot help it. I take my bag and leave the house.

'Deb?' Shrey says as he picks up the call.

'Yes, I am coming to office.'

'You are? Everything fine now?' he asks.

'Yes,' I say.

It is embarrassing to admit to your guy friends that you are bothered with such petty things. People die every day. It takes only one gesture to lose all respect as far as being macho is concerned. You can lift ridiculous weights in the gym and stop trains with bare hands all your life, but the moment someone spots a pink stuffed toy in your hand, you are screwed for life. The blast was the pink stuffed toy for me. I faltered. I am screwed for life.

After all, for everyone else, it was just a bomb blast, and I was at least 500 feet away! I spent fifteen days locked up like a scared little kid. I have lost all my machoness.

I look out of the auto. It has been long since I stepped into one of these. But now, for a few days, this will have to be my mode of transport. My car was burnt beyond recognition. Call me a sissy, but I was a little sceptical about the auto too. Who knows? Another bomb carrier?

The auto takes a different route. It takes a left, and I see the blast site from a distance. The cars are still lined up in their burnt state there and my car is amongst them.

'Bhaiya, can you drop me there?' I ask him and point to the parking lot.

The auto driver nods and heads there. I pay him ten rupees more than the fare and get down. He smiles. I had hoped I would feel good after helping a stranger and making him smile—something I couldn't do that day. But nothing changes. Money can't buy you happiness. But it does buy terrorists stuff to make bombs with. Now I am pissed at myself. *Why can't I think about anything else?*

I walk towards my car. Everything has returned to normalcy. The blood has been washed off the streets. People have found places to park their bikes amidst the burnt cars. There are hawkers on the streets again. I am sure some of them are missing.

I walk close to the car and look around. It is burnt and black. I don't know what I am doing there. I turn and watch life go by. I look at people and think—*Are they going through the same?*

I trudge towards the place where the bomb had gone off. The ground is black, charred and there is a huge crater there. I could have been there, I think.

I no longer want to go to office. I take a deep breath and start walking close to the pavement. There is a guy cleaning the street. I wonder if he was around that day. He seems unfazed. Life goes on for him.

'*Dekh ke!*' the cleaner shouts out as I stumble over a dustbin.

'Fuck,' I say to myself. My shirt is ruined and I curse the road. It is just not one of my better days. The road cleaner helps me up and I smile at him. I thank him and keep walking ahead. Suddenly, a voice calls out from behind.

'Bhaiya!'

I look back to see the cleaner running to me, waving his hand frantically. He is carrying a notebook in his hands. He shows it to me and asks, 'Is this yours?'

I look at it. It is a diary, which is in tatters. The back cover is totally burnt and its edges have been consumed by fire. I stare at it for a while. It must have dropped out of the dustbin I had just stumbled over. I look at it again. I want to shake my head and walk away, but I can't.

'Yes, this is mine,' I say, taking the diary from him, and thank him. I take a ten-rupee note out of my wallet and hand it to him. He smiles, thanks me and walks away. I clutch the diary and wait on the side of the pavement for an auto. The sides of the pages of the diary crumble in my hands and are reduced to ashes.

The sun has come out and I start to sweat. I look at the diary. It has nothing written on the cover, except the year—*2010*—

which is faded. There is no auto in sight. I sit on the pavement and flip through the contents. It is nearly full. The handwriting is not the best, but it is neat and deliberate. The first few pages are damaged beyond recognition. The top-right corners of the pages keep crumbling into charcoal.

I stare at the burnt diary. This is the diary of someone who must have gotten seriously hurt in that day's blast, I think. Not many people survived the blast; I was one of the few who did. The diary is in bad shape. It doesn't look as though the person to whom it belongs would have survived the blast. I open the first unburned page. There is no name.

Just the initials—*RD*.

'You're late,' Shrey looks at me and says.

'I know. Got stuck,' I say. I clutch the diary inside my office bag. It is still there. I have kept myself from reading it.

Shrey and I had been to the same college, Delhi College of Engineering, now rechristened Delhi Technological University. We had a crazy time there. It was during those days that I had started dating Avantika. She was studying at Shri Ram College of Commerce (SRCC) and was even then as lovely. We have a come a long way from then. It's been many years now. Man! I almost feel like a granddad.

Anyway, between Shrey and me, he has always been the bright one. My mother loves him and all my ex-girlfriends have always found him very attractive. Clearly, I don't see what those girls did. Well, Shrey is tall, dark and fairly handsome. His hair is like thin noodles like those African-American disco dancers and it gives him character. The most striking thing about him is his disregard for the impossible. There is nothing in the world he thinks he cannot do. His overconfidence makes him almost cocky. In one crisp sentence—*He is a freak*.

He has lived in Paris, Goa and other places in strip clubs and with beautiful women for quite some time. After a lot of sex with random European women, he thought he should slow down. And so, he flew back to Delhi. As soon as he did that, he wrecked my life. I was working with American Express and writing books in my free time. The books were doing fairly well and my life was perfect. But, as always, he had different plans for me. And, like a fool, I followed what he said.

A month later, we started our own venture—a publishing house. Starting Chrome Ink Press was his crazy idea. Despite everything, I know this guy is really talented, because I am now making more money than I would ever have had in my old job. Yes, it is hard work in a way, but it's amazing.

But today, I am in no mood to reflect on how my life has changed ever since Shrey decided that my old life was not the life I should lead. Right now, the initials 'RD' are troubling me. My worst fears, the recurring dreams, have just come true. Someone died that day, someone that could have been me. And I have his or her diary in my hands.

There are about a million mails in my inbox but I couldn't care less about them. I take the diary out of my bag and put it inside the first drawer of my table. The burnt edges make me shiver. The hand that held it that day must have been torn apart. The hand may've belonged to one of those bloodied faces that had asked me for help that day and for whom I did nothing.

'So? Still haunted?' he asks.

'Haunted?'

'The blast, Deb. Avantika told me. These bloody terrorists!

Why can't they just go home and fuck their wives and sleep peacefully? What's even more surprising is that no one has come forward to claim responsibility. I think it's the goddamn government,' he says, his brain running ahead of himself.

'Government?' I ask.

'Yes! With this whole Anna Hazare protest, maybe they're just saving their ass. They are taking our minds off the protests and the agitations. A few people killed here and there don't matter, do they?' he says with absolute conviction. I am sure he heard this on some news channel. It makes some sense, though.

'Maybe.'

'Oye, I need to leave to meet someone from the *Times*. Will you be able to handle everything here?' he asks.

'Yes, I will.'

That is our code for a date. We have a few people working under us and we don't want them to think that we go out during office hours for movies and dates. Because that's something we do a lot! So whenever we have to go out, we say we have to meet 'somebody from the *Times*'. I wave him goodbye, he checks his noodle hair in the mirror and leaves.

There is not much work. There is *never* much work. I sit in front of the laptop and check my Facebook account. Facebook is boring when you're dating the prettiest girl there will ever be.

I don't want to, but I still end up doing what I've been avoiding since morning. I fetch the diary from my drawer and open it. RD.

I turn over to the first page. There is a short note. I close it immediately. I am not supposed to read it. I am supposed to return it to the rightful owner, but the rightful owner is probably dead. I open the first and the last pages of the diary and look for an address. There is none. It leaves me no choice. I start to read it.

15 June 2010

'Just as she walked past me, I felt the world come to a standstill, the birds stopped chirping, the wind stopped blowing and the sun stopped shining . . . It was only her, it was only me.'

She looked beautiful. I see her with other guys and I feel envious. I'm sure no one around her likes her as much as I do. It's been a week since I first saw her, and she only looks more beautiful every time I see her. I saw her at the water fountain today. It made my day.

I wish to see her again tomorrow.

Okay. Now, I cannot stop. Personal diaries have always been a weak point for me. Avantika and I had one of our biggest fights when she did not let me read hers. The only part I was interested in was what she thought about me in bed, whether I was bigger than her previous boyfriends, whether I was a better kisser . . . *That* sort of stuff. Well, after a lot of histrionics and girlish tantrums, she let me read it. I just read the words *big* and *fabulous* somewhere in the paragraphs and I was happy. I'm sure she added them after I told her I wanted to read the diary. She threw away her diary the very next day. There are certain privacy boundaries that even people in relationships shouldn't cross. Like Facebook passwords, mail passwords and personal diaries.

Anyway, I flip the page over and see another short note. How can I stop? I almost died along with this guy.

28 June 2010

'Every day that I don't see her, is a day not worth remembering. Because ever since I first saw her, she defines my life.'

I saw her again today. Not just saw her. I followed her today. I hope she does not have a boyfriend. Even if she does, it would not matter. She is so beautiful. I see the guys who surround her all the time. They are all creepy. I hope she thinks so too. All of them tried to give her their old books. I even saw a few of them exchange numbers. I wish I were one of them. But I have already sold my books. Maybe I could get new ones for her. And scribble down short, sweet notes for her on every page. But I don't want to be one of those creepy guys surrounding her. I will let it be.

I wish to see her again tomorrow.

I can read a lot faster than this, but I don't want to. For every page that I turn I think that this person might be dead. It is a little unsettling. I have already imagined him in my head. He's probably a geek with big spectacles and oiled hair. The kind who hide behind concrete pillars and stalk the girls they have a crush on. I don't want the person in my head to end up dead. I flip through the diary, skimming the pages to find out whether he has written his name anywhere. No signs. No numbers. No addresses. *Nothing*.

I move on to the next day. The page is a little burnt on the sides. I try not to imagine what must have happened to the hand that held that diary.

2 July 2010

'I don't know whether my love is shallow or unfounded since we have never talked. But unrequited, untold love is the purest form of love. There is no pretence in that.'

It has been two days and I have not seen her around. I wonder where she is. She looks like someone who studies a lot and doesn't miss any classes. Maybe she is on a date with someone. Maybe not. I hope not. I will ask her name tomorrow. The guy at the stationery shop will say if he'll be able to find that out for me. I don't even know which section she is in. I have missed seeing her the last two days.

I wish to see her tomorrow.

Okay, now this guy is creepy. He doesn't have a life. Stalking somebody *this* badly? Who does that? My interest dwindles a bit. Though I feel a little sorry for him. I have been through what he went through. I was a geek once. Not that a lot has changed. I am still an ugly geek, so I know how that feels.

Please don't let this guy be dead, I think. But it's a hollow thought. No one could have survived the impact of the blast after being so close to it. The diary is stark evidence of that.

Anyway, I keep reading.

17 July 2010
'I don't agree that if you are intrigued by a girl, you fall more in love with her. The more I know about her, the closer she comes to me. I want to know everything about the person I love.'

Thank you, God! I saw her again today. The stationery guy had a lot of information about her. Her name is Ragini and she has left Lady Shri Ram College to come here. She is in third year too. That means I can't give her my books. She moved in with her aunt here after her parents shifted to London this year. Maybe she is from a rich family, but I don't care about that.

I like the name. I am saying this name repeatedly in my head ever since I heard it. It sounds good. The stationery shop guy asked me to go and talk to her. He is a little crazy. She is pretty as a fairy. And I am . . . well, anyway. I know I don't stand a chance. But some day, I will talk to her. Till that time, I will just look at her and feel happy. Happiness. Yes, that is what she looks like. I like her. She is like the warm morning sun on a cold winter morning to me.

I wish to see her tomorrow.

I am drawn to his story now. He might not be great with words but there is a certain honesty about him and what he writes. I can instantly feel a connection. It's almost like I have written those words for Avantika. It is lovely and terrifying at the same time. I can't be dead. I can't leave Avantika behind. I feel sorry for him. Ragini would have been proud to read this, right? A guy so selfless in his love? Pure and untainted. Not a speck of lust.

It's not seen these days, is it? Guys don't count days to when they would talk to a girl they like; instead, they try to guess when the girl would kiss them or make out with them. Avantika and I had kissed on our first date itself and had made out in the second, but I loved Avantika. I could have waited for an eternity for those things to happen. I was just lucky that I didn't have to. I am so glad I did not have to stalk her like this guy.

The *dead* guy. Every time this thought comes to my head, I am scared. What if she'd got married to the guy? 2010, right? That's almost two years back! What if *the dead guy* eventually gets married to this girl, Ragini? *Fuck.*

Just as I flip over to another page, a barrage of mails floods my inbox. *Work.* I close the diary, put it back in my drawer and get to work. The downside of running a publishing house is that you get many junk mails. And you don't know they are junk till you've spent at least twenty minutes on each of them. Even today, there are a few manuscripts from new authors lying in a stack, waiting to be reviewed. Some of them are just-okay, some of them are really good and some of them will take years to finish. Picking out that perfect manuscript written by a sensible author is a tough task. It's more about luck than anything else, but I love doing that.

I flip through some manuscripts. They are all college love stories. Yes, they are done to death, but they work! And I still like them. I lean back into my chair. This is a lot better than being at home and waiting for Avantika to get home and get out of her clothes.

Just then, Avantika calls and it brings an instant smile to my face, like a small kid's eyes light up outside a candy shop. Five years and nothing has changed. She still makes me the happiest I can ever be. She still makes my world go round.

'Deb?' she asks.

'Hi! What's up?'

'Umm, nothing really. Are you okay? Have you eaten?' she asks. She has reason to be concerned. I have been acting a little strange over the last fortnight.

'Yes, yes,' I say.

'Are you working?'

'Yes.'

'Okay. See you in the evening then,' she says.

'Wait, Avantika! Tell me something—if you find a personal diary on the road, will you read it?'

'I will not,' she says. She is almost instantly pissed off. 'There is a reason why it is personal.'

'And . . . what if the person is dead?' I ask.

'What?' she says. There is some noise in the background. 'Listen, Deb, I need to go. Can we talk about it when I get home?' she asks sweetly.

'Sure,' I say and disconnect the call.

I feel traumatized, disturbed. This could be the diary of a dead man. His last written words could be in my hands. It might have things that he had wanted to tell his friends, girlfriends, family . . . and might have never said before. That's too much pressure. I'm a little scared now of what's to come.

I try and put myself in his place. If I were to write everything I feel about everyone in a diary and die, would I like my diary to be read? *Yes, I would.* I would like my last words to reach the people I love. They have a right to know what they meant to me. I wouldn't miss any chance to tell Avantika that I love her. Or my parents. Even Shrey, for that matter.

I get back to work. Shrey has not come back from his meeting with 'somebody from the *Times*' yet. I am sure the conference table is his bed and the discussions are limited to both of them saying just one word—*Yes! Yes! Yes!*

Five hours have passed by and it's already six in the evening. I leave the office and look for an auto. I have the diary with me. I cannot wait to get back to it. I sit in the auto and open the diary, even when a part of me doesn't want to. I know it will take me just an hour to finish the full diary and I don't want it to end so soon. But the curiosity is killing me. I open it and start reading slowly.

25 August 2010
'A whiff of her perfume, a tiny chirp from her sweet lips and just one look from those almond-shaped eyes make my day. I need nothing else.'

Ragini. I tried to stand really close to her at the bus stop today. She was alone. I wanted to talk to her, but didn't know what to say. She looked beautiful and I stood there staring at her. The sun reflected off her glazing long black hair. I followed her into her bus. People around me saw me stare at her. I didn't care. I got down where she got down. It was pretty far away from my place, but I couldn't care less. I walked behind her till she entered the gate of a building. Sea View Apartments. I walked back to the nearest bus stop and caught the next bus home.

I wish to see her again tomorrow.

I google Sea View Apartments on my phone. Nothing substantial comes out. They have apartments of that name all across the country. In at least fifty cities. I shut the diary. I still don't know which city this guy lived in. I get restless. The auto drops me off at my place and I can't wait for night to fall so I can read the rest of the diary. It's too early to tell Avantika anything about it. I don't want to come across as a freak and I am a little scared how she will react to me reading someone else's diary.

⌣

Avantika is sleeping. This night is slightly better than the past ones. I am in the balcony again, staring at wide open spaces. I clutch the diary. I am torn. Stories excite me, but stories that end too soon sadden me. I don't want this to end. The diary I hold in my hand has a story with a lot of value to me. The guy who wrote this diary is dead. I could have been that guy. If I had written a diary and died in that blast, someone else would be reading it. Maybe him. And it would have killed me had he not read it. My last chance of reaching out to my loved ones would have gone waste.

So, in a twisted manner, that guy and I are connected. I am the last person to read what he last wrote. I am probably the only person who will ever read this diary. It's a huge responsibility. I have survived and he has not. But he lives through the diary I hold. He lives through what he tells me in this diary.

Yes, we all snatch the diaries of our friends and browse through them, but this is different. This diary has the last words of a dead man. I open it again with trembling hands.

7 September 2010

'I don't think colours and hues make her look beautiful. It's the other way around.'

I think she noticed me stare at her today. I had waited for her bus to stop outside our college. She wore green and fuchsia pink. And looked resplendent. She has made quite a few guy friends and I am jealous. While they sit near her, smile and laugh with her, all I can do is sit at a distance, alone, and stare at her. Today, I sat on a bench right next to her. Her voice is sweet. Like little birds chirping on a bright Sunday morning. Her shining eyes and honey-sweet voice are like windows to her pure, clean soul. Maybe I will talk to her tomorrow. Maybe she will chirp for me. Only for me. I can't get my mind off her. Her face, her simplicity, her voice, her slender fingers, I just can't stop thinking about her. It's like I am possessed. I am hers. I wonder what she is doing now. Did she really catch me staring at her? Does she know I exist?

I wish to see her again tomorrow.

I finish reading the diary when it's one in the night. I am wide awake and I notice that I have put bookmarks in a million different places. I can't put in words how I feel about it. As I read the diary, it was as if I was the dead guy and Ragini was Avantika. It seemed like *my* diary and *my* story. I am enraged that I didn't get to tell the girl I loved the most that I loved her and now I am dead. It's frustrating and I am exasperated. It's like a novel with no end. Or a movie without the climax scene. And it's just grossly unfair. It feels like my own story has come to an abrupt end.

I have read the full diary, but still found no addresses, no numbers and no clues for me to know who the guy was. It's infinitely irritating. I just have to know who he is and I will do anything for that. It's my only chance at redemption, the only chance of helping one of the many people who died that morning. It's my only chance to make those images in my head go away forever. I will not let this go. I will find an end to this diary. *I have to.*

I start reading the diary again—from start to finish—with higher concentration this time round. I don't want to miss a single thing. This time, I start taking notes to find out who the guy was. Within an hour, I have finished reading it again.

The Diary

16 September 2010

'You're in love when she's around and when her voice alone is your guiding light, your only motivation in your life. I am in love.'

I will never forget this day. I cannot forget this day. This day defines me now. I hadn't seen her for many days before today. It was just another morning and I was a little restless. Dejected, I reached the bus stop at the time she used to and waited for her to come, hoping against hope. She came, I looked at her and she looked amazing. I don't think she saw me. The bus came and there was a mad rush to jump into the bus. She was standing right beside me as we waited for people to board the already crowded bus.

I went out of the line and motioned to her that she should get in first. There was way too much jostling and she couldn't get in. The bus started moving and her eyebrows made a small frowning hill on her head. She looked adorable. She glanced at me and whispered an apology. 'Sorry'—the first word she said to me. I thanked the bus driver in my heart and smiled at her. We waited for the bus, but I knew the next bus wouldn't come for the next twenty minutes. I shifted in my place. I knew I wouldn't get a better chance to talk to her. I have been in relationships before and it's not as if I can't talk to girls. But with her, it's something different.

I looked at her and waited for her to look at me. When she looked at me, I said a feeble 'Hi' and she replied. The pressure of starting a conversation was on me and I was getting very nervous. I asked her if she was in my college and she nodded. She added that she had seen me around. I wondered if she knew that I was stalking her, but she told me that she knew me from a students' council meeting. She sweetly complained about the buses and how far she lived from college. I nodded and added in. Her sweet, chirpy voice made me forget all about whatever was going on around us. We introduced ourselves. She asked me where I lived and I remembered an apartment near hers and lied.

The next bus came a little too early. We both got in. She got a seat and I stood. She offered to hold my bag and I gave it to her. We smiled. It seemed like one of those daydream sequences I had had about her and me, but it was actually happening. We didn't talk much as the bus was jerking too much. We reached our bus stop and got down. She looked at me and asked me if I took this bus every day. I nodded and her smile seemed to say—will see you around. She walked away. I wish I had taken her number. But I have no complaints. I got to talk to her today.

I wish I could see her tomorrow.

'Deb?' A voice calls out from behind. It is Avantika. I always like her best when she is half-sleepy and all messed up. That's when I feel the luckiest. Even when she is not at her best, she is still the best-looking girl I have ever come across. I feel like the guy from the diary, looking at someone I love like a cowardly geek.

It's three in the night. I'd slept while reading the diary for the third time that night. The pages are now creased from where I had folded them. I have made some notes on my cell phone and some on little scraps of paper. They make no sense at all. I am very anxious and I cannot get what I have read out of my head. It is very disturbing yet enamouring. All I know is I have to find Ragini. The mysterious girl from the book, the girl who screwed up, the girl who has to know about this guy, RD, and his undying love for her.

'Why did you get up?' I ask. I slip the diary behind me to prevent her from spotting it.

'Won't you sleep?'

'I guess I will,' I say and hug her. For the first time in the past fortnight, I feel sleepy. The images are still there in my head but they are blurring a little. Suddenly, my head is filled with images from the notes in that diary. The guy. His best friend. The pretty girl. The unfortunate sister. The inconsiderate guy. There are no faces in the pictures in my head, there are no places, but there is a story. The story of a person who is now dead. The dead guy left a story behind. A story that I have to make sense of. It is incomplete and I cannot let it be that way. The girl has to know.

I write for a living and every time I write a book, the only thing I look forward to is the ending. A book without an ending makes no sense. It is the same with this diary. It is incomplete. The first and the last few pages are burnt beyond recognition. Maybe they were all blank, but I want to know and I will find out.

Even if they were blank, Ragini, the girl from the diary, needs to know about this guy's love for her! I hug Avantika that night and sleep like a baby.

The next morning, I wake up with a start. I am clutching and groping around on the bed for it. *The diary*.

'What happened?' Avantika asks as she dusts her face with make-up. Not that she needs any. She looks better without it.

'Nothing,' I say, not wanting to sound like a creep.

She tells me she has served the breakfast on the table and that she needs to rush. She is working very hard and I don't like her working her ass off. She should work her ass off for me . . . if you know what I mean. Anyway, she leaves and I get the diary from where I had hidden it. It almost draws me towards it. I turn over the pages I have already read thrice.

I finish breakfast and rush to the office. I take an auto and it takes the same route it had taken that day. For a second, I feel like getting down and walking around the place where I found the diary, but I decide against it. I have horrendous images in my head of this guy burning to death. I don't want them to get more vivid. I can almost feel him around me, asking me, 'So, now that you've read my diary, what will you do about it?'

There is a lot of pending work in office and Shrey is going to meet that 'someone from the *Times*' again. It's strange to see him go for a second date. Maybe he's taking his work very seriously. He is working too *hard* this time. He leaves me with a few manuscripts to go through. But none of them interests me.

I have already found the perfect manuscript. It is on my desk—the diary. The only problem is that it doesn't have an end. The last few pages are either missing or it just ended abruptly. Ever since I've read it, all my mental energies have been diverted to its content. It's nothing phenomenal, but the sheer circumstance around it is so powerful. What lies on my desk are a dead man's words. Could a story be more perfect?

There were some books that I had written before I started my own publishing house and they did well, but I don't write much now.

I pick up the diary and flip through the pages. The writing is ornate, slow and deliberate. It hardly seems like a guy has written it. I guess the guy always wanted to show this diary to Ragini. The writing is too pretty to not show off.

I like this guy. He's creepy, but he isn't that creepy. I have tried to decode everything that's there in the diary and made notes on a sheet of paper. It's like a jigsaw puzzle with the major parts there but all the tiny, critical parts are missing. No city, no names, no addresses, no phone numbers. It looks like someone is playing with me. The questions keep troubling me.

My mind creates this image of a guy madly in love with a very pretty girl. It feels so picture-perfect. But as I feel the burnt edges of the diary, I feel unsettled. His hands were blown off from this diary. Somehow, I have assumed that this diary is about a guy who doesn't get his girl and that's why he carried it around. It makes perfect sense. If he was with the girl when the blast took place, why would he keep the diary with him? But I have to consider both possibilities. What if both of them died together? Could it be that? What if this was their last remembrance they'd left behind? Of all the people, *I* get the diary.

I google news results of the Chandni Chowk blast. The death count is rising. It's now one hundred and twenty-seven dead and fifty-seven injured. Initially, there were three hospitals that all the blast victims had been taken to. I call up the first hospital. I pose as someone from the media and take down the names of twenty-three people who had died there. After the third hospital, I realize it's futile.

'Can you give me the names?' I ask the disinterested guy on the other side of the phone.

There should have been twenty-nine names listed in the third hospital. He gives me three.

'The rest? Twenty-nine people should be on the list. I called all the hospitals and have got just ninety-eight names,' I say.

'People get transferred to different hospitals within hours of when they get here. Some of them are reported, some of them are not,' he answers.

I pester him to give me more details, but he says he can't help me. Overeager and scared relatives transfer patients to better, private hospitals as soon as possible. So, the number of people dead is reported on an estimate basis. I hang up, fuming, not knowing what to do next. The tease was thrilling, but now, it's annoying. I want to know who the hell this RD is. I am pretty sure he is dead, but I want it in writing.

Shrey walks in a little while later.

'Working?' he asks. His ruffled hair is more ruffled. This time his hair is strange not because of his botched-up genes. This time I am sure it's a girl. The glow on his face is more evident than a pregnant woman's. He smiles and waits for me to ask him about the love bite I spot on his neck, which is big, red and very prominent.

'Yes, and you have been working *hard*, I suppose.' I smirk.

'You wouldn't believe!' Shrey comes and jumps on my table. I hate it when he does that. Twice he has broken the glass top. Twice.

'Do I have an option of not listening?' I ask. I know I have no choice. He would still tell me. I don't mind his sexual escapades, though. They are usually very entertaining till the point he decides to dump the girl. Because after that, it's just sad and pathetic.

'You've got to meet her!' he says. 'Every time we meet, it's like freaking amazing sex.'

'You had sex? C'mon! Even I didn't have sex today, and I am engaged. This is just unfair.'

'Not only that! We did it in the washroom. Can you beat that?'

I have done that, but I let him have his moment of glory. Why would Shrey even think he has done something that I have not? Yes, I am very possessive and proud about my very healthy sex life. Any insult to my sex life is a direct insult to my lust for Avantika, which I think is unmatched and phenomenal by any standards.

'Washroom! Nice. But in the afternoon? How?'

'We got drunk. And she needed help to walk up to the washroom! She just pulled me in and we did it.'

'*She* pulled you in?' I smirk again.

'Okay, whatever,' Shrey says and I hear the glass top creak under his weight. 'The manager came and shouted while we were still at it!'

'Then?'

'We just said that she was vomiting and he went away. All in all—awesome day, awesome girl, awesome date,' he says and smiles creepily. 'Look! Look!'

'What?'

'She sent me a picture! I am sure she's still drunk,' he says and pushes his phone in my face.

'I don't want to see!' I push it away. But I catch a glimpse from the corner of my eye. She is in a really low-cut dress and is hot. *Slutty* hot. Too big a cleavage for my taste. I am more of a nice-ass guy.

'I am meeting her again tonight. We are going drinking first and then a movie. But I don't think we will be watching it. We will be making one.'

'Just make sure you don't make babies.'

The last girl Shrey had gone out with ended up pregnant. And he paid for her 'treatment' through company accounts. The expense was accounted under 'indirect expenses'. Why can't he just keep his pants zipped up? Horny bastard. But it's good to have him around. He lives a crazy life and does things that are hard to digest or believe.

Anyway, he gets back to work and so do I. Life's easy these days. I am not working for anybody and I make my own rules. Well, almost. I do have to pay for abortions sometimes, but yes, more or less, I can dictate what I want to do.

I leave the office after a few hours and come back home. A friend of Avantika's is throwing a birthday party at her place and she's invited us. The friend has married a pot-bellied, ugly guy who doesn't even reach my shoulder. And I am 5'10", which is not a very high scale anyway. But then, of course, he is *rich*. That adds another foot to his height.

It's going to be another boring party, but Avantika told me she's going to dress up and I *never* miss a chance to see her dress up. I put on the cleanest, whitest shirt I can find. She dresses up exquisitely and makes me look like ragged beggar. I look at her and ask her, 'Do you wish you were dating someone rich too?'

'Why would I? I am already dating the richest guy. You give me everything I have ever wanted,' she says and smiles at me.

A little later, we get inside the car. She is driving today. There's nothing hotter than a girl driving a big car. Plus, she is wearing a really short dress and I want my hands on her porcelain-smooth skin and not on the hard leather of the steering wheel.

'Avantika, the only reason you go to these parties is because you like dressing up!'

'Everyone likes dressing up,' she says and puts the car into gear.

'But you dress up to make other people realize that you're prettier and hotter than them.'

'That's just a by-product.' She smiles and winks at me.

'I tell you every day that you're the hottest! Why isn't that enough for you?'

'It is, baby. We will stay there for just an hour, pucca,' she assures me.

'Can't we just stay home and get you naked?' I ask and run my fingers over her bare thighs. I hope she gets turned on. She doesn't. She gives me a cold stare instead. I still don't take my hand off—too stubborn, too horny.

'Be a good boy till the party ends and I promise I'll be a very bad girl for the rest of the night.' She winks.

The smile on her face tells me that things will get nasty tonight. I take my hand off. Soon, we'll be doing much more.

My mind drifts off. The diary. I still haven't decided whether I should tell her about it or not. It's kind of killing me. I take out my cell phone and start to find anything that I can on the internet. I have searched the name 'Ragini' a million times on Google, Facebook, Orkut and MySpace, but nothing substantial has come out. There are just too many girls with that name. The only concrete information I have is that this guy was from Imperial Academy, Dehradun. But there is one sentence that can tell me more—'I used to call him Pappu, to show him down, but he was the champion, his name etched on the achievements board of 2007 as the All-Rounder of the Batch.'

I search the name of the school on Google. They have a very elaborate website, but I can't find any list of toppers or rank holders. We drive on. I can hardly stop myself from making her stop at a deserted road and 'ruffling' her hair, but there is still time for that. We reach the place. It's a humungous house at Aurangzeb Road, Delhi. Fucking huge.

I look at Avantika. I don't have a big house, but at least my girlfriend is hot. Within minutes, I am bored. There is no beer in the party. Only expensive whisky, wines and whatnot. I sit in the corner and watch television when my phone rings. It's Shrey. As usual, he's in trouble and sounds frantic. This time, I don't mind.

'I hope you're not lying,' Avantika says as we get inside the car.

'You can ask Shrey! He called and said he needed me.'

'But why?'

'He banged his car into a divider,' I say.

'So can't he call a taxi? Or a crane? Why us?'

'I don't know.'

Avantika sounds really pissed. I am wishing he really fucked up his car or I would be the worst loser. No sex. Maybe no breakfast tomorrow too. We reach where Shrey had asked me to come. It's really deserted and I am scared. It really shouldn't be a silly prank or I will be so screwed. Or *not screwed* at all.

At a distance, I see two pairs of headlights. I drive towards the cars. As we go closer, I see things more clearly. Shrey's car is *smashed*! Thank God! I hope he's a little hurt too. I can act upset then and Avantika can give me a consolatory handjob. Yes, I know I am pathetic.

'Fuck! That is his car, right?' says Avantika in shock.

Yes! It wasn't a prank. I will get laid tonight.

'Yes,' I say and park our car nearby. I ask Avantika to stay in the car as I see a police car near his. Girls and policemen is a bad combination. For the police, every girl out in the streets after six in the evening is a slut. I walk up to where Shrey is standing. He is still smiling. On his right is a frail girl, who looks pretty young and she is shivering in fear. A disgusting, pot-bellied policeman is taking down information on his pad in Hindi.

'Sir, he is Tiya's brother. Ask him. We're getting married next month,' Shrey says in a very timid voice. He winks at me playfully.

'You are?' The police guy looks at me.

Before I can say anything, the young girl comes and hugs me. 'Bhaiya!'

'Ummm . . . I am her brother,' I say and point to the young girl who has held me tight around my waist.

I see Shrey smile. The girl is a better actor. She keeps clutching me, as if hanging on for dear life.

'You two can go home,' the policeman points at the girl and me. Shrey nods and tells us he will come home and explain *our* parents everything. The girl's arms are still around me. We walk towards the car. Avantika looks strangely at us.

'What's going on?' Avantika asks as soon as we get inside the car.

'No fucking idea!' I say, and we both look at the young girl in the back seat.

Suddenly, she is calm and composed and stares right back at us. Before I can say anything else, she asks me to turn the air conditioner a notch up. I am a little offended by her audacity.

'He was teaching me how to drive. We started making out and I didn't see the divider,' she says nonchalantly and keeps chewing on her bubblegum.

'Why are the police here?' Avantika asks.

'We banged the car, that's why! And they think I'm under eighteen, so they wanted to call my parents. That's why Shrey called you guys. And that's why you're my brother,' she says with absolutely no change in the expression on her face.

'How old are you?' Avantika asks her.

'Seventeen,' she says.

Fuck. Is this the girl from the washroom? She's not even eighteen! Old pervert.

'Then what are you doing with him?' Avantika asks, shocked.

'I love him!'

'*Love?*' Avantika asks. 'He's just using you! He just wants to sleep with you.'

'But he has already slept with me.'

'He has?'

'Quite a few times and he's still with me. And Avantika di, he's really good in bed.'

If you ask me, she looks at least twenty. And she is too hot to be seventeen. But that's not what I'm concerned about. I am stunned at the ease with which she started discussing her sex life with Avantika. I don't know why, but girls discuss *everything*. It's very disturbing.

Anyway, Avantika isn't too interested in the discussion. In fact, she's furious and takes it out on the car. She puts it in gear and goes full throttle on the accelerator. I'm a little scared now. I don't have a car any more, and if things go like this, Avantika's car would not be in a good condition either.

'Where are we going?' I ask.

'Home,' she says.

'And where is she going?' I point to the girl in the back seat. Tiya, Shrey had called her in front of the policeman. But nothing Shrey says in front of a policeman can be considered truth.

'She's coming with us,' Avantika replies.

'And Shrey?' the girl asks.

'I don't give a fuck,' Avantika says. She's angry and she pushes the pedal all the way down. She shouldn't do that. She is a girl, after all; people expect her to drive badly and bang into dividers and not weave seamlessly through the traffic. But, I have to admit, I am a little turned on.

A little after we get home, Shrey drops in. We are sitting in the drawing room and no one says anything. I steal a glance at the girl. Despite the dead serious look on Avantika's face, the girl is unfazed. She sits cross-legged next to Shrey and is least bothered. I hadn't noticed it before but she is quite tall—around five-eight—and a little too skinny for my taste. She looks a little like those anorexic models on Fashion TV, though with a bigger cleavage. But her face still has a kid-like glow. Her long hair is a mix of black and golden brown, and strangely enough, she is only seventeen.

'I didn't know Tiya wasn't eighteen!' Shrey says finally. I guess her real name is Tiya, after all.

'How does that matter?' the girl protests.

Everyone is looking at Avantika to react. She looks like a mafia don presiding over a gang meeting. Her cold stares are scary and her posture is menacing. I know why Avantika is taking it so seriously. Avantika has a screwed-up past. She had gotten into drugs and alcohol pretty early in her life. She's had many flings before me and she blames them for the years she lost to drug abuse. So every time Shrey starts sleeping around with someone young, she freaks out. And this girl is *seventeen*! I can tell she's very angry at Shrey and Tiya.

I don't think I'm getting laid tonight.

'Come. You're sharing a bed with me,' Avantika says.

'Why?' Tiya protests.

'Because I'm asking you to.'

'Why should I listen to you?'

'My house, my rules. Though you are free to go home. I can call your parents and they will be more than happy to pick you up from here,' Avantika says.

'Fuck.'

'Now come with me,' she says and takes her away. The girl looks at Shrey, blows him a kiss and winks at him. He responds. I look at Shrey. I so want to kill him! I had things planned with Avantika and he just came and ruined everything.

'You're such an asshole,' I say.

'Why? I didn't know, okay? She said she was nineteen!' Shrey insists.

'Whatever it is, had it not been for you, I would have been getting laid, fucker.'

'Had it not been for Avantika, I would have been getting laid too. Why does she have to behave like her granny?' he says.

I give him a warning stare. We don't exchange a word and get into bed. Such a waste.

'You think they're doing something?' Shrey asks with a smirk.

'Fuck off.'

I fantasize about Avantika and what we would've done and slowly drift off to sleep.

When I wake up, I find that Shrey and Tiya have already left. Avantika still looks angry about what happened last night. I think she's making a big deal out of it so that she doesn't have to sleep with me. Maybe she doesn't lust for me any more. I look at myself in the mirror. I am not that bad-looking. She has made out with worse versions of me—like when I had a paunch and really long rope-like hair! And once when I had kept an ugly beard as I thought it was cool. The beard is still there, a little less bushy though. It's there to hide my ugly face.

Despite my attempts, she doesn't talk much and leaves for office. Every time Shrey does something like this, I have to bear the brunt of Avantika's anger. When will she understand that no one, absolutely no one, can make Shrey mend his ways?

As soon as Avantika leaves, I open the website for Imperial Academy, Dehradun, again. I call on the numbers given there but there is no response. It seems like it has been an eternity since I've read the diary and the suspense is killing me. But I'm very bad at resisting temptation—naked girls (read: Avantika!) and books without endings. I can't help but want to open them both. A very dirty pun intended.

I want to know more about the dead guy, what his name was, where he lived, what he did, everything. All I know is that he is obsessively in love with a girl. And such love needs to be confessed and not hidden. It has never done anyone any good.

Even if Avantika left me, I would tell her every day how much I love her—till my last breath. Ah! I am so in love with her. There are days when I just sit and stare at her. Those are the days when I feel really lucky. She is so perfect and so freakishly beautiful. Suddenly, I can't recall the last time I'd told her that I love her. So I pick up the phone and dial her number.

'Hey!'

'Deb? I'm working! I really can't have phone sex right now,' she says very seriously.

'Is that the only thing I call you for?' I'm a little taken aback. When I had picked up the phone to dial her number, the only thing I'd felt was love, but she is branding me a lusty bastard!

'Yes. When was the last time you called me and said something nice?' she whispers into the phone.

'I called to say that *now*!'

'*Of course* you did,' she says sarcastically.

'Oh c'mon! I *really* did.'

'Deb, you don't have to lie. It's okay. I know you love me. Yes, you try to get me naked half the time, but I love you for that too. You are my boyfriend and it's always great to have a boyfriend who gets turned on by a mere touch. Makes life a lot easier.'

'But I do love you!' I protest.

'Yeah, yeah,' she says. 'And yes, I might need to go out tomorrow morning to Mumbai for a couple of weeks. A project is stuck there.'

'What? *Tomorrow*? For *two weeks*? And you tell me now? Tell them you can't go!'

'Just a few days, Deb. Okay, I really need to go,' she says and disconnects the call.

Almost immediately, I find myself in depression. A couple of weeks without sex? I mean, *love*? No Avantika for the next two weeks? That's disastrous! I haven't learnt to be without her. She makes my life possible. This just can't be. She will have fun in Mumbai and I will rot here in Delhi and wait for her?

I am angry and unreasonable. Well, she has work there . . . but whatever. I am not staying here and missing her. This is unfair. I know my senses are overreacting and I know why. I am restless to find everything about the guy. And Avantika is the only thing that has kept me and can keep me from thinking about it. I will go crazy thinking about that mysterious girl, the dead guy, and the burnt diary if Avantika goes away to Mumbai.

23 September 2010

'I don't believe in putting a timeline on love. It will happen when it has to. It doesn't start on a specific date, nor does it end on one. It's eternal.'

It had been five days that I had been waiting for her at the bus stop. Every morning, I woke up at six, took a morning bus to her place and waited for her at the bus stop. I had started to think that it was stupid of me . . . until today. Today was different. I waited. Like every day, I had woken up at six, put my best shirt on, sprinkled cologne all over, and waited at her bus stop from seven. At eight-thirty, I saw her. Her hair was wet and she looked fresh, like a drop of morning dew. As soon as she reached the bus stop, I waved a big 'Hi' and she acknowledged it with a lovely smile. We sat next to each other on the bus. I have stalked her for quite some time now, so I knew she could talk and she didn't disappoint. And once she started talking, she just didn't stop. While she talked, I told myself, 'This is the best sight in the whole wide world.'

She told me about her days in Delhi and how much she missed them. She spoke about everything she likes about her city and everything she hates about mine. I listened. She asked me which school I was from and as soon as I told her that I was from a boarding school, her eyes widened and she begged me to tell her stories about my school. She told me that she has always been very fascinated by elitist boarding schools—Doon, Mayo's, Welham, etc. I wished I could tell her that she was too fragile and too tender to be told stories from my boarding school. I still remember my first day. Mom cried a lot, but Dad was confident that it was the best for me. I had mixed feelings about it. I thought it would be exciting, but I knew I would miss Mom and her home-cooked food.

But soon, everything changed. I was twelve and I was being sexually abused by three older kids in the common bathing area. For about a week, I was constantly teased by those seniors. I didn't bathe all of the next week as I was too scared to go anywhere alone. But one day, I saw them in my dormitory and I panicked. We were alone. The minute they came close to me, I picked a compass from my geometry box and drove it through the hand of one of the boys. I pushed it till it came out from the other side of his hand. The other two boys looked in horror and ran even as their friend lay on the ground, bleeding and writhing for help.

The school authorities got to know about the whole incident and all three of them were expelled the very next day. Mom wanted to take me back home, but I had a newfound confidence. Suddenly, I was famous in my boarding school. I commanded respect. People saw me as a guy who was frail and weak, but could still fight for what was right. I told Mom I would be okay and she wished me luck with tears in her eyes. Dad was proud of me.

It was one of the best days of my schooling life, but I couldn't have told her about it. Instead, I told her about my best friend in school. I used to call him Pappu, to show him down, but he was the champion, his name etched on the achievements board of 2007 as the All-Rounder of the Batch. We were the best of friends—before we drifted apart.

We reached college and I didn't want to lose sight of her. I wanted her to stay right in front of me, to look at me, smile at me and enrapture me with her silly, long tales of how her best friends ditched her, how her heel broke on an important occasion, and so on and so forth. I was so in love with her. We exchanged numbers, and I have been staring at it ever since. I couldn't study the entire day. I was thinking about her during the classes, outside the classes, on my way home and till the time I started writing this. I am in love. It's a strange feeling and I have never been happier.

I wish I could see her tomorrow.

1 October 2010

'Every time her eyes look at me, I am scared that she would see through me. I am scared that eventually I am not a perfect human being and, unlike her, I have flaws.'

It has been days since she gave me her number but I haven't mustered enough courage to call her. She has been busy with her Western Dance practice for the college festival, three hours every day, in the college auditorium. I have watched her dance and she looks the happiest when she's dancing.

Finally, after so many days, I caught her on the bus back home. It's amazing how perfect she looks every day. She looked tired from her dance practice, but that didn't stop her from talking. She asked me if I had a girlfriend and I blushed and shook my head. I didn't take her question too seriously. She couldn't have been interested in me. Or maybe she was. I don't know. I dropped her home and wondered if she had dated before. I was already jealous, even before she could tell me about it.

I wish I could see her tomorrow.

It Gets Interesting!

It's been four hours since I've been in office and I still don't know how to approach it. Ever since Shrey and I had started working together, he has been pestering me to take a vacation. But I've always turned it down as we both can't take leave from the office at the same time.

But when Avantika left this morning, I felt like going on a vacation myself. Not really a vacation, more like an investigative journalism mission sort of thing. It sounds super cool in my head, like what those men in Hollywood movies do. I just have to find out more about this guy.

All I know is the nickname of his best friend and where he did his schooling from. I have to know more. I rub my hands together in excitement and mentally start packing my bags for a road trip. I have been waiting for the right moment. I don't want to sound like I have an agenda in mind. I don't want to sound stupid going on a road trip to trace a dead guy's girlfriend.

Shrey has been busy staring at the screen for quite some time now. He is pretty good at the number-crunching stuff and handles all the accounts for us.

'Shrey, did we make any money last month?' I ask.

'Yes,' he says with a smile on his face. These days, he answers gladly whenever I ask him anything about the sales of our books.

'So, didn't we decide we would go on a vacation when things started to look positive? I mean, I remember you saying that.'

'You asshole! I've been saying that for ages!' he says and looks away from the computer screen. There is a glint in his eyes almost immediately.

'I am not saying that I want to go. I am just saying that this is what we decided,' I say.

'Fuck you, man. Let's *go*! Like *right now*,' he says and sits on his table. It's the kind of reaction I always expect from Shrey. He always overreacts, does something dramatic and immensely cool and then says something about sex.

'Imagine, Deb! You, me, and *loads* of girls! Shitloads of sex,' he says. There comes the sex part.

'I am engaged. And nobody is sleeping with you.'

'I just got laid a week ago. And, for your information, I would have had that girl under my desk if it were not for your stup—' he pauses before letting the word *stupid* slip away. Good for him. 'I mean—Avantika.'

'She was seventeen, Shrey. Grow up. Date your age, man.'

'Grow up? That's what! She had grown up. Didn't I show you the picture? The cleavage one?' He comes near and thrusts his cell phone in my face again.

'You're a pervert.'

'And you're a saint? When was the last time you talked to Avantika with your eyes not on her breasts?'

'Avantika is my girlfriend. I can stare wherever I want to,' I protest.

'Blah. You're one horny bastard yourself and you judge me for who I sleep with? Anyway, that's not the point, Deb. Let's go out. It's been so long! When was the last time we went out like buddies?'

'Umm, three years?'

'More than that. You have been seeing that hot girlfriend of yours for five! And we haven't gone out since. Just you and me,' he says.

'Just *you and me*? Are you wooing me? You do know that I have a dick, don't you?'

'Yeah, I know. A small one, at that.' He smirks.

'Blah.'

'Whatever. Go home and pack. We're leaving in two hours. My car. It's CNG-fitted, so our expense on petrol won't be that much. And think of a place.'

'I will,' I say.

'What's our budget like?' he asks.

'You're the baniya here. You decide.'

He sets us a limit at ten thousand bucks each and extra emergency cash at five thousand per person. I don't get into his calculations. He says—just in case his calculations go wrong, we will come back when we run out of money. He tells me that the rule no. 1 of road trips is: you do everything on a shoestring budget and don't spend a single rupee more than what's required, even if it means sleeping on railway stations. Shrey has done a lot of backpacking around India and abroad, so he knows.

I don't argue with him on things like these. As I said, he does things that sound cool. It comes naturally to him. Not deciding where to go while making a plan, not making a plan at all, risking a long drive on his broken-down car—cool things to do, things you only see people in movies do. Maybe he fakes his coolness. But if he does, he does a damn good job of it.

'So? Two hours? Your place?' he asks.

'Sure,' I say and we shake hands.

'Don't be late or I will screw you over. And you'll be driving then.'

'No way. I am not driving that shitty car of yours.'

'It's not shitty. It's a vintage. You wouldn't understand.' He pulls a face.

'I don't *want* to understand. Bye now. See you then,' I say and leave.

As I drive back home in Avantika's car, I know where we are going—Dehradun. I feel a strange sensation when I hold the diary. I will be tracing the path of a dead man, who told me his story through these pages. I will live his life through these pages. It is exhilarating. Invasion of privacy, yes. But he is dead now! And who cares about privacy anyway? The thought that I will be at all the places where he has been and I will see the things he has written about is thrilling. For the first time in years, something other than Avantika excites me.

I pick up the diary and flip through the pages again. I realize that by now I know exactly what's written where. For one last time, I try to find something that would lead me directly to the girl, or the dead guy, but I'm sure there is nothing.

I pack some essentials and a few toiletries in my laptop bag and leave my place. Over the years, I have learnt that taking too many clothes on a road trip doesn't help. It's better to buy 'I Love India' T-shirts along the way. Plus, with Shrey in the picture, you never know where you'll end up, so it's better to leave all your expensive clothes behind.

When I walk out of my apartment, I find Shrey already waiting for me in his death-trap car, which he'd bought six months back. I had tried to dissuade him from buying the piece of scrap that he calls a car, but he didn't listen. It's a 1989 Jeep with worn-out door knobs and a creaky suspension. He has spent a fortune trying to restore the car, a fortune he could have invested in a really nice sedan. Somehow, he doesn't give a shit.

I envy people who don't think about what others think. Caring about what others think is the biggest jail one can put oneself in. Shrey has never cared; he is smiling in that rotten cage of metal, like he has already planned things that would eventually land us in trouble. I see no baggage and he smells of cheap deodorant. This is going to be a *long* trip.

'So? Where to?' he asks.

I pretend to think for a little while and say, 'Umm . . . err . . . Dehradun?'

'Dehradun it is!' he says, puts the car into gear. The car stutters to a start, clouds of black smoke splutter out of the rust-eaten exhaust pipe and we are off! He doesn't even ask why I chose Dehradun. I don't mind that too. I wouldn't have had an answer and I don't want to sound crazy. Sometimes, I am just scared how little Shrey cares about things. Not a single second thought before doing anything at all. I always feel a little old and docile in his presence. Like someone who has already lived the best days of his life.

An hour passes by and he still doesn't ask why I picked the place. Maybe he bought that I'd picked a place at random. As we leave the city behind and reach the outskirts of Delhi, a sense of calm prevails. It feels great to be away from the hustle and bustle of the city and driving in the pleasant breeze. Now I get why people go on vacations.

Within an hour of leaving work behind, I already feel rejuvenated. I am sure Shrey feels the same because he has been looking at me from time to time and smiling. Either that or he has arranged for hookers/strippers at Dehradun. We make our first stop after driving continuously for three hours. I still haven't touched the steering wheel and I don't want to. I just don't trust his car. It looks like a contraption to kill people really slowly and painfully.

'Crazy, huh?' he says as he orders mammoth quantities of food for himself.

'What?'

'This trip. Finally, you have managed to come out of your girlfriend's lap and into the real world.'

'Fuck you.'

We share a muted laugh. It's like we are back to our college days. Only that our topics of discussion in college used to hover around boobs and porn, while just yesterday I found myself discussing the Indian foreign policy with him. Growing up is a painful process.

Anyway, I order conservatively from the extensive menu of dals, chicken and rotis. There are still five hours of driving left and I don't think I would get a decent washroom for miles. But, obviously, Shrey doesn't mind. He can go with a bottle into an open field and do the needful. I feel like a woman—clean and organized—after living with a girl for the past several years. Girlfriends tend to slowly turn you into a woman. You find yourself using moisturizer and lip balm after a few days. Shrey, on the other hand, is very unkempt, and almost lives like a prehistoric caveman.

'Avantika is the reason for the vacation, isn't it?' he asks.

'Are you crazy? Well . . . Okay, just a little bit,' I say and look at the car parked at a distance. My bag is still there. I feel a little insecure. There are no locks on his car and I don't want to lose the diary.

'You're paranoid, Deb. Can't you live just one day without her?'

'It's not that,' I say and stuff a slice of carrot in my mouth to end the conversation. Shrey makes it sound very gay to be in love with someone. Maybe because he never found what I did with Avantika.

I try not to eat much, but the food is so delectable that I end up eating a lot. My stomach growls as we walk back to the car. The sun is about to set and the roads are getting deserted. A few taxis and a few trucks here and there. I'm a little worried as his car makes threatening noises every once in a while. Sometime later, I doze off.

⌒

'Get up!' Shrey barks into my ear and I get up startled.

'Huh?'

'We have reached,' he says.

'Already?' I ask. It doesn't look like I've been sleeping for long. I look at my watch and notice that it's been four hours since we left Delhi. The drive is six hours long, but with Shrey's car we had put our estimate at ten hours. I look around. It's a deserted place with just one stand-alone motel. *Hookers?* In the middle of nowhere? I am exasperated and Shrey reads my face.

'No, the car broke down,' he says, his face smeared in grease and oil. Obviously. The car broke down.

'Shit. Now what?' I say. I am not shocked. I had prepared myself for it. I just hope it blows up after we leave and we have to hire a new car.

Shrey tells me that he has talked to the motel owner and he'll arrange for a mechanic early next morning. And for the night we'll have to stay there. I make a face but I'm not bothered. I desperately need a bed to crash into.

'Tomorrow, 8 a.m.,' the old man at the reception says and hands over the keys. We go up the rickety stairs of the old motel and reach our room. Everything is falling apart—the stairs, the doors, the walls. It's a motel where truck drivers spend their nights and hence it's at a bare minimum.

We enter the room. It stinks of sweat and alcohol. I don't mind, though. I am too tired to care. Soon, we are both snoring in that filthy room. In the middle of the night, my slumber is broken by the sound of a few steps outside our door. The sound becomes fainter but I can't sleep any more. I have had too much sleep already. I get up, walk around the room and I realize that I have gotten used to the stink and the filth.

I call up Avantika.

'Reached?' I ask.

'Just now,' she says.

'Where are you staying?'

'They have put us up in the Taj,' she says.

'Aha! Big corporate hot shot, eh!'

'Just a generous client,' she says. 'Where are you? Reached Dehradun?'

'Not yet. Shrey's car broke down, so we are staying in a very filthy motel for the night. Umm . . . I miss you. I wish you were here. It would have been fun.'

'Eeks! In that filthy motel?' she says.

'*Haan haan!*'

'Kidding, Deb. I would've loved to be there!' she says. 'Next time, it's just you and me? What say?'

'How can I ever say no to that?'

She giggles on the other side of the phone. I'm sure she's tired so I ask her to go to sleep and disconnect the call. It's been quite some time that Avantika and I have gone out together. The last time we went anywhere was Goa and man, was it awesome! Three days of a heady concoction of alcohol, love and lust! Incredible, legendary stuff.

I look out from the window, reminisce about all the good times I have had with Avantika and think about whatever is going to come. I have a smile on my face. Being loved and wanted is the most amazing feeling in the world . . . it's like a whole new experience. No matter how far we try to run away from it, it only gets you closer. As they say, it's better to have loved and lost than not have loved at all.

Even today, if Avantika walks out on me for some reason, I would only smile for whatever she has made me feel over the years . . . in my heart and a little below, in my pants. Yes, I always add an unnecessary sexual comment after my love-sapped talk. It makes me feel manly and non-gay.

It's been three hours and Shrey is still sleeping. I run out of things to do to prevent myself from getting bored. Shrey and I had decided that we wouldn't bring laptops along, so I have nothing to do. I can't wait to reach Dehradun. I pick up the diary. I read it for the fifth time, cover to cover. *This would make a great story*, I tell myself and go back to sleep.

The sun is out and we're back on the road. This time, I am driving and it's a torture to drive that car up the rugged slopes of the hills. The only consolation is the weather, which keeps getting cooler and nicer. How much one misses the love of his or her life is directly proportional to how good the weather is! Obviously, I miss Avantika a lot right now!

'So what do we see here?' Shrey says as we enter Dehradun.

'A few boarding schools,' I say.

He looks at me with terror in his eyes and asks, 'Why? Why would we visit *schools*? We have been there and it wasn't fun.'

'I have always wondered what boarding schools are like.'

'What do you mean "what boarding schools are like"? They are boarding schools, man. Buildings, dormitories and classrooms. Why do you want to see them?' Shrey asks.

'Just like that.'

'I am not fucking doing that.'

'I never asked,' I say and negotiate a steep hairpin bend on the rocky road. *Imperial Academy, Dehradun*. That's the reason. I can't tell him that, though.

A little later, we enter the beautiful city of Dehradun. We check into a small, cheap hotel and Shrey says he needs to rest for a while. I am sure he has something else on his mind—girls, hookers, something.

But I don't have a minute to waste. I wash my face, change into fresh clothes and hire a local taxi to take me to Imperial Academy. I can barely keep my excitement hidden. The city with its narrow, winding lanes and fantastic views is breathtaking, but I have other things on my mind. For now, I just make a mental note that I have to come to this beautiful place again.

Half an hour later, I reach Imperial Academy, the biggest boarding school in Dehradun. A fake story to the guards and I am allowed to enter. My heart rate kicks up as I move beyond the humungous gates that I had seen previously on the Internet. I walk around the campus. It is huge. Lush gardens, huge buildings and big classrooms. It is nothing like the school I had gone to.

The winter holidays have started, so the place is nearly deserted. There is no one around to ask where the lists and the felicitation boards are. All the rooms and buildings are locked. I ask the sweeper who is mopping the already clean floors and he tells me that the administration staff will be there in another half an hour. I pick a spot beneath a huge tree and take out the diary from the bag. I check it again. It clearly says that RD (the dead guy) was proud that Pappu got the best all-rounder award in the year 2007. I just need to find that out and all will be solved.

I flip through the pages and every time I do that, it's like a whole movie playing before my eyes. I have no idea what the characters look like, but I have given them faces in my head. A little later, I find a few people loitering around the corridors and opening locks. I close the diary and walk about the school campus, looking for the reception.

A few teachers pass by me and I wonder if someone knows this nameless guy from the diary. I walk around the corridors and enter the great hall where all the student photographs are hung year-wise. I look around for felicitation boards that the dead guy wrote about. There are none. I become restless and look for somebody who can tell me. I leave the room and go into the next one. *Bingo!* In front of me, there are about twenty huge, dark-brown boards with hundreds of names painted in white.

I check the years. 2002 . . . 2003 . . . 2004 . . . 2005 . . . 2006 . . . 2007 . . .

There are twenty names on each board, honouring the students for different accomplishments—Toppers, Best Dancer, Best Debater, etc. My eyes scan for the All-Rounder of the Batch.

I start reading the names on them and there it is—*Pappu*, or the All-Rounder of the Batch in 2007—*Piyush Makhija*.

I look at it for a little while. The guy who will lead me to Ragini and finish the unfinished story of RD. But I need to know more about Piyush Makhija. I google the name. Nothing conclusive comes out. I look for the administration room. Luckily, there is a woman sitting at the counter.

'Hi,' I say. 'I needed some information on a student.'

'Where are you from?' the woman asks.

'I am from the press,' I say and offer to give her my card. She refuses. This trick always works.

'What information do you need?'

'Telephone number? Or address of a student?'

'Name?' she says and turns to the computer.

'Piyush Makhija, 2007 batch,' I say.

She types in the name and something flashes on the screen. She picks up a pad and writes down an address and a phone number. I take that piece of paper, thank the lady at the counter and leave. As I cross the room with the boards again, I dial the number. It's a landline number. There is an engaged tone and I'm told the number doesn't work. I try again. Same result.

I look at the address. It's a Haridwar address. I've never been to that city. And I'm sure Shrey hasn't either. He is quite an atheist, so his going to a religious town is out of the question. I smile to myself. It seems like we just got the next destination for our road trip.

～

As I move out of the school with an air of victory and fulfilment, I realize that I have quite a few missed calls from Shrey. I get into a taxi and get back to the hotel as fast as I can. But as far as I know him, he would be out looking for cheap alcohol or easy women to hit on. I try my key on the lock, but the door doesn't budge. I try it again and it doesn't work. I wonder if Shrey is inside. I knock. No answer. I knock again. There is no answer again. I shout out, 'SHREY!'

Yet again, there is no answer.

I look into the keyhole. It's blocked and I can't see anything. I hear footsteps inside. First a few, then many. They are hurried and none of them seem to be coming towards the door. I hear some more. There is someone with him. God! No! A hooker in Dehradun? I can't say that it's totally unexpected, coming from Shrey. I knock harder. Finally, I hear footsteps approach the door.

'What the heck were you doing?' I ask as he opens the door and I barge in. He is in his Superman-printed satin boxers.

I look around for a girl. The bed is all ruffled and there are lipstick stains all over the bed sheet. I can't see the girl. There is a green, lacy bra at a corner of the bed. Incredibly sexy lingerie for a prostitute. It seems like if this girl is an escort, then Shrey has spent a lot on her. The door to the bathroom is closed.

'Shrey! Even here? Where did you buy her?'

'Buy? I didn't buy anybody!'

Soon, my questions are answered as the bathroom door opens and I see the girl to whom the lacy lingerie belongs. She is the girl from that night! Tiya—the seventeen-year-old. Damn. The girl who kept me from getting laid that night. Oh, I hate her. Life's short and every opportunity lost to make out with Avantika spells catastrophe. One of the big reasons why I got engaged was to avoid taking Avantika's permission before taking her clothes off. So if a girl spoils one making-out opportunity, she is taking away one reason to be alive from me. It's unpardonable.

'What are you doing here?' I exclaim as I see her. She is wrapped in a white bed sheet. I'm pretty sure she's naked underneath.

'It's my birthday,' she says dispassionately.

'Let her at least get dressed,' Shrey says. The girl gathers her skimpy clothes from around the room and disappears behind the washroom door. I look at Shrey and I just don't know what to say. He looks at me like a pet that has pooped in the living room. He's guilty, but his face says he couldn't help it.

'What the hell, Shrey?'

'In my defence—she turned eighteen last night!' he says.

'But what the fuck is she doing here?'

'She missed me. I told her I was going to Dehradun and she landed here! I didn't know she'd come,' he defends himself.

'You've got to be kidding me,' I say.

'Well, I just told her that I wished she were with me on her birthday. I didn't know she would actually come. I said it without any intention of calling her here. You know how I wanted this trip to be just you and me.'

'Screw you, man. You're such a pervert,' I say.

'Me? I caught you with a picture of Avantika in your cell phone in the office washroom.'

'Firstly, I wasn't doing anything and secondly, even if I was, she is my fiancée. I am allowed that.'

'And Tiya is eighteen. I am allowed what you are,' he says and lights a cigarette.

I sense that there is no point in having that conversation. I sit on the bed and wait for the girl to come out. I am not angry at Shrey any more. Tiya is eighteen; she is allowed to have frenzied hormones and wear lacy lingerie.

We all have been eighteen at some point in our lives. Avantika and I could barely keep our hands off each other for a good part of the first three years. Those were some crazy days. We're not proud of the kinky things we did . . . umm . . . Naah, we are!

Avantika is a lot less horny now. She is more into vegetables. I mean that in a very non-kinky way. Ever since we've moved in together, all she cares about is where she can find the best vegetables and get me fatter.

Finally, Tiya comes out. I have to admit that in my head I forgive Shrey. Tiya is too young to be this hot. She is in an off-shoulder top and a pair of stockings and she looks stunning. She goes and sits where Shrey is. Shrey passes on the cigarette to her and she takes a long puff. Crazed hormones and sky-high confidence is a very heady mixture.

'I'm eighteen,' she clarifies before I can say anything.

'And your parents know where you are?'

'Stop being such a grandfather, Deb,' Shrey interrupts.

'Did your parents know everything about Avantika from the start? Your night outs? Your wild sexual escapades?' she asks me with an evil grin on her face.

I look at Shrey and he says, 'I told her everything.'

'Whatever.'

I have nothing to say. I see the two of them kiss and I miss Avantika. She is definitely hotter. And a better kisser too. Huh.

'By the way, Happy Birthday Tiya,' I say.

'Birthday? Whose birthday? Ohh! That was just a way to make Shrey miss me.'

'*What?*' we echo.

'Nah, just kidding. It is my birthday. So, thank you.' She smiles at me. Tiya is a little too cocky for my taste and her age. Shrey and Tiya kiss again and I begin to feel a little uncomfortable. There is no space for a girl on our road trip. This is just wrong. I tell them that I have a long phone call to make and I leave the room. I see the door close behind me. Shrey is going to make out and that makes me jealous.

'Hey, what's up?' I call up Avantika and ask.

'Nothing much. You tell me. You're on a road trip, not me. Missing me much?'

'A lot.'

'Aha. Shrey isn't interesting enough?' she teases.

'He is busy making out,' I say. 'Tiya,' I add after a pause.

'*What?*'

'It's her birthday today. She turned eighteen and came over.'

'But! I thought they don't talk,' Avantika says.

'Seems like they do,' I say.

Avantika sounds pissed off. She hangs up to call Shrey, who doesn't pick up. Avantika calls me back and tells me that Shrey is an asshole and I should tell him that. She tells me that I'm responsible for it too and disconnects the call in anger. It's not my fault, but I still send her a text saying I am sorry and I will try to be better.

I again have nothing to do. I don't know how long Shrey would keep on with that kid in the room. I walk the streets of Dehradun, clutching the diary of the dead man. I finally have a lead, and I feel good about it. Who knows? Maybe I'm just a phone call away from getting to Ragini and well . . .

5 October 2010

'If there is one truth that could make the person you love never talk to you again, would you tell him or her? I would rather not.'

This time every year, I am haunted. I feel like a monster today. I don't want to go to college. I would like to keep myself away from her. At least today, I want to be miles away from her.

I am a different person now, but the day still haunts me. I was in ninth grade and things were going good for me. I had always been good in studies, but those days, I had my growth spurt and I was one of the biggest guys in class. I was still seen as the guy who had attacked three seniors and the respect for me was intact. But as I grew taller and stronger, I became a bit of a bully. No one questioned me and what I said had to happen. All teachers were big fans of mine and used to disregard any complaints against me because I scored well.

Slowly and steadily, all the arrogance turned into anger. I used to be furious all the time and made quite a few enemies. I was used to being alone and enraged. The summer of that year, I went back home for my vacations. My parents noted a change in me, but as it always happens, if you're scoring well, no one cares. They gave me their old car to drive around during the vacations. I met all my old friends and, needless to say, they were all impressed. I was taller, smarter, lived in boarding school and drove a car. That day we were all at a friend's place and he had bought an entire bottle of vodka. None of us had tasted it before.

I, being the man amongst them, took the initiative and gulped down the contents of my glass. It was terrible, but I didn't let it show. A little later, a few of them started puking and we had to stop drinking.

I left his place because Mom kept calling incessantly and wanted me to come home as soon as possible. As I put the car into gear, I could feel that something wrong was going to happen, even though my house was barely a five-minute-drive away. The images had blurred. The road looked like a wavy black river. As I drove, a truck kept honking and flashing its lights behind me. The horn was irritating and I decided not to let him pass. Seconds later, the truck and I were racing, and trying to leave each other behind.

A few kilometres down the road, there was a blind turn. Both of us had slammed on our brakes and turned sharply. I had noticed that there was a man at a distance standing in the middle of the road. He would jump out to safety, I had assumed. Three seconds later, the man had frozen in front of our headlights. He didn't know what to do. I didn't want to stop and be defeated. I pushed the pedal all the way down and whizzed ahead of the truck. Seeing me come faster at him, the man jumped out of my way and right in front of the truck. The truck driver didn't want to be beaten either. The man was crushed under the wheels of the truck.

I looked in the rear-view mirror. The truck had stopped. The driver got off the truck. He looked around, panicked, held his head in despair, got back into his truck, and drove away in a mad frenzy. I drove back home. I didn't even go and see if the man was dead. I was scared. I was fifteen. I had killed a man . . . I was a monster. I thought no one saw me that day. I was wrong.

God saw everything that had happened and punished me in equal measure when I first met Nivedita, a few months after that day. What happened to her is totally my fault. Ragini will never know this. I will never tell her. She is a gentle soul and I don't think she will ever talk to me if I tell her this.

I wish I can see her tomorrow. I wish she doesn't see the monster in me.

17 October 2010

'It's amazing how promises like "I will be there" are made and broken in a matter of days. For me, though, promises are meant to last forever.'

I have not dated in a very long time. Unless I am in love, I see no point in dating. I am not dating Ragini, but I am certainly in love with her. We had gone out today. For the first time we had met somewhere outside college. She asked me if I drink and if I had ever tried it. I shook my head and told her that she shouldn't try it either.

I have never tried a drink since that day. No matter what happens, I stay away from it. But Ragini wanted to try it today and I shot it down. Seeing her face droop made me regret that day even more. There is no such thing as drinking responsibly. The moment the first drop of alcohol enters your bloodstream . . . I have seen what can happen, and I will never be a part of that again.

Ragini's fascination with my days in boarding school has not died down and she asked about my schooldays even more today. I told her about Pappu and our days in the football team. Ragini asked who was a better player and I said Pappu. He was way better than me, but since I was the more aggressive one, I was made the team captain. Though we always won matches because of him.

I can't really say when we drifted apart. I guess he had problems with me being chosen as the captain. And I used to be a little jealous that he always scored well. Also, he was the better-looking guy, scored better marks and was everyone's hero. He was revered in our school and by the girls from the boarding schools nearby whereas I was just an angry bully who was somehow good academically.

Ragini asked me to call Pappu and mend things with him. But it has been five years now and we haven't talked. And I don't think we would. I can't call him. He must have even forgotten me. But I have not. I don't know why I am talking about all this. I should concentrate on better things. Ragini. I love the way she rests her chin on her knuckles and hears me talk.

I wish I could see her tomorrow.

We're Not Taking Her!

O ur argument regarding Tiya reaches a crescendo and we are almost at each other's throats. We're shouting outside our hotel and a lot of people are staring at us.

'Are you crazy?' I say out aloud. Shrey makes a face and pulls me away from his car. 'She is not coming with us, Shrey. This isn't happening.'

'But why not?'

'She is a *girl*. She can't go on a road trip. It's not safe. Plus, we stay at really dirty places.'

'She would be more comfortable in a filthy room than you. Stop being so sexist. And I really want her to tag along. She's special,' Shrey counters.

'She is seventeen.'

'Eighteen. And how does that matter? I really like her. This could be something new and meaningful.'

'You always say that, Shrey. Three weeks later, it's all history. All that will remain will be a few naked pictures of her. I am not ruining our trip because of her,' I say.

'This time it's different. I am telling you. Just trust me,' he insists.

'Doesn't she have to go home?'

'She told her parents that she's going to BITS, Pilani, for their cultural festival for seven days. But I don't think she'll be with us for more than a couple of days,' he says and I know he's lying. He thinks he is very convincing but he smiles a little every time he thinks I am buying whatever he says.

'Fine.'

Fifteen minutes later, I already regret my decision. I am driving his shitty car while he's making out in the back seat. Why do I even listen to him? I know why—because he leaves me no other choice. *Asshole.* I stop by at a restaurant to grab something to eat. I am hungry as hell.

'Where are we going next?' Shrey asks.

'I don't know,' I say. 'Are you sure you're done with Dehradun?'

'I have seen enough. I hate this place. So many fucking schools. This is where childhood is murdered!'

He has hardly seen anything. As I sit there and eat, Shrey and Tiya leave the table and click some pictures. Tiya is an amateur photographer and has one of those huge cameras with big white-and-black-striped lenses attached to it. She looks a little hot in her fitted tee, hot pants and the big camera hanging on to one side. I am still irritated with her presence. She shouldn't be here.

I don't feel like eating much. I take out the diary and I know it's the only thing that can get my mood right. I keep the slip of paper with the Haridwar address inside the diary. I clasp it and my heart is thumping loudly enough to be heard by people around me. I read the name on the slip again—Piyush Makhija, the best friend from school—and wonder what he would say about the dead guy. How would he react?

'I think we should go to Haridwar,' I tell them.

'Haridwar?' Shrey asks, a little shocked.

'Yes,' I say.

'Are you sure? You do know that it's only temples, flowers and diyas there, don't you?'

'I know that. I just want to see what the city is like. I've heard a lot about it and it's just an hour from here,' I say.

'What do you think, Tiya?' Shrey asks and looks at Tiya. Tiya looks at him with let's-make-out eyes.

'Anywhere with you,' she says and smiles.

We leave the place and get inside our car.

'I am not driving,' I say.

'Why not?'

'I drive and you guys make out. Not happening, Shrey.'

'Asshole. Fine then, we leave in the evening?' he asks.

We nod. Shrey takes the driving wheel and we leave the restaurant to go around Dehradun and hang out at some notable places. Shrey occasionally slips his hand from the gear on to Tiya's bare legs. He keeps caressing them till the car starts to make strange noises.

A little later, Tiya unties her hair, props her head by the window and puts her long, never-ending legs on Shrey's lap. She closes her eyes and lets her hair blow across her face. Shrey looks at her and smiles lovingly. Maybe this girl really is special to him.

After about twenty minutes, we switch places. I drive for the rest of the day. Shrey and Tiya keep busy clicking pictures of each other throughout. For the first time, I see Shrey posing for pictures without making a face. And I notice that Tiya is a brilliant photographer.

'Are we there?' Shrey asks as I stop the car near a new hotel. He has been busy making out for the last half an hour. We check into two separate rooms and he tells me he needs an hour with Tiya, alone. I don't hang around them much. They've waited all day to reach a room and do something and I can give them one hour.

We decide to leave for Haridwar after that. I check if I still have the address. I come to my room and flop on the bed. I realize how dependent I am on Avantika. The minute I see a couple holding hands, exchanging short, sweet unsaid messages or making out, I can't help but think of her. I miss her so much. I have no idea how long-distance relationships work. What do you do when you miss him or her like nuts? I call her.

'Hey,' I say. 'Where are you?'

'Just got back to the hotel room. I am so exhausted, Deb. I wish I were on a road trip too.'

'Then come! I'm getting bored anyway. Shrey and Tiya keep doing stuff and I feel left out.'

'Aww! That's sweet. But I am going back to Delhi tomorrow. There is some work there so they cut short the Mumbai trip,' she says and I feel sorry for her. I don't like her working so hard.

'Stop working so much. I think it's time for you to retire and never be away from my arms,' I say.

'That's so sweet. Don't make me want to be there. I have so much work.'

'Leave work, Avantika. We need to go out and have fun!'

'You mean we don't have fun now?' she asks.

'We do. But we don't do crazy stuff any more,' I say. I really want her to come and I try to incite her. It's stupid; I know she has better things to do than to accompany her boyfriend on a senseless road trip.

'If it were possible, I would've come. I am leaving for Delhi today. My flight leaves in an hour.'

'Hmmm.' I make a puppy sound, but she doesn't feel pity. I don't blame her.

She is surprised to hear that we are going to Haridwar and even more surprised to hear that it was my idea. She is a little sceptical but doesn't say anything. We talk for a few more minutes and hang up. Usually, how much a couple talks on the phone goes down as the relationship progresses. In our case, it has just increased exponentially. I go to sleep at six and it's ten in the night when I wake up. Shrey and Tiya still haven't left their room and I knock on their door to wake them up.

~

'All set? It's been four hours,' I ask Shrey as he scrambles for his clothes and bags. We check out of the hotel soon after. Since its Shrey's turn to drive, I doze off in the back seat. After a while, I hear the car stutter to a stop.

'Huh?' I wake up. I slept throughout the drive. I am a little surprised to see Tiya in the driving seat. *Isn't she too young to drive?*

'You were driving?' I ask.

'I am eighteen and I have a licence. And it's real. You want to check, *daddy*?' she says and looks for her handbag.

'Okay, whatever,' I say.

Shrey and Tiya laugh. Shrey whispers into her ear, 'I thought I was your daddy.'

Tiya bites his ear. I have to admit I kind of like this girl. She reminds me of the Avantika I've never seen, the Avantika who is now forever lost behind the smoke of hash, the dust of cocaine and the hallucinations of heroin. She still has those tattoos she got made on her lower back and her arms in those delirious, foolish times. She used to do cocaine and ecstasy on a daily basis. Syringes and white powders ruled her life. Many guys, junkies like her, came and went—used her and dumped her. The serious boyfriends—one landed up in jail, the other lost both his legs in an accident—were rich bastards and drug addicts who did nothing to pull Avantika out of her misery.

By the time I met her, she had left all that behind. The short dresses, the mad parties and the heavy make-up she had hid beneath during those years. By then she had joined Spirit of Living and was much better. I still can't figure out what took her so long to come out of it. She is so gorgeous! Why didn't anyone see what she was going through and pull her out of it? Avantika—the quintessential tragic beauty.

Tiya is like her photocopy, only less pretty. I applaud her devil-may-care attitude, but I'm a little scared for her. Avantika survived her reckless phase, but not everyone is as fortunate. We keep on driving and spot a signboard that indicates we are close. Soon, we reach the city of diyas, incense and the sacred river, and Tiya parks the car near a really shitty hotel.

'Here?' I ask.

'Why not?' Tiya says and takes out her bag from the car.

Shrey smiles at me. It really seems like I am the girl and not Tiya. I check my phone. There are thirteen missed calls. *Avantika*. It's a little strange, I think. I call her back, guessing that she must have reached Delhi, but I am in for a shock.

'Hey!' I say as I take my bag out of the car. I ask them to go along, knowing well that they would get down to business as soon as they reach their room, and tell them I will follow later.

'Where the fuck *are* you, Deb? And why don't you pick up your phone?' Avantika says.

'I left my phone . . . I mean I dropped it in the car,' I say. Yes, sometimes my girlfriend, though she is as adorable as a newborn, scares the shit out of me.

'Have you reached? Don't tell me you haven't reached Haridwar yet! It's just a one-hour drive from Dehradun!'

'Yes, we have. But why?' I ask, a little taken aback.

'I am here.'

I blank out. It takes me a few seconds to comprehend what she is saying and then I ask, 'Haridwar? You are *here*? When? *How?*'

'Yes! I wanted to surprise you, but you were just not answering your phone,' she says.

'You have still surprised me! Where are you? How? Weren't you going to Delhi?' I ask as I pace around the car. I am ecstatic.

'I changed my mind. I came here instead and you—'

'But where are you right now?' I ask.

'Hotel Goodwin,' she says. 'But you spoilt it all. I had prepared everything. Hot water tub, candles and everything. Now all that's left is molten wax, cold water and an angry girl, which is me, of course.'

'You're kidding, right?'

'You would have had the time of your life, Mr Debashish Roy,' she says. I can almost see her winking from the other side of the phone.

'Fuck. You can't take all that away from me,' I squeal.

'It's your fault.'

'I'm coming.'

'Whatever,' she says and disconnects the call.

Fuck.

I look for the keys of the car and find them on the dashboard. I rev up the engine and drive through the crowded roads of Haridwar. The city is lit up with candles, diyas, tiny LED lights from China and it looks beautiful. But I am incredibly pissed off. I couldn't possibly have missed it. Damn the phone! I ask around for directions and reach the hotel. It's a big hotel. I call her and she doesn't pick up the phone. It seems like she's having her own sweet revenge now.

'There is someone by the name of Ms Avantika who checked in earlier this evening? Room number?' I ask frantically at the reception.

'F,' the receptionist says and points to the lift lobby.

I rush through the corridors of the hotel, get on the elevator and reach the room. It's safe to say that Batman would have taken longer to reach there—I was *that* quick. The door is unlocked. I take a deep breath and push the door open. I'm more eager and nervous than a newly-wed virgin bride who hasn't even seen porn yet.

There is no light inside. I am panting by the time I reach there. My breath is heavy and my eyes are still getting used to the darkness. I look around and she is nowhere to be seen. The bed is covered with satin sheets—red and white. I see light emanating from below the washroom door. My mind tingles as I construct images in my head. I open the door slowly and the sight is exactly what my mind had conjured up . . . and better!

There is a huge bathtub filled with glittering soap bubbles, lined on all sides by candles of different colours and sizes and the air filled up with intoxicating fragrances. I spot her behind those bubbles with her one leg, wet and smooth, lifted atop the bathtub. The soap hides her but I know what waits behind those shimmering soap bubbles—the succulent bosom of the prettiest girl ever, waiting to be devoured by me. She looks radiant in the glow of the candles around her. Her eyes are smouldering and they invite me, mock me and disarm me. Oh. And disrobe me.

She doesn't say anything. Neither do I. Minutes later, I am with her inside the bathtub, holding her from behind and our lips are in a warm, wet embrace. All that I had imagined, and probably she had too, when I was driving down to her hotel, does *not* come true. We aren't overcome by lust but love.

I just want to hold her close and never let her go. As she kisses me deeper, I can see a few drops of tears run down her cheek. I can feel what she feels. We've never been apart for more than a day at a stretch and it is painful. I am happy to see her and my grasp around her bare waist is not out of my physical desires and needs, but it is to tell her that I would never want to let her go.

We don't make out. Yes, we start, but both of us just keep telling each other how much we missed the other being around. I never thought I would ever be talking to Avantika while she was naked, but I am today.

'It's a shame that I lit these candles, prepared the bath and . . . we didn't even do it,' she says.

As she says it, I realize—and probably she does too—that it is actually an insult to our sex life, and almost instantly, we are all over each other. An hour later, we find ourselves on the bed, naked, wrapped around each other and in those satin sheets. It was good. It was more out of love than lust. The stares lingered for a little longer, the touches were more deliberate, the kisses were more passionate, and the moans were replaced by *I love you*. It was exhilarating. We didn't have sex. We *made love*. There is a distinct difference.

'How much did you miss me?' she asks and puts her hand on my chest. I am still panting. It is challenging to make out with Avantika. I am exhausted. Making out with her is like a pleasurable and dirty version of *Man vs Wild*.

'A lot,' I say.

'Aww! You're the best,' she says and kisses me.

'You're better!'

'I know that,' she says and winks at me. We lie there for quite some time.

'So you cancelled Delhi?' I ask her.

'I had no choice; I missed you. I took the flight to Dehradun and hired a taxi to come here. Strangely, I reached before you could.' She smirks. 'And I wanted to see how much fun you're having on your road trip! Where have you guys put up?'

'Umm, it's a small place. Outskirts of the city,' I say.

'Why don't you come here? You are here for a day or two, right?'

'Yes, but it's a road trip. The ground rule is that you don't spend money unless it's really necessary. This place is really expensive. Plus, we have Tiya with us. She insists on spending her own money and she wouldn't be able to afford this hotel,' I say.

'Then take me to your hotel,' she says.

'Sure,' I say.

We laze around for a little while and she gathers all her stuff. Twelve suitcases! I wonder why though. She looks good in anything she wears.

'Are we going in *this*?' she exclaims as we put her suitcases in the car.

'Shrey insisted.'

We drive away and I text Shrey that Avantika will be joining us. There is no reply from his side and I am too busy staring at Avantika to care. She looks beautiful as the moonlight reflects off her long black hair. As she looks in the distance, I wonder if she is thinking about me. If she is, will she always be thinking about me? Sometimes thoughts like these trouble me. What is a girl like Avantika—who is so perfect in every sense—doing with me? She deserves someone much better. I am an ugly guy who writes and publishes trashy campus novels. She can do much better than that.

'How far is it?' she asks.

'Just there,' I say and point out to the hotel.

'Are you *serious*?' she asks and crooks her nose. She looks adorable doing that.

'Yep.'

We stop at the gate and unload her suitcases. The bell boy of the hotel refuses to pick them up for free. They are huge and heavy. I fish out a hundred-rupee note and he smiles.

'Seriously? This is where we're going to stay?' she asks again.

I nod and ask the manager for a room. The manager informs us that Tiya and Shrey moved into the last room available and that he might allow us to share that room if we pay a little extra. We do so and instruct the hotel guy to take the luggage to Shrey's room. The waiter dumps all the suitcases in front of the room and goes away. He is half-dead and has a broken spine for sure. We knock on the door and Shrey opens it after the third knock.

'Where the f . . . fu . . . fuck were you, man?' Shrey shouts out as he opens the door. 'And Avantika! Welcome to our trip! And our hotel . . . and our room.'

I look at him. He looks strange. I look at Tiya. She looks stranger. *Oh fuck.* They are drunk! Like majorly drunk; they look like they're about to pass out. Their eyes are rolling over and they have silly smiles plastered across their faces.

'Did you drink?' I ask and Tiya waves a bottle from behind. She looks sloshed and her head keeps bobbing from side to side.

'You can't be serious,' Avantika says and enters the room.

I get down to my job—the suitcases. Shrey and Tiya look at me with wide-open eyes as I pick the suitcases one by one and bring them inside the room. 'How many?' Tiya mocks in her drunken state.

'Twelve,' I say as I huff and pant. Still seven to go. My back snaps into two, my body revolts against the weight.

'Actually, it was a long business trip. So, I had to,' Avantika defends herself.

'Long trip? You were there for three days,' Shrey adds and both of them, the drunken fools, laugh.

I want to join in the laughter but I can't laugh at Avantika. She is my baby. Everything she does is forgiven.

'Shut up, Shrey. I was going to be there for two weeks,' Avantika says. 'And *you*! You should be home.'

'I am eighteen. I can run away from home if I want to,' Tiya says and takes a gulp from the vodka bottle.

'It seems fun now, but you're going down the wrong road, trust me,' Avantika says with authority in her voice.

'*Achha?* We will see what happens! You're just jealous that you're not young and fun any more. Twelve suitcases for a three-day trip! Even the three of us combined don't have more than four.'

Avantika looks at the tiny four bags, those that belong to the rest of us, collects herself, and says, 'You're going to puke soon.'

'No, I'm not!' she says and the vodka bottle finds her lips again, this time for a little longer.

'Isn't she super hot?' Shrey says and hugs her. Avantika looks uncomfortable. I think she has taken what Tiya just said seriously. She sits on the bed and I hug her.

'Is something wrong?' I whisper in her ears. She shakes her head unconvincingly, flicks her hair and looks away.

Suddenly, Shrey shouts out, 'OH SHIT!'

We look at him and notice that Tiya is starting to shudder. She has both her hands on her mouth and her eyes are bulging; she is going to puke. Shrey moves away from Tiya and Avantika rushes to her side. She helps Tiya to her feet and walks her to the washroom, while I pray to God that she doesn't puke anywhere outside it. Avantika closes the door behind them. Shrey and I look at each other and exchange a dirty expression. It's disgusting when girls drink and puke. Only guys have the right to be disgusting. We play that part better. Plus, you can no longer kiss a girl once she has puked! Ugh. We hear sounds from inside the washroom and initiate small talk to drown out her coughs and other detestable noises. Tiya automatically becomes a little less hot for me.

'Tiya has some balls, man,' I say.

'Yes, she does. She talks back to Avantika. And no one does that! *Not even her boyfriend.*'

'Very funny. But yes, she is crazy . . . and not in a good way.'

'C'mon, she is so much like Avantika used to be! I still remember your college days. Those insane make-out sessions, the wacky night outs . . . I've always wanted all that. Avantika should have dated me and not an ugly geek like you,' he mocks.

'Who says we don't have insane make-out sessions now?' I say, offended. I don't care if someone calls me ugly, because that's partly true, but I'm very touchy about my sex life.

'Whatever. I love the way Tiya is. The things she does. It's freaky! Yes, she is a little young . . . but that doesn't matter, right?' he says.

'But she *is* mad! She got drunk in fifteen minutes and puked. She doesn't have any freaking sense.'

'Fuck you, Deb. She will learn.'

'Let's see,' I say.

We lie back and wait for the girls to come out. After about half an hour, Tiya stumbles out and we help her on to the bed. She looks half-dead. Avantika tucks her inside a blanket and looks at Shrey with murderous eyes.

'Shrey, are you mad? She is just a kid. And you're encouraging her stupid decisions,' she says.

'I tried to stop her.'

'You did? You just stood there and grinned. I've never seen someone more irresponsible. If you love her, then don't ruin her life. And if you don't, please find someone who is immune to your stupidity. If you have a little sense left, you better start taking care of her or leave her. I don't know if you realize it, but you can and you are destroying her.'

Avantika's outburst shakes us up a little. She gets on the bed and asks the two of us to manage something on the ground. Then she switches off the light. I look at Shrey and curse him. I could be hugging Avantika right now. As I'm going to sleep, my phone rings. It's a text from Avantika.

Am I getting old? Boring?

I reply.

Are you crazy! No! ☺

The phone beeps again.

I wish you could hug me right now. Love you, Deb. ☺

1 November 2010

'What good is intimacy if you don't love the person you are intimate with? I have never understood it and I never will.'

Ragini is slowly taking over my life. She is all over my internet space too. I added her on Google Talk and the little green light, whenever I see it, makes my day. Today, we talked about relationships, even though I wanted to avoid it. I wasn't scared about telling her about my past relationships, I have nothing to hide, but I was scared to know about hers. Anyway, we started to talk and she wanted to know everything about Sumi, my first girlfriend.

She was Pappu's ex-girlfriend. Sumi and I came close when Pappu and I had drifted apart. Pappu was a big flirt and I don't blame him. When you're young and popular, it's hard to stick around in one relationship. I was surprised when one day Pappu, drunk and out of his senses, abused me, and told me that I had snatched his girlfriend away from him. Anyway, Sumi was short, very fair and quite nice. I had really started liking her. We were together for two years and broke up in twelfth grade. She was in St Thomas and the school had really strict rules for twelfth grade students. We didn't get much time to talk and be together. So we split. It was nothing unpleasant. We were friends for long even after the break-up. But we haven't seen each other for long. I think I should call her one of these days.

Ragini was surprised, even chuckled, when I told her that I hadn't kissed Sumi, or any other girl for that matter. She didn't believe me when I told her that I felt physical intimacy is something that should be shared only between two people in love. And I know I love Ragini—not because she is pretty, has beautiful eyes and smells like the first blossom of spring. I love her for the person she is. The way she crinkles her nose when she sees a beggar on the street, how she closes her eyes whenever we cross a holy place, how she listens to whatever I say and acts empathetic . . . there are many reasons to love her and not one to not.

I have never shared anything about my life with anyone.

Somehow, I have always maintained the bully exterior while inside I have been a little boy craving for love and attention. Ragini asks questions and things about me that no one else has ever asked or cared about. Today, she asked me about my parents and why I never talked about them.

My relationship with my parents was not always strained. I had spent a considerable time at boarding school, but the years of separation is not why I am angry; I am angry for Nivedita. Nivedita is my sister. She does not exist for my parents, though she means everything to me. Nivedita was eleven and I had just turned fifteen when she was brought into our house. It was a few months after that man had been crushed to death under the wheels of the speeding truck. I was told that her biological parents, my maternal uncle and aunt, had died in a car crash, and Nivedita had suffered severe brain damage. Her growth had been stunted and she couldn't talk or even walk like us. She was confined to a wheelchair and could only smile. For all practical purposes, she was dead. I had never met her before. They used to live in Dubai. The first time I set eyes on her was at the airport. She was in a wheelchair. She smiled at me and we forged an instant bond.

I used to ask many questions in those days. Why couldn't she talk? Why couldn't she walk? Why does she just stare and smile?

That's all Nivedita did—she smiled. She was virtually dead for everyone, but not for me. I spent that summer sitting by the side of her wheelchair, holding her hand and talking to her. Everyone else thought she had only one smile, but I could count millions of different ones. I knew what each of them meant. I told her everything and her smiles were the only responses that mattered to me. We used to spend hours together and she was the very friend I needed. She was the treasurer of all my secrets and my guiding light.

But a few days after my vacation ended, my parents packed her off to a mental asylum. I did not know about this until two months later. I fought, cried and threatened, but nothing worked. They were not going to get her back. I cried for days on end. Then I stole some money and visited the asylum in Gandhinagar, Gujarat. It took me two days and five buses to reach there. When I first saw her in the mental asylum, her body weak, frail and slumped over the wheelchair, I cried uncontrollably. I asked her to take care of herself and promised her that I would see her every fifteen days, and in return, she smiled as if to tell me that she missed me.

Ever since that day, no matter how busy I am, I go to that place every fifteen days to meet my sister, my only family. My relationship with my parents has not been the same since. I am not sure whether they realize this or not and I don't care. I love my sister and she is all that matters. I wish to shift out of my parents' house and get her out of that place. I don't like her being there alone.

I told Ragini all this and she cried. She said that I was a nice person and that she was lucky to have me as her friend. I saw no sense in that sentence. I was the lucky one, not her. It was four in the morning and she had to sleep, but she said she would try to meet me tomorrow.

I wish I could see her tomorrow.

3 November 2010

'I would never want her to be referred to as my girlfriend, a term too polluted and often abused, because she is much more than that. Why call her anything else when she has a name so beautiful?'

Every day I find myself more in love in with her. Every day that passes by draws me closer to her. Over the last so many days that we have been talking, I have been meaning to ask her what I mean to her, if I do mean anything at all. I want to ask her whether she sees me as a potential boyfriend, but I will not, because I don't believe in the terms 'boyfriend' and 'girlfriend'. These terms are too frivolous and are just used to introduce people. I believe more in the word 'soulmate'. It makes so much sense. When you're in love, it's meant for life, isn't it? If not, then what defines love? A cup of coffee shared together? A drink? A night of merriment and intimacy? I don't think so.

I am not in a hurry to propose to her because that's another thing I don't believe in. I just want to tell her that I love her. If she loves me, it's okay. If she doesn't, I can't force her. I don't know how to put this across to her.

Yesterday, we bunked our classes and went for a quiet lunch, just the two of us. She ditched her zillion other friends for me and it felt nice. Apart from feeling wanted and loved, it tells me that I am important to her. I really don't know where this relationship is heading, but I have a good feeling about it. I don't know what she means when she looks at me and says she's glad she found me, but I know that somewhere in her heart, she feels the way I do. It could be a fool's dream but it makes me happy.

I look at other couples and feel sorry for them. I see the guy whisper in the girl's ear when they enter a movie hall and I know they want to make out during the movie. What I feel for Ragini is very different. I love her. That's the only emotion she evokes. I just want to be with her and hear her talk and listen to me. Everything else is incidental and unnecessary. I don't think a kiss shared between us would in any way be superior to a long conversation between us. Having said that, I don't think I will turn down a kiss either.

She wanted to tell me something today. She said it is serious and I would judge her and leave her. She is silly. The only thing that can make me leave her is she herself.

I wish I could see her tomorrow.

Haridwar

A warm breath grazes my neck, and I hear a soft whisper in my ear: 'Get up.' Avantika looks at me and smiles, her hair falls over my face and she smells of expensive moisturizers and shampoo.

Shrey and Tiya haven't woken up yet. I get up and follow Avantika to the balcony, where she has already ordered tea for us. The tea tastes horrible but the early morning breeze is amazing. We look inside and Shrey has already moved to the bed. He hugs Tiya, who purrs in her sleep, and kisses her on her neck. Avantika looks at them and smiles. I wrap myself around Avantika and hold her close.

'That girl is crazy,' she says.

'I know. I don't know what Shrey is doing with her.'

'Naah, she is a nice girl. She apologized yesterday,' she says.

'She did?'

Avantika nods.

'Deb . . . why Haridwar?'

'Umm, just like that,' I say.

'You can hide it from them, but not from me,' she says, as scepticism drips from her eyes. I try to lie but I've never lied to her. I give up. I knew this was coming and I was wondering last night what's taking her so long.

'Fine, I will tell you.'

We sit down with our legs hanging from the ledge and I start to tell her everything that has happened since the day of the blast. She is partly shocked, partly interested. But mostly, she thinks I have gone mad.

'Why didn't you tell me before, Deb?'

'I didn't want you to think I'm crazy.'

'I think I would have,' she says and smiles. 'Why are you doing this? Are you okay?'

'See? That's why I didn't tell you. You think I'm crazy, don't you?'

'Aww. I don't, Deb. I just want to know why. I can ask that, right?'

'Of course, you can, but I don't know,' I say. 'I just want to know about this guy. I just think it could have been me.'

'Don't say that. Nothing will ever happen to you.'

'But, Avantika . . . I have you. You know what I have for you. You know what my parents mean to me and what Shrey means to me. If tomorrow I am not there any more, you can tell them that. This guy died without telling anyone. Piyush, his girl . . . I could have been him. I could have gone without telling you how much I love you. This story is not yet finished,' I say.

She has tears in her eyes. She doesn't give a shit about the guy in the diary, she cares about me.

'I would've known you love me,' she says and I kiss away a sole teardrop resting on her cheek.

'I know it's crazy but I want to find the girl from the diary and hand this over to her. The guy deserves it, don't you think?' I ask.

'I am coming with you.'

'Don't you have office tomorrow?'

'That can wait. It's been so long since we took a vacation. Maybe this will rejuvenate me. And make me a little younger. Maybe fun too,' she says a little sadly.

'Aw! You will always be sixteen to me.'

She smiles. 'Deb, can I read it? The diary?'

'How can I ever say no to you?' I say and fetch it from my bag.

As soon as I give it to her, I see the small pearls of tears accumulate at the corners of her eyes. I know what she's thinking. The burnt edges of the diary bring vivid and scary images to one's head. The person who possessed it burnt to death and the diary was probably what he was holding in his dying moments. It's a powerful feeling and you can only feel it when it happens to you.

I keep her close as she starts to read the diary. I wrap a blanket around us as it's a little chilly outside. She looks at me intermittently and she can barely keep herself from crying. It's as if her eyes keep asking me the same question—'Is he really dead?' It's amazing how much sympathy *the dead guy* evokes.

Anyway, I like these moments. Traditionally, the guy is supposed to take care of the girl he's in love with. But with Avantika, it doesn't work that way. Avantika has always been a strong woman and never needed my help in doing anything. She is as good with screwdrivers and laptops as she is with her make-up. But in these moments of vulnerability, like the one right now, I feel like a man. I can hold her, hug her and tell her that I will be there and I will make everything all right. I have always waited for times like these when I can make her feel like a little baby who needs to be cared for. Usually it's only me who needs a lot of care.

Avantika and I had prepared for the CAT (Common Admission Test) together—the exam to get into most of the elite management colleges—and I know that she is a fast reader.

She used to be lightning-quick with the English passages we had to read through to answer multiple-choice questions. But she takes her own sweet time reading this diary, stopping and rereading certain sections.

She reads the entire diary, looks at me and says, 'I am coming with you.'

She doesn't say anything else, but her eyes tell me everything. She hugs me tighter and sobs slightly, and we sit there, wrapped within the warm blanket and she dozes off. I hug her tighter, watch her sleep for a little while and doze off too.

꩜

'At least tell us where you are going?' Shrey asks us as Avantika and I step into a taxi to go and meet Piyush.

'Later,' we say and wave at them. Shrey stands there confused and Tiya smiles at us meekly. She has both her hands on her head; her hangover is still pretty much kicking the shit out of her. The taxi drives away from them and Avantika snatches the piece of paper from me.

'Have you called?' she asks, pointing to the piece of paper with Piyush Makhija's name and address.

'The number doesn't work.'

She still calls on that number. Same result. We move through the streets and Avantika waves and asks about the address from anyone she can get hold of. People stare at her for a while, then shake their heads. No one has seen the place. Finally, after going to all the wrong places, we reach the house we're looking for. It's nothing like what we'd imagined.

We stand outside a house, wrecked by weather and time, the walls covered with overgrown algae and stripped of their plaster—the bricks lying almost bare. The address is barely visible. Imperial Academy, Dehradun, is a school for rich kids and this is not what we had expected. The house looks deserted. I point to the address plate. It's the same place for sure.

'Are you sure they still live here?' she asks, almost disappointed.

'Let's see.'

I ring the bell and there is no answer. We wait for a couple of minutes and I ring it again. I look at Avantika and she shakes her head. This can't be a dead end. I am dejected. Just as we're about to leave, we see an old man walking towards us. His clothes are in tatters; time and old age seem to have taken a toll on the man.

'Hi, Uncle. Is Piyush there?' I ask.

'Beta, you are?' he asks.

'We are his friends from school,' Avantika says.

'No, beta. He lives in Bhopal. He works there. Come inside. Have something,' he says and opens the door.

'No, Uncle, thank you. We were in the area so we thought we would meet him,' I say.

'Can we get his number? Or address?' Avantika adds.

'Yes, sure,' says his father and insists on us coming inside. We politely refuse. He goes inside and returns with a card in his hand.

'Here,' he says and hands it over to us.

Avantika takes it from his hand. 'Thank you, Uncle. Umm, does he come here often?'

'We haven't seen him in a year,' he says. 'He is working hard. His mother has not been keeping well. She needs a lot of medical care . . . lung cancer.'

The old man has tears in his eyes. They are of pride and sadness. He has a good son, but a dying wife. Life throws such immense riddles at you. I look at him for one last time and feel lucky about myself. In moments like these, I believe there is God. We smile at the old man and take his leave.

'Show!' I say and snatch the card from Avantika. 'So, are you going to call?'

'Should I?' Avantika asks.

'Why not? Go ahead.'

Avantika calls on the number and there is no answer. The call goes to voicemail and it plays a recorded message.

'Hi. This is Piyush Makhija. I will not be available till the 22nd of September on this number. I'm sorry for the inconvenience. If it's urgent please call on the office landline at 0755-56457332 or else record your message after the beep. I will get back to you as soon as possible. Thank you. Beep.'

We call on the number thrice and it goes to voicemail every time we do that. We call on the office landline number and his colleague tells us he is visiting the power plant site and cell phones don't work in that area. He adds that he'll be back by tomorrow morning.

'What do we do now?' Avantika asks.

'Twenty-second is tomorrow, right? So we stay here today. And we call him tomorrow and ask about Ragini?'

'How long is the drive from here to Bhopal?'

'Wait,' I say and google 'Haridwar to Bhopal' and it says, 919 kilometres. 'It will take approximately thirteen hours to get there.'

'So, we can be there by tomorrow morning?'

'If we leave in a few hours, yes, we can,' I say.

'We can go there then.'

'But we can call him tomorrow too? Why go all the way to meet him?'

'Deb, it's a road trip, right? And there's nothing to do here. Just an overnight drive away. What say?' Avantika suggests.

'Seems like we're going to Bhopal, then,' I say and smile at her. It's hard to turn down her requests. She looks so adorable when she asks for anything.

'Wouldn't Shrey mind?' she asks.

'He wouldn't ask.'

We get back into the taxi. Avantika keeps staring at the address and the phone number for quite some time.

'It's good that we're going there. I wanted to see what he's like,' she says.

'Why would you want to see what he's like?'

'I think I have a little crush on him. He's so sweet.'

'Crush? You read two lines about him, Avantika.'

'I'm kidding! But I'm curious,' she says, smiles and looks away from me. I really don't get her at times. But then again, she is a girl and girls are not meant to be understood, they are meant to be loved. I do that job well enough, I guess.

⌒

We get back to our hotel room. We don't see Tiya and Shrey around. They must have gone out, I think. I haven't shaved for the last four days and Avantika has been complaining.

'Deb?' Avantika asks and enters the washroom as I start to shave.

'Yes?'

'Where are their bags?'

'They aren't here? They must have gone out. The car was still outside.'

'But where are the slippers? Toothbrushes? Everything?'

'Huh?'

Before I can process anything, my phone rings. It's Shrey.

My hands are smeared with shaving foam, so Avantika picks up the phone, holds it near my face and puts it on loudspeaker.

'Hey, Deb! We had to leave, man,' he says, 'We hired a bike and we're going somewhere. Tiya will decide in a while where we're going. I've left the car for the two of you.'

'Going, as in?'

'On a trip of our own.'

'*What the fuck!* Why?' I ask and try to turn the speaker off. But Avantika doesn't let me do that.

'Just like that.'

'Just like that, Shrey? You get Tiya along first. And now you abandon me? This is your idea of a road trip?'

As I say this I can hear Tiya *woo-hoooing* in the back seat of the motorcycle, through the speaker. I don't know why girls do that. Years of pillion-riding behind Shrey and I haven't ever made that eardrum-piercing sound. *Girls!*

'Deb, it's just that Tiya and I wanted to spend some time alone. And with Avantika, umm, she isn't that comfortable.'

I see Avantika's face droop. I try to switch the speaker off again, but Avantika slaps my hand away.

'Comfortable as in?' I ask Shrey.

'Avantika acts like her mom. Tiya is young. And free! She wants to have a little fun, like get drunk and not be told what's right and what's not. Avantika is a little . . . like *us*. Old.'

'Fuck off, man,' I say.

'Whatever, Deb. Anyway, I know you'll have fun. It's you and her alone. What else can you ask for?' he says.

Avantika keeps the phone on the washbasin and walks away.

'Oh yes. Thanks for that! Why didn't I think of that? This should be nice,' I say loudly so that Avantika hears and feels good about it. She doesn't react.

'Bye,' Shrey says.

'BYE, DEB!' Tiya shouts from behind. The call disconnects. *Fuck.* Avantika shouldn't have heard that. She sits on the ledge of the balcony and looks outside. I go and sit next to her. She stands up.

'I will go take a shower,' she says.

'Should I join in—?'

'Don't even think about it,' she says and looks at me with murderous eyes. I take these looks seriously. She walks away. Avantika makes me horny all the time, but she scares me more.

She shuts the washroom door behind her and I sit there imagining her under the shower. I know that's not something I should be thinking about. I should be thinking about damage control. And, c'mon, Avantika is not old. She's just twenty-three! And she is like a little wild cat in bed. How can someone call her *old*? Just because Tiya is younger and crazier doesn't make Avantika old, does it?

I walk into the room and lie down on the bed. I look around to see Avantika's suitcases all around me. Twelve of them. Maybe something has changed. She has grown up a little. I still remember the two days we spent in her old classroom at SRCC. We had just started going out and both of us were big fans of cheap thrills.

She had always wanted to make out in her college classroom. So one day, after class, we had hidden inside the college and got ourselves locked in with a blanket and few packets of chips and water! The next day, the college staff had gone on a strike. So we were locked in her classroom for two days with just a blanket and hardly any food. And lots of love, of course.

So now, seeing these suitcases around me . . . yes, something has changed. She is not the crazy nineteen-year-old any more, but she is not a boring twenty-three-year-old either. I can't keep up with someone like Tiya, so I'm glad Avantika has slowed down as have her crazy instincts. But then, how can Shrey cope with Tiya? Oh crap. Am *I* getting old?

I wait for Avantika to come out of the shower. I lie down and feel like sleeping. Maybe I am getting old. This doesn't sound so good. Avantika comes out of the shower, wet and gorgeous, though her face still wears a dead expression.

'So, we leave for Bhopal, right?' I ask. Despite everything, I still can't shake the diary off my head. I know she's sad and I should say something sweet, but the diary just keeps making me restless and I can't make the journey alone. Bhopal is too long a drive from Haridwar and there's no way I can do that alone.

'Home,' she says.

'Delhi? But why?'

'I have work,' she says and dries her hair.

'But we were going to Bhopal. We have to find this girl. You can't just let it go,' I protest.

'You carry on. I just remembered I have some work to take care of in Delhi.'

'See, if it's about what Shrey—'

'It's not,' she says.

'You know he's an asshole, and—'

'It's *not about what he said*!' she shouts. I don't know what to say. She gets back to drying her hair, still pissed. 'It's not his fault. I am getting old. You should go on this fun trip with Shrey and Tiya. I will go back to Delhi.'

'But, Avantika—'

'Just do what I say,' she says and gives me one of those dead serious looks and I don't have a comeback for it. It's very hard to argue with her. She is breathtakingly beautiful and ruthlessly authoritative. It's impossible to stand up to her.

I watch her dress up and manage her suitcases. I pack my small bag and pretend to be busy. I'm not sure whether she's angry or sad, but whatever it is, I can't do anything about it. I'm ready to leave.

She stands there and puts on her lipstick. Avantika always looks great in formals but I can't tell her that today. Her movements are slow and deliberate. She looks worried. It seems like she has taken Shrey very seriously. I don't know how to set it right. What makes it worse is the fucking diary. I have no idea what I'll do next. I don't know if Shrey and Tiya would want to join me and I certainly can't go back to Delhi. I *have* to go to Bhopal.

'Deb,' Avantika looks at me and says. 'Go to the reception and ask the guy to carry these suitcases to the car.'

'I will take them,' I say and start to pick one of them.

'Deb, leave it. Do as I say. Go, wait in the car. Send the guy up, I will come down in a while,' she says dryly but authoritatively.

I have no choice. I pick up my bag and head downstairs. On the way out, I pay the receptionist and ask the waiter to get the suitcases. My brain is a wreck and I have no idea how to put this trip back on track. Fifteen minutes pass by and there is no sign of the waiter or Avantika. I call her on her cell phone but there is no reply. Is she crying? Is it that big a deal? I stick my eyes on the hotel door and wait for her to come out. I try to construct sentences in my head that I would say to console her and get her to accompany me to Bhopal. I wait endlessly. There is no sign of her. Until . . .

I feel lost. Is this . . . ? *No way!*

A girl walks out of the main door of the hotel who looks like Avantika but starkly different. It takes me time to place the face that is staring back at me, but I now remember clearly—she is the one I have often seen in my dreams, intentionally and sometimes unintentionally.

The girl is in a dirt-grey vest tied above her navel baring her washboard-flat stomach, light-brown hot pants and a big buckled belt. Her long legs, perfectly shaped and toned, glisten in the morning sunlight. There is no sign of any fat on her body. Her stomach, flat and shiny with a perfectly round navel, seems to be made out of granite. The vest accentuates her breasts and the hot pants are such a cruel tease. Her long, black hair is untied and blows in the direction of the wind. There is no make-up on her face, her eyes are hid partially behind yellow-tinted sunglasses and she is smiling wickedly. As she walks closer to me, I feel threatened by her sheer sexiness. Her smouldering eyes never lose eye contact with me, although I mentally strip off her skimpy clothes.

There are very few times when a girl looks better with clothes on than naked and this is one of those moments. She looks stunning. Like a model walking on a ramp. A showstopper in her last show ever. Half her sexiness is in her walk, her flat stomach and her sultry legs, and the other half is in her eyes.

She comes near and steps into the car. She leans back on the passenger seat and rests her long, bare legs on the dashboard. It keeps getting better. I am dazed, fascinated and shocked, all at the same time. I am whirling down an unending pit of mind-boggling hotness. Finally, I find the courage to speak.

'My girlfriend is in the hotel, but I am ready to dump her for you.'

'Do you like me better?'

'I think so, but I love her.'

'You will learn to love me too. Now, stop staring and drive,' says Avantika and puts her shades on her head.

'Your suitcases?' I ask.

'What suitcases?' She winks at me.

And people say that the spark in a relationship dies out after the first few months. Ha!

8 November 2010

'Why should it matter if someone else touched her in the past? Does it hurt because she has been violated and is impure? Or does it hurt because she was in love with someone other than me? For me, it's the latter.'

There must be a bond greater than friendship between us that made Ragini talk about her previous relationships today. Ragini's voice quivered as she told me about the guy, her best friend in school, whom she had loved with all her heart. I asked her if she still had feelings for him and she shook her head. But I knew something was wrong and I insisted. She said I would judge her if she told me everything and I made her believe that I wouldn't.

Ragini was the house captain and the guy was the vice president of the students' council—it was a match made in, well, ninth grade. They held hands, made handmade cards and did their homework together. As years went by and innocence became more of an abusive term than a virtue, intimacy started creeping into their relationship. This was in eleventh grade. In twelfth grade, Ragini got pregnant.

It wasn't until her second month that she got worried and realized that something was wrong. The guy developed cold feet and asked Ragini to 'manage' on her own. Ragini's close friend, Nigel, a handsome boy whom Ragini had always liked, came to her rescue. He had just started college then and was more mature.

Nigel helped Ragini get an abortion. Her eyes had tears as she narrated the incident that could have left anybody emotionally scarred for the rest of their life. I could only imagine what she must have gone through. She was only sixteen—an age where young girls start to have minute little crushes—and she went through an ordeal which could have withered even the sanest of adults.

I told her that she is the bravest girl I have ever met and she smiled at me. Her hand grazed past mine, leaving me short of breath, and then she held it and thanked me. She told me that she had not been able to share this with anybody else. I am sure she tried to imply that I was special to her. She doesn't say it, but I am sure she wants to. Maybe she will do so tomorrow. She had to leave today, so she did, and left me behind, missing her. I am sure we have a connection. Or else why would she share something that she has not shared with anyone else?

I wish I could see her tomorrow.

13 November 2010

'What do you do when the person you love the most loves someone else? Do you stop loving that person? Or do you love that person even more? It's the latter for me.'

Ragini called me yesterday. I wish she hadn't and I wish yesterday didn't exist. I have never been inclined to meet any of Ragini's friends and she had never asked. But when she called me and pestered me to meet a friend of hers, I knew I had competition. The person had to be really special. Even before I met him, I had only contempt in my heart for him.

I saw him, the second special person in Ragini's life, and I was not happy with what I saw. He had tiny fingers, I noticed, but apart from that, he looked like what everyone labels as Boyfriend Material. He stood well over six feet tall, had a sharp jawline and a sinister bad boy smile. He told me he had just graduated and was working with a big bank in Bangalore. He used to be a neighbour of Ragini's in Delhi before he relocated with his parents. He should have been in Bangalore right then, but he said he couldn't and told Ragini—while I stood there and hoped he wouldn't say what I feared he would—that he missed her and couldn't stay away. He told her that he had come just to meet her.

It turned out that Ragini had always been in love with Nigel, she tearfully admitted, and Nigel had broken up with his girlfriend because she couldn't bear Nigel being so close to Ragini. Their teary reunion and confession of love brought tears to my eyes too, though my reasons were a lot different from theirs. But I am not that selfish. I would still love her and be happy for her. It would take a lot more than Nigel to make me not love her. And anyone would say that Ragini and I would make a better couple than Nigel and her. Nigel is too tall for her. And he's Christian . . . What about Ragini's conservative parents?

As they sat in front of me and held hands, shared private jokes and anecdotes from their days in Delhi, I felt jealous.

The only silver lining to the dark cloud was that he left today. He had to rejoin work and he said he would be back soon. I am not looking forward to that. I don't know whether it's my mind playing tricks, but Ragini looked even more beautiful today. Had I been Nigel, I would never have left.

Ragini looked happy and I was happy for her. They were made for each other. They were perfect. They were the best of friends and had seen some tough times together. It's a perfect fairy tale. Nigel loves her too. It's evident in the glint in his eyes and the warmth in his touch. Nigel deserved her. And she deserved him. I was an outsider the day I had started stalking her, and maybe that's how it's going to be.

Ragini asked me to start dating someone too. I tried not to tell her that she was the only one I wanted. As I sit on my bed and write this, I can feel a few tears trickle down my cheek and wet the diary in which I am writing. I plan to be okay tomorrow. We are meeting again. She wants to catch a movie though she is not sure whether she can bunk her class. I wish she does. I don't know if I will be as special to her in the days to come as I am now.

I wish I could see her tomorrow.

Piyush Makhija

It's becoming embarrassing now. I can't take my eyes off my own girlfriend, the girl I've been dating for five years. My jaw had dropped the moment I'd seen her walk out of the hotel door and I have not returned to normal yet. I thank Shrey for it. Avantika and I have been driving for the past six hours and it is the best drive ever. She has mastered the art of seduction. Though, I should add here that my threshold is shamefully low. At times I have gotten seduced seeing her brush her teeth.

But today is *off-the-charts* awesome. Avantika has been slipping her hands in . . . *everywhere*! I liked her anyway but I like the *new* her more. But it's bothering me. She does not have to pretend in front of me. That's not what people in love do, right?

'You really don't have to do this. I think you're still fun and awesome.'

'Why do you think I'm doing this for you?' she says and looks at me.

'I don't know. I mean, Shrey said those things and you—'

'I am doing this for myself,' she says. 'Shrey was right. I have grown up. I shouldn't have. I have been the sane, mature person in our relationship. Maybe it's time to switch places. I will be the stupid, irresponsible one now.'

She winks at me. Her winks are like the lull before the storm. Sometimes it means let's-go-home, other times it means you-are-so-owned . . . and so on. I wonder what it means this time. I have to admit that I'm a little scared. I have seen the 'Tiya part' of Avantika and it's infinite times crazier than anything Tiya does. I don't think I can keep up with that now.

Slowly, the sun turns orange and sets across the horizon. We have taken a million detours and I'm still not confident that we are on the right track. The maps are all awry and the people around are as clueless as we are. But they still try to help us by giving us wrong directions. Silly helpful people.

A little later, we find ourselves on a long road that doesn't seem to have an end and our car is the only one for miles around. Shrey's car can give way any time and I'm sweating just thinking about it. I look at Avantika and her eyes are closed. She is least bothered that there is absolutely nothing in sight. No motel. No dhaba even.

'Do we drive through the night?' I ask.

'Why not? I can drive if you feel tired,' she says and looks at me. She really isn't concerned.

'Are you serious?'

'Yes,' she says. 'Anyway, there's nothing in sight. We don't have an option.'

Contrary to what I'd expected and hoped for, she doesn't panic. Instead, she asks me to switch and takes over the driving wheel. She puts on her iPod earphones and starts to drive along.

Soon, the only light in the pitch-black night are the headlights and the stars above, and the only sound is the rumble of the car's engine. The darkness around us is a little disturbing.

Try driving on a deserted road with the car's headlights off. I can bet it's the most uneasy you would ever feel. We are all used to the *light* around us; *darkness* unsettles us.

Avantika, I am sure, is not thinking about it. I look at her and she is bobbing her head to the music on her iPod. Soon, I am asleep.

I wake up with a start. I look groggily all around and notice that Avantika is still driving.

'Finally!' she says.

'What time is it?' I ask.

'Five.'

'*Five?* And you have been driving?'

'Yes,' she says and smiles. She has driven through the night. Six hours.

'Six hours?'

'Yes.'

I ask her to stop the car and she does. We brush our teeth and wash our faces with a few bottles of mineral water we had picked up on the way. I take over the driver's seat.

The sun is slowly coming out and there are some trucks at a distance. My neck hurts for I had slept awkwardly. Avantika, on the other hand, behaves like it's just another day. Even though she hasn't slept the entire night, and her hair is a mess, she looks amazing. Those svelte legs and her perfectly sculpted body is just what you want to see early in the morning. The warm morning sun pales in comparison. She leans back on her seat.

It's only been fifteen minutes when I see the diary on the dashboard with the bookmarks inside it. It's so distracting. At certain levels, it takes me back to my college life. The screwed-up life and times of the dead guy bring back some strange memories. I drive on.

Avantika has dozed off and my mind wanders to the times I've spent with her. I see many couples around and I don't know how much they love each other, but I know for sure that our love is *way better*. She completes me. No matter where I go, what I do, she is always on my mind. Anything I do or strive for is meaningless if I don't have Avantika by my side. Cheesy as it may sound, life without her is meaningless.

I know I'm not the best-looking or the smartest guy Avantika can get, but one thing I know for sure, she won't ever get someone who loves her more than I do.

Three hours more of driving through empty, wide roads brings us to Bhopal. The city is still sleeping when we get there. We cross a few mosques, a huge lake and a couple of parks. But I know we wouldn't be doing much of sightseeing on this trip.

I stop outside a small hotel, ask the receptionist for the rates, negotiate a little and finalize it. Avantika is still fast asleep. I pick her up in my arms and carry her to the hotel room. Apart from the fact that I just love watching her sleep, I think carrying her in my arms is an incredibly romantic thing to do. I am sure it's something she will brag about to her girlfriends.

I tuck her inside the blanket and lie down right next to her. Almost immediately, I fall asleep. It's nearly noon when I wake up. Avantika is already up and around. She has a cup of coffee in her hand. She is looking out of the window and looks enchanting.

'When did you wake up?' I ask her.

She looks at me lovingly, comes near me and sits on my lap. 'It's been a couple of hours.'

'Why didn't you wake me up?'

'You look cute when you're sleeping,' she says.

Aha! That's exactly what I think about her.

'Thank you.' I blush. It's been years but still I turn into a red tomato every time she says something nice about me.

'Aww! Look at you.'

'What?' I say.

'You're blushing, Deb.'

'No, I'm not. I am a guy. I don't blush.'

'*Achha?* I thought it was cute. Anyway, if you say you weren't blushing . . .'

'No! I was.'

We both laugh aloud.

'Oye, I was waiting for you to get up. Let's go meet him. I can't wait,' she says and I nod. I can see the diary in her hand. Obviously, she's been reading it again. Suddenly, her face droops and she looks away.

'What?'

'We need to meet Nivedita too,' she says. I nod again.

~

I can see that Avantika is more curious than I am about meeting Piyush. We stand outside the office Piyush works in, holding his business card. We are about to know the name of the guy whose initials are etched on the diary. Needless to say, I am freaking excited.

It's a smallish office, and I see the designation—'Design Engineer'—on the card. I hope he isn't busy and gives us time. After all, we have some bad news to give him. His best friend from school is dead. That's got to mean something, right?

I follow Avantika into the premises. She always takes the

initiative for all the things that require extreme confidence and I usually just hide behind her.

'Hi, I want to meet Mr Piyush Makhija,' she says. 'I've come from his hometown. His father sent us.'

The receptionist looks up at Avantika, dials Piyush's extension number, and lets him know. She asks us to wait in the adjacent room. I wonder if Avantika is thinking what I am thinking—what will we say to him?

A little later, a guy dressed in a crisp, white shirt and a well-ironed pair of trousers walks into the room. He has a slight paunch, but his bright, fair face distracts me from it. He looks intelligent and hard-working in his rimless spectacles and cropped hair. So, this is what hot guys from school grow up to be?

I don't know, because as a kid, I was the fat, ugly one, who used to be ridiculed all the time. I was a favourite for all the bullies in school, and used to spend days crying on the last bench.

He gives us a confused look but puts his hand forward.

'Hi, I'm Avantika,' she shakes his hand. 'And this is Deb.'

'Where are you from?' he asks. He looks confused.

'Your dad gave us your number and address,' Avantika says. 'Actually, we wanted to know something from you.'

'Yes?'

'We found a diary,' she says and pauses dramatically. 'It's of a friend of yours from school. We wanted to know something about him.'

'Diary? I don't get it,' he says. The look on his face tells us that he thinks we're two crazy people.

'Did you hear about the Chandni Chowk blast?'

'Oh yes, I did. What about it?'

'A friend of yours died in the blast. Deb survived and found this diary.'

'My friend? Who? I don't—'

She hands over the diary to him. He looks at the diary, looks at us, and then flips over to the first page. He runs his hand over the initials and doesn't look up. He has recognized the initials and the person to whom this diary belonged. He flips through the pages and his eyes tear up. He keeps turning the pages over without reading, and feels the burnt edges of the pages. We hear him sigh. The death of a best friend can take some time to sink in. After quite a while, with tears in his eyes, he looks up and says, 'Are you sure?' We nod.

'Can you tell us his name?' Avantika asks.

'Ritam Dey,' he says softly.

RD.

He pauses for a little while and asks how we got to him and we tell him everything. We show him the sentence in the diary that led us to him. He hands the diary back to us. We look at him with expectant eyes, hoping he could lead us to Ragini or Nivedita.

'Don't you want to read it?' Avantika asks.

'Had he wanted me to read it, he would've told me. And we didn't end on a good note. So, I should probably not be reading this.'

'What can you tell us about him?' I ask.

He starts, 'We first met at the boarding school right after that incident with the guys . . .'

He continues and tells us that Ritam was from Mumbai and that's where he lived before coming to the boarding school. Piyush tells us that Ritam was an aggressive football player and that's why he was drawn to him. Together, they made the most lethal forward attack that Dehradun school football had ever witnessed.

'We made a great team on the football field. In the three

years in which we played together, I don't think we lost a single match. We were unbeatable. I can't believe he's dead . . .' His voice trails off.

'We are sorry,' Avantika says.

'He was a nice guy.'

He tells us more about how they first met, grew and bonded as friends. Piyush's voice trails off in the middle a few times as the news of the death of his best buddy from school sinks in slowly. He is in tears. I know how he feels. When I first saw Piyush, I had replaced his face with mine and imagined Shrey being dead. My heart shrank to the size of a peanut and I could barely keep my tears in. Yeah, I'm sensitive. Just that I don't cry during movies.

'He really missed you,' Avantika says.

'It's in the diary,' I say. 'He thought you ignored him.'

'Why would I?' Piyush asks.

'You were popular, a better player, better in studies and had a pretty girlfriend. He thought you forgot him in all that.'

He takes a deep breath and sighs. 'Sumi liked him,' he says. There is a hint of nostalgia and a little flavour of first love, and the first heartbreak, in his tone.

'Sumi liked him? He thought she came to him because you had started ignoring her!' Avantika says.

'No, it wasn't that. Even when Sumi and I were together, Sumi liked him better. But Ritam was always a bully and Sumi was scared of him.'

'So? What happened?' I ask.

'She said she was falling out of love with me. She wanted me to talk to Ritam about her since we were the best of friends. I still loved Sumi so I didn't want to do that. I was too arrogant to hear that my girlfriend liked someone else. Worse still, my *best friend*! I told her that Ritam and I didn't get along well. I stopped talking to Ritam to make her believe that. But she just didn't stop talking about him. So, I started talking to other girls to make her jealous, but it didn't work. One day, she left me and went to him . . .'

His voice trails off again.

'And?'

'She never came back and I lost both of them,' he says and looks at the diary. It looks like he wants to read it.

'He wrote in the diary that he is sorry that he envied you and stopped talking to you. He missed you,' Avantika says.

'I missed him too, but more than that, I was angry at him for dating my ex-girlfriend. I know it wasn't his fault. We were best friends and I stopped talking to him. I shouldn't have done that.' A lone tear rolls down his cheek. I like him instantly. Tears usually don't lie. They are the most honest form of expression. He continues to tell us fondly about their football victories. Piyush talks for long and speaks very lovingly about his friend.

'It was very hard to understand Ritam at times,' he says. 'Sometimes, he used to act all angry and rough. But on other occasions, he used to seem like a very docile guy. It was amusing.'

'Do you have a picture?' Avantika asks.

'Not right now. But I might have one at home.'

Damn. Digital cameras—a few years too late.

'So, you weren't in touch with him after school at all?' I ask.

'No,' he says. 'I went to Rourkela for my graduation and got busy. My mother was not keeping well, so I had to take care of that too. Everything else took a back seat. There have been times that I have looked for him on social networking sites, but have never found him.'

While we are talking, the receptionist enters for the third time. The first two times she had said that there was something important from Piyush's boss. This time it looks urgent and something that can't wait.

'I really have to go. How long are you two in Bhopal?'

'We are leaving tonight,' I say.

'Oh, okay,' he says.

'We will let you know if we stay for longer. We would love to hear more about him,' I say.

'So, whom are you meeting next?' he asks.

'We wanted you to tell us that,' Avantika says. 'Do you know he had a sister?'

'Yes, I do. I don't remember the name . . . Umm . . . Oh wait—Nivedita, right?'

'Do you know where she is?' I ask.

'I'm not sure. I've never met her,' he says.

'Did you know she is crippled?'

'What?' Piyush takes a little time to comprehend what Avantika had just said.

'You didn't know?' Avantika asks.

'He had once asked me for money because he wanted to see her in Gandhinagar. I thought he was lying and I refused. We had a huge fight that day. I didn't know—'

He looks like he regrets it. Until just a moment ago, he still thought that Ritam had been lying about the crippled sister. He feels sorry and it shows on his face.

He looks at us and asks, 'Can you make me copies of the diary? Of the parts I am in?'

'Sure. We will leave it at the reception.'

'Thank you,' he says feebly.

Before he leaves, Avantika asks him if he knows where Sumi is or what her full name is.

'Sumi Das,' he says. 'I have no idea where she is . . . Sumi and

Ritam were my only good friends in my schooldays. If you meet Sumi, please tell her that I really cared about her.'

Just as he is about to leave, Avantika asks him—just out of curiosity—what Ritam looked like. It is awkward for him to describe another guy at first, but then he tells us that Ritam stood at about five-ten, was strongly built—hardened from football practice, I presume—and had a sharp jawline on which he was often complimented. He hugs us both and leaves the room. Avantika and I look at each other, feel sorry for Piyush, and ask the receptionist to make copies of the first few pages of the diary.

'Mumbai?' I ask Avantika.

'Gandhinagar first,' she says.

'And we don't have to call him the dead guy any more.'

'Yes. Ritam sounds much better.'

Nivedita.

Avantika has a heart as big as anyone you can imagine. Her office project is lagging behind and she is getting a little restless with the road trip. She has to get back to office, but I know she wouldn't do that before she meets Nivedita. I can tell that she really wants to meet her. Gandhinagar—another thirteen-hour drive stares us in the face. I wish we could've taken buses like Ritam did every fifteen days to meet his crippled sister. But, instead, we have Shrey's creaky, rotten car.

15 November 2010

'When you know that your happiness is like a sacrificial lamb for the happiness of the person you care about, you should realize that you're in love. The most incurable form of love.'

Ragini has been a little sad since the past few days. I knew the reason but I insisted she tell me and she did. It was not something I enjoyed doing but I found my bits of happiness in my own small way. I imagined her talking about me the way she talked about Nigel. How lucky I would be if I could make her eyes sparkle the way Nigel did. I wanted to be the guy she loved, but life had other plans.

The sparkle didn't last too long. After a while, she started to cry and said she missed him too much. She told me that Nigel had been trying to get her an internship at the bank he works in but things were going nowhere. Our vacations are scheduled to start in another fifteen days and it was too short a time to go through the entire procedure for securing an internship. I don't know how I feel about that. I have mixed feelings. I would be happy to see her happy. I would be sad to see her happy with someone else. After a little while, she stopped crying and smiled at my efforts to make her smile.

I wish I could have frozen that moment in time. I wish I had, because the very next moment, her phone rang and it was from Nigel's company. During the entire duration of the phone call, she looked at me with wide-open eyes, bit her nails and smiled at me. She shrieked like a little kid after disconnecting the call and hugged me. Her application had been accepted. Being in love is difficult. When she was right in front of me and smiled, I was glad. Now that I am alone, I am consumed by my loneliness and the hollowness of the times to come. She was going to Bangalore. And not to meet Nigel just once but to stay. For two months. Her little gamble had paid off.

Nigel called to confirm the news. Suddenly, she was ecstatic. She passed her phone to me and Nigel asked if I too wanted to apply. I turned it down. Ragini begged me and insisted I come with her. I said no. It hurt me to say so, but going with her would have hurt more. And she would not need me anyway. She would have Nigel to take care of her. He was all she ever needed.

I feel like being alone for a while. But still, I wish I could see her tomorrow.

18 November 2010
'And when you agree to hurt yourself for the happiness of the other, you know you're never going to stop loving that person.'

Ragini was supposed to be happy, but she wasn't. After all, the way things were panning out, it seemed like even God was in on their plans. She said she was in a bad mood and would be okay soon. I didn't buy that. Something was wrong and I had to know. I probed. She broke down and held on to me for dear life. She asked me if I considered her a good friend and whether I would do anything to help her. I feel lost when she asks me questions like these. Sometimes, I am very tempted to tell her the truth, but pull back thinking it's too early and too stupid.

I told her I would do anything to make her happy. She stopped crying and told me that her parents weren't allowing her to go to Bangalore alone. Unwillingly, I asked her how I could help. Her parents had told her that she would be allowed to go only if someone else from the college was going to Bangalore for the internship too. With tears in her eyes, she asked me if I would. I was the reason for her tears. It was because of me that those beautiful eyes had shed tears, the cute nose had crinkled and the sweetest girl in the world was sad. I was angry at myself for it and I made up my mind. Yes, I would accompany her to Bangalore. I couldn't have been selfish and said no to her. While she smiled, my life came to a standstill. Two months. Nigel and Ragini, in front of my eyes. I shudder to think what would become of me.

All the paperwork is to be done and we have to leave in ten days. I didn't see Ragini in college later today. She was way too excited about going to Bangalore and had lots of shopping to do. After all, she had a boyfriend to impress. Since the day her internship was confirmed, she has changed. She looks . . . hot, yes, that's what people would call her. She has done something with her hair . . . the natural waves and cute curls are missing. All that is left is stick-straight hair, which falls all over her face and gives her a sharp look. The sweetness is gone. Did Nigel ask her to? I knew she loved her curls and would never destroy them. Maybe I am thinking too much.

She told me all about her day and how much fun she had shopping. But after a while, she fell silent and had a dreamy look on her face. On our way back home, I saw her look out of the window, wordlessly. She had stopped talking. She must have been tired. But her eyes weren't. They were still dreamy and thinking about someone. And as I saw her look out of the window, I noticed her lips curve into a little smile. I wish she would remain like this, happy, forever. Even if her happiness was because of someone else.

I wish I could see her tomorrow.

To Gandhinagar

I find us packing our stuff as soon as we get to the hotel. The adrenaline is getting to us. We are finally getting somewhere. Though the thought of Ritam's crippled sister saddens us. But at least we have a name. *Ritam Dey*. That's a start. I am sure we will be at Ragini's doorstep soon.

'Are we leaving already?' I ask. 'It's a nice city. Can we rest a while? Have a few walks along the city lanes? Nice dinner?'

'Deb,' Avantika says and throws my bag to me.

'What?'

'Nivedita. It must have been weeks since her brother hasn't met her. What if Ritam's parents didn't let Nivedita know? What if they never tell her that Ritam is never coming back?' she says with concern.

'I was just kidding. I wanted to see how kicked you were.'

From what I inferred from the diary, Ritam's parents had never bothered to contact Nivedita after they sent her away. It's a little strange to take his name over and over again. *Ritam*. Earlier, it was just *the dead guy*. But now, he has a name and a personality to go with it. It makes me feel even closer to him. It's like I know him now, like he's a friend ... a friend I am responsible for, a friend who died an unfortunate death, leaving behind his story in a diary.

Fifteen minutes later, we are already in the car. We both buy 'I Love Madhya Pradesh' T-shirts, for a hundred bucks each, as we leave the city and throw our old ones (We Love Haridwar) in the dustbin. She ties the T-shirt a little above her navel and we continue our journey on the open, dusty roads again.

It's a fifteen-hour journey and I check our supplies—mineral water, packed food, chips, knives, condoms, etc. Life seems crazy now. Come to think of it, only a week back we were a boring couple who used to sit at home, watch television, order pizzas and have a lot of sex. And this morning, we didn't even think of taking a shower together. I don't know how that's a good sign in a relationship, but that's what's happening. And I have come to love it.

While I drive, Avantika fiddles with the diary and reads parts of it again and again.

'He was a sweet guy,' she says and looks into the distance. 'Ritam Dey.'

'Hmmm.'

'It's so nice, right, Deb? He doesn't even think twice before agreeing to go to Bangalore for her.'

'Yes,' I reply shortly.

'Neither did he react when Ragini told him everything. She had an abortion at sixteen, and Ritam could only say how brave she had been? This is true love,' she says.

'Yes, I'm sure it is.'

'You don't find guys like that any more,' she says.

'You found me!'

'Shut up, Deb!' she says.

'*What*? I would have done the same for you,' I protest.

'You wouldn't have.'

'I would have,' I say. 'You told me that you had kissed many guys before me. I never reacted to that.'

'Because you knew I was never in my senses when I used to do it. You can't call them kisses,' she says while referring to the times she used to kiss random guys at parties under the influence of drugs.

'Whatever.'

'And the only time I lied to you about kissing someone other than you, you left me.'

There is an awkward silence. I have nothing to say. Why don't girls ever forget anything? Two years back, Avantika and I had broken up and it was because of me. We were in the Management Development Institute (MDI) doing a management course. One day, I had gotten drunk and kissed a classmate of mine. Avantika had stopped talking to me for a little while, but we were back together within a few days. I'd apologized and she'd forgiven me.

During those days in between, when she was apart, she hung around with a guy named Kabir. It was only after we got back together that she told me they had made out. In a fit of rage, I dumped her! I walked away from her and vowed that I would never come back. I told her that she disgusted me and I would never like to see her again.

Our distances increased and she started staying alone in college. She kept apologizing, but it was way too hard for me to forgive. I used to see her with Kabir on occasions, and I used to feel sick. That's when I started to spend a lot of time with the girl I had kissed—Malini. She was hot and very intriguing. She had come to India from Canada after spending a few years there and I was the only person she spoke to. She helped me through the times when I used to be angry and disappointed. We had a sort of a relationship and we even made out a few times, though both of us knew that she would never replace Avantika.

The silence and the awkwardness in the car make me uncomfortable. I have always tried to avoid conversations about Malini or that period when Avantika and I were not together.

'Do you still think about Malini?' Avantika asks.

'No, I don't.'

'You're lying, Deb.'

'I do, sometimes. She was a friend. It was a tough time for me and she helped,' I say.

'It was tougher for me . . .'

'I know. But you didn't have to lie about it,' I say. I had met Kabir months after Avantika and I had broken up. He told me he had never ever kissed her, let alone make out with her. Avantika had lied about it.

'Do you think it was easy for me to lie?'

'Then why did you?'

'Deb, I was in love with you. I was ready to spend every waking moment of my life with you. I had the right to know whether I meant as much to you as you meant to me. When you kissed Malini, I forgave you almost instantly. Whereas when I told you that Kabir and I had made out, you just left me like that. You told me that I disgust you. How do you think I felt back then?' she says.

'I am sorry . . . I was just so mad at you.'

'Never mind. I don't want to think about it,' she says and looks away.

It was a horrible time for me. Avantika was in Mumbai when I got to know that she had lied about it. The very next day, I was on a flight to Mumbai to woo her back. It took me months before Avantika finally agreed to date me again. It's not that I didn't miss her when I believed that she had cheated on me. I still missed her as much, if not more. I still have a text saved that I had written for her in those days.

If I'd only known,
That this is the last time we've met,
I would have stopped the break of dawn,
And stopped the sun to set.

If I'd only known,
That I wouldn't ever see you again,
I would have framed a picture of you within,
To end my suffering, to end my pain.

If I'd only known,
That this is the last time I sit by your side,
I would have told you how much I loved you,
Keeping other things aside.

If I'd only known,
That we would never hold hands again,
I would have held them strong,
And never let anything go wrong.

If I'd only known,
That you would always stand by my side,
I would have fought the world for you,
Breaking all the walls through.

If I'd only known,
That your love was true,
If I'd only known that you would come back soon,
I would have waited for you to come by.

If I'd only known any of this,
That you were what I was breathing for,
I would have breathed my last for you,
Seen you enough and bid you adieu.
While all I can do now,
Is sit here . . .
. . . and wait.
Love you.

If I'd only known.

Anyway, I look at Avantika and have nothing to say. Ritam was a better person than I will ever be. He had accepted Ragini just the way she was. Well, I have my flaws. No one's perfect, after all. Except Avantika, of course. She is flawlessly divine.

'I love you,' I say.

'I know you do,' she says and smiles at me.

Ever since that blast, I have never missed a chance to say that to Avantika. Who knows what will happen the next moment? And *I love you* needs to be one of the last words that I say to Avantika. So I have made it a point to tell her that whenever I get a chance, just to be sure.

The drive is long and tiring. The first nine hours are still okay. We take shifts and drive, but after that, we are exhausted. It's a tough job driving Shrey's car. But we are lucky it hasn't broken down yet. We park it and move into a hotel, at two in the night. I see the bed and all I can think of is sleep. I crash, arms and legs wide open.

Suddenly, it seems like we've been doing this forever—driving through empty, unchartered roads, falling in love with each other all over again, staying in dirty hotels and meeting new people—it's like a new lease of life for us. I am beginning to love this. It's addictive and it's fun. It will be tough to get back to our routine lives after this ends.

But today, I am just fucking tired. While I look like a roadside labourer, Avantika still manages to look smashing. I don't have the energy to change, so I go to sleep like that. A little later, I sniff something fabulous—Avantika. She snuggles up next to me inside the blanket. She has taken a shower and smells fantastically fruity.

She turns towards me, kisses me on my nose and whispers, 'I love you.'

'I love you more,' I reply. She smiles, snuggles closer and I put my hands around her.

'I love you.'

'I love you more.'

'I love you so much.'

'I love you so much more.'

'I love you so freaking much.'

'I love you so freaking much more.'

Yes, we are silly and we like saying these things to each other. We are in love and we are allowed to be like that. People who are not in love can just be jealous and say things like, 'They are so creepy!' or 'Shit. So cheesy.' But I don't give a shit. It's not my fault that you don't have a super pretty girl as your girlfriend. But I do, and I will dance naked in a dress made out of leaves and shout that I love her, if it makes her happy. Slowly, we drift off to sleep.

We've been sleeping for long when my sleep is broken by the heavy beating on the door.

'Kholo!' The voice says from the other side. Once. Twice. The voice keeps getting louder. I wake up Avantika.

'Huh?'

She hears it too. The bangs on the door keep getting heavier and more determined. We get up. I am a little scared, but Avantika is not. She checks her face in the mirror coolly. I hold her hand as she walks to the door and shouts, 'Kaun?'

'POLICE!' they shout from the other side.

What?

We look at each other. Although we haven't done anything, but with the Indian police, you never know. You might be innocent and still spend years rotting behind bars. Yeah, that's how 90 per cent cases are closed. So, yes, we are scared.

'Yes?' says Avantika as she opens the door.

There are two rustic-looking men standing outside. Moustached, not too old, and with slight paunches. I am confident that slowly and steadily their paunches will grow to become hot-air balloons. And their teeth will be stained red and yellow. For now, they are marginally presentable. They must be new in the force.

'COME OUTSIDE. We need to see IDs,' one of them says in a stern voice.

'Fine,' Avantika says rudely and goes to fetch the IDs.

The two policemen look at me. One of them looks at Avantika lewdly. I want to poke his fucking eye out. He looks at me and raises an eyebrow.

'*Ladki kaun hai?*' he asks me.

'I'm getting married to her. We're engaged.' I wave the ring.

'Hmmm,' he says with his eyes stuck on her.

'*Kya karte ho?*' he asks.

'I am in the media. The press,' I say. I don't work in the media, but it helps me get out of sticky situations. It's a no-brainer. No one messes with the media. You never know when Aaj Tak people might come out with cameras shouting '*Sabse Tez*' and label anyone a sex offender or child killer—whatever catches their fancy. So, yes, that works.

Finally, the policeman takes his eyes off Avantika and looks at me. We don't exchange a word. I smile. My smile says, 'Yes, Media, you asshole. Eat that!' Policemen *never* mess with people from the press. Soon, Avantika comes with our IDs and hands them over to the policemen. He looks at the IDs and looks at us, matches the faces and hands them over to us.

'We are sorry for the trouble, but you have to come downstairs and sign the entry register and submit photocopies to the receptionist. It's standard procedure,' the policeman says politely.

'It's harassment,' Avantika says arrogantly.

'Madamji, it's procedure.'

'Fine,' we both say. Our tones indicate that we are not at all pleased by what he has asked us to do.

We close the door behind us and walk down the dark, creaky and narrow stairs of the hotel. As we approach the reception, we see twenty more people there, all cribbing about how they had to wake up in the middle of the night and how the procedures are all fucked up.

We get in line. Then we overhear a heated argument in the room adjoining the reception. I ignore it and look how far the line has moved. There are still five more people ahead of us. The old people are taking ages to write their names down. The noise from the adjoining room just keeps getting louder. Everyone turns to see what's happening inside. I look in the direction where everyone else is looking and I'm taken aback.

What the fuck!

Shrey?

'That's Shrey, right?' I point to the little window of that room.

Avantika turns to look and is equally shocked. 'Yes! What's going on there?'

'Let's go,' I say, hold her hand and walk towards the room. Friends in need are such pests. We instinctively go out of our way to help them. It's often involuntary and lands us in trouble. But we just don't learn.

I knock. No one listens. I knock again and enter. There are five people in police uniforms who stare right at us. Two of them are the ones who had come to our room. I look at Shrey and he looks at me and freezes, his hands hanging in mid-air as he stops in the middle of an animated discussion. In a corner is Tiya, and she looks at us, equally shocked.

Their eyes say what ours do: *'What the fuck!'*

There is silence for a little while after which the most senior policeman asks, *'Kaun hai ye?'* He almost barks with authority.

'Press se hai!' one of the policemen says.

'Boliye?' The senior guy nods and asks us. *'Kya chahiye?'*

'We know them,' I say.

'They are with you?' he asks, his voice not softening.

'Yes,' I say.

'What are their names?' he asks and looks straight at me.

'Shrey and Tiya. They are with us,' I repeat.

'Do you know the girl is just eighteen? Should she be out like this? Do you know what these two were doing? Chhee! Is this what your parents teach you?' he asks. He gets into a preachy, irritating dad mode.

'We are doing a project. She is an intern and is working with us. And, sir, we know she is eighteen and hence can take her own decisions,' Avantika says sternly.

'You kids these days think you can do anything—'

'We are not breaking any law,' she says even more sternly. And when she does that, no one—absolutely no one—can stand up to her. She looked freakishly dangerous and mean.

'Fine,' he says as he gives up. 'Take their details and let them go.'

We move out of the room. And as we do that, Shrey whispers in my ear, 'Press? Since when?'

'Fifteen minutes ago.'

'Shit! Why didn't it occur to me?' He looks at me with respect.

We stand in line, write down our names and submit our IDs. All the while, the five men in uniform hang around us. The four of us keep faking conversations about international conferences with ministers and MLAs. We make sure they hear us.

Once we enter the room, Shrey says, 'What the hell are you two doing here?'

'Apparently, saving your ass from getting kicked,' Avantika says smugly.

'Seriously, man. They were about to call her parents. Luckily, I didn't say anything about what we were doing here,' Shrey says.

Tiya, who had not spoken anything till then, suddenly runs to Avantika and hugs her. She starts to cry. Avantika looks at her, puzzled, for a while. She smiles, pats her and assures her that nothing will happen.

'They scared her, man,' Shrey says softly. 'They were about to call her parents. They said she will have to go back to Delhi with them.'

'She didn't say anything?'

'No, luckily. Thanks, man. One minute more and she would have said sorry and cried . . . we would have been so screwed,' he says.

'But what was the argument all about? What the fuck were those guys talking about? Why did they get hold of you?' I ask.

'They caught us making out,' he says with a smirk.

'What? Where?'

'We were doing it in the balcony. One of them saw us and thought there was some sex racket thing going on in the hotel. So they wanted to call her parents and check,' he says.

'You're a sex-starved bastard,' I say.

'Look who's talking!'

'This is different. And I don't do it in the balcony.'

'Unlucky you,' he says and winks.

I make a mental note to self—*do it in the balcony*. And I am a little jealous. Anyway, Avantika asks Shrey where they are headed. Shrey and Tiya had picked Ahmedabad as the next city but had lost their way.

They ask Avantika if they could tag along. She smiles and tells them they are most welcome to do so. Shrey asks us why we picked Gandhinagar and we avoid the question. It's been a long night and we go to sleep. Avantika with Tiya and Shrey with me. We are not taking any chances. The balcony make-out would have to wait another night.

I text Avantika—*Have we ever done it in the balcony?* ☺

She replies—*We will. Soon.* ☺ *Good night. XOXO.*

⌒

The next morning, we leave early. Tiya is still sleepy, so she sleeps in the back seat, while Shrey drives the rented motorcycle alongside our car. It's a 1987 Harley Davidson, collector's edition, and it looks ragingly hot. The engine makes more noise than an airplane's turbine and it looks powerful and imposing. Too bad, I would never get to drive it.

My parents have always been paranoid about two-wheelers. They never let me even pillion-ride one, let alone ride it. They used to tell me ghastly stories about brutal accidents and I used to believe everything they told me. Consequently, I never learnt to drive one. Pretty shitty, I know.

It's been a couple of hours since we've been driving. The sun comes out a little. The weather keeps getting more pleasant and the views more spectacular.

Tiya wakes up after a while, rubs her eyes and asks, 'Where are we?'

'Umm, no idea,' I say.

'Amazing!' she says as she looks around, stands up on the back seat and stretches her arms, just like they do in the movies. Avantika and I look at her, a little scared that she might fall off, a little jealous because she is the first one to do that. She takes out her huge camera and starts to click pictures. Avantika and I smile for a few pictures. She makes us look good in them. Her talent in undeniable.

'STOP!' she says suddenly. I screech the car to a halt.

'What?' Before Avantika can even say that, Tiya is already sitting behind Shrey and hugging him tight.

Shrey gives her a cute yellow helmet, she puts it on and they race ahead of us. Avantika looks at them and sighs. I hold her hand and tell her I love her. That's how I try to make up for my flaws. I tell her that I love her and assume that it works. I know she wants to sit behind and be driven around on a gorgeous motorcycle, but she has a useless boyfriend like me.

Meanwhile, Tiya stretches her arms and leans back dangerously on the bike, but I think it must be fun. We enter the state and are just a few hours from where we have to go. Avantika switches places with me and we drive on. The weather, the setting, the scenes around us—perfect to fall in love all over again. We stop at a roadside eating joint and order for ourselves. Last night now seems so far back in history. Time's flying by and I love this life.

'It's a freakish coincidence that we're back together,' I say as I start to eat.

'What if they called your parents?' Avantika asks Tiya.

'Chuck it now,' Shrey says.

'I would be screwed,' Tiya says. 'But I don't like them anyway.'

'They are your parents,' Avantika preaches.

Avantika has always been a very family person. Well, at least she has *wanted to be*. That's why my mom, sisters and everybody—they all love her. But my family is her only family apart from her real brother. She belongs to a family of rich businessmen and she was always treated like a piece of furniture. Her parents wanted to get her married off as soon as she graduated but she ran away. She never liked her parents either, so she feels bad for anyone without a family. So when Tiya shows apathy towards her own parents, Avantika is visibly disturbed.

'So what? They treat me like shit. They never let me do anything,' she says. 'And they keep fighting all the time.'

'So what? There are problems in every family,' Avantika says.

'I can't take it. Can we talk about something else, please?'

'You're going to regret it.'

'I'm young. I'm allowed to make mistakes,' she says and smiles at Avantika.

'There are some mistakes you can't undo.'

'Whatever.'

We get back to the food. Tiya and Avantika have been at loggerheads ever since they first met. They are like the same poles of a magnet. So similar that they continue to repel each other. Avantika will not stop acting like her mom and from how things have gone till now, Tiya will not stop screwing up. But everything aside, it's a little amusing too.

We finish our food, pay the bill and head back to our vehicles for the last part of our drive. I throw the keys towards Avantika because it's her turn to drive. She looks at the keys for a while and throws them to Shrey. Shrey looks strangely at her.

'But—'

Before Shrey can say anything, Avantika takes the bike keys from his hand and sits on the motorcycle. She takes the cute yellow helmet and puts it on. She puts the key into ignition, turns it and kicks the pedal hard. The beast comes roaring to life. A gear shift and the bike starts moving. Our eyes pop out as she takes to the road with fierce acceleration. We look at each other and run to the car. Shrey puts the car in motion and we start following the bike as it whizzes through the traffic. Shrey and Tiya throw questions at me with their eyes.

'What? I didn't know she could ride a bike,' I say, equally puzzled.

We start to follow her, but she is moving too fast. Fifteen minutes, a few trucks and cycles on the road slow her down and we catch up with her.

I shout at her, 'Since when?'

'FOREVER,' she shouts back.

I ask her to stop and she does. I get down from the car and jump on to the bike. We start moving again. It's a little sissy to be pillion-riding a girl, but when the girl is immensely sexy, it doesn't matter. I get to hold her close, my chest touching against her every time she brakes, and say dirty things in her ears. I look at her in that cute yellow helmet, the aviator shades, the denim hot pants, and the black tank top and I am mesmerized. Her hair blows in the wind and smells heavenly. I hold her from behind and plant a kiss on her neck, with a lot of tongue in it.

'I didn't know you could drive,' I say.

'Neither did I. I used to drive long back. Just wanted to see if I could still do it.'

'Seems like you can.'

The entire ride is awesome. I pull back from letting my hands wander all over her satin-smooth body and from biting into her neck. I do it from time to time, but then her driving goes all awry.

It's nearly lunchtime by the time we reach the quiet and dusty city of Gandhinagar. We follow the usual routine—find the cheapest hotel and check in. We are dead tired. Thankfully, Shrey and Tiya check into a different room and Avantika doesn't kick up a fuss.

I flop on the bed and Avantika goes for her shower, smears moisturizer over her already creamy legs and snuggles up next to me. We are both tired and hungry. No matter how sexy it is to ride a bike, it's always back-breaking. I run my fingers over her perfectly arched and smooth back and she purrs lovingly. She asks me to keep doing that and I happily submit. It's amazing how she drove today. It was as though she has always been driving a bike that heavy.

'Why did you do it?' I ask her.

'Do what?'

'You know, Avantika. Drive the bike. To stamp superiority over Tiya?'

'Yes,' she says.

'But we know you're better, hotter and everything else she can never be.'

'Aww! Thanks, baby. But it's not about that. That girl is a kid. She needs to know what's right and what's not. You can have fun and do crazy things, but you don't have to be stupid. And she is being stupid.'

'Is that it?' I ask.

'And I think I'm just a little jealous too, Deb.'

'Jealous? Why?'

'She just doesn't give a damn! She can just go about doing silly things and it doesn't make a difference to her. We can no longer do that, can we?' she says.

'Are you crazy? We can't? Did you not drive a bike across the most difficult and busy roads ever? Not even she can do that. You're the best. She can never come near you.'

'This is why I love you so much!' Avantika says and hugs me tight.

'Not even close to how much I love you, though.'

4 December 2010

'When you see the person you love move away from you, what do you do? Do you panic? Or do you keep loving and hope that things will be just like they were before?'

My heart sank when our train reached the railway station in Bangalore in the evening that day. Nigel had come to pick us up. I looked away when I saw them hug. He took us to our accommodation, which is in the same building where Nigel lives with his parents. Ragini and I are staying in two different rooms on the same floor. We met Nigel's parents for a bit too. Sweet people. After that,

I excused myself to my room, saying I was tired. It had begun to look like I was hindering their privacy, so I took their leave.

I came to my room and unpacked. The image of them hugging was still in my head. I was having a few doubts about the kind of person Nigel is, but I thought I should let it go. Who am I to say anything, right? He has not done anything wrong anyway and has been a perfect boyfriend. And the look on his face when he saw Ragini was reassuring. He seems equally in love with her. Who would not be? But I felt something was wrong. Maybe it was all in my head.

I did not hear from Ragini the rest of the day. I had felt like going to her room several times and I did that a few times too, but every time I came back without knocking. I did not want to be an unwanted interference. I didn't even know if she was there. Maybe she had slept off. I sent her a text message wishing her a good night. She didn't reply. These two months are going to be the hardest, I told myself. I couldn't sleep that entire night.

Today is my fourth day in Bangalore. And apart from the initial neglect I faced on the first day, right after we had arrived, she has been sweet to me all through. The first two days of our internship have passed by without anything interesting happening. I think that is how things will be here. It is really dull and boring. But I guess I am the only person getting bored. Ragini has a smile plastered across her face through the whole day. I like her like this. Just that I do not get to see her much. She is either working or with him. Every second of her free time is accounted for. All for Nigel. I saw him in the office today. Before I could do or say anything, I saw him make his way to where Ragini was. He whispered something in her ear and I saw her turn a little pink. She looked immeasurably adorable. They left soon after that. I did not need to ask where they were going. I did not even want to know. I was happy with the short, semi-formal wave Ragini gave me before she walked out of the office doors. She looks so hopelessly in love with him. Nigel is an extremely lucky guy. I hope she spends more time in office tomorrow.

I wish I could see her tomorrow.

8 December 2010

'As the days pass by and I see myself getting engulfed in loneliness, my mind wanders off to the days when I used to see her and that used to be my biggest pleasure. I want more now. I am spoilt.'

I have not seen her in the last two days. I do not know whether she misses me. She is probably busy being in love. I miss her. I miss her smiles, her chirping, her eyes . . . I miss everything about her. But I know she has other better things to do than to spend time with me. She has come here for a reason. And that reason is Nigel. It's only fair that she gives him proper attention. I do not have the right to complain.

Two days ago, I had seen her in office, tense and worried, and she was walking around in circles. Once again, I committed the mistake of asking her what's wrong. She told me she wanted to go out with Nigel. He had something planned for her . . . a secret . . . or maybe she just did not want to tell me. Anyway, that's not the point I am trying to make here. She had wanted to go out with him, but our supervisor had assigned us a lot of work. It would have taken her a full day to complete it. She did not have a full day to waste. Nigel's surprise was waiting for her.

She had looked at me with her big, puppy eyes and my heart melted immediately. And that's where I had come in— her foolish knight in shining armour—and offered to help her with her work so that she could leave early. But she was still having a lot of trouble. She did not know anything about what needed to be done. It was obvious since she hadn't been paying attention in the orientation classes in which we were trained. I asked her to leave and told her I could handle it alone. And she left, but not before asking me to explain everything to her when she got back. She must have been feeling guilty about neglecting the internship so badly. I hope she had noticed that I was being neglected as well.

Two days and she hasn't yet returned from her date. It is midnight now. I think I should sleep. I do not need to worry about her. She is with Nigel. He would take care of her. Anyway, I had texted her and she had texted back saying that everything was perfect. Perfect. I should stop being the pestering friend who worries too much about everything. But I can't help it. I hope she is all right.

I wish I could see her tomorrow.

Nivedita

Shrey and Tiya are still sleeping when we leave the hotel for the mental asylum where Nivedita is admitted. We had looked up the address yesterday and everyone we asked knew where it was. Avantika and I have hardly talked since morning. We are a little unsure of what we'll say to Nivedita. Not only that, we don't know what to expect.

According to his notes, Nivedita doesn't talk or understand anybody other than her brother. She talks through her smiles, which only Ritam understood. We won't be able to tell her anything. And even if we do, what will we even say to her? I sweat thinking what I would've done had Avantika not been with me.

'This is going to be strange,' I tell Avantika.

'I know.'

We enter the building. It's an old one, probably standing since the early 1890s. We ask the receptionist if we could meet Nivedita. She asks if we are from her family. We nod. She brings out a register, goes to the alphabet N, painfully slowly, and then gets to Nivedita.

It has a log of all the visits made to her. Our eyes light up as she turns the register towards us. All the entries are of one name—

Ritam Dey. We check the dates—he used to come there every fifteen days, except for a few occasions. The last day he visited the asylum was two days before the blast. Avantika and I look at each other and we feel sorry for Nivedita. She will never see her brother again and she probably has no idea about it.

'Ma'am? Do you know Ritam?' Avantika asks the lady.

'Yes,' she nods.

'Did Ritam come alone to meet Nivedita or with someone?'

'Alone,' she says and gets busy knitting her sweater.

'Thank you so much.'

The lady shows us to the visiting room and we wait there. It looks like an expensive place; the waiting room itself is done up in expensive wood and well-designed wallpapers. A little later, a ward boy in a white uniform wheels in a girl, wearing a slightly old and worn-out hospital gown, in a grey wheelchair.

The head of the girl is tilted towards one side and she looks at us with deadpan eyes. The ward boy wheels her towards us and stops inches away from Avantika. Nivedita's face is expressionless. She must be around nineteen, but her hair is a little sparse and I'm guessing it's due to the medicines. Even though Nivedita is thin, frail and slightly pale, I'm sure she must have been a very pretty girl. Her bony frame is quite visible from outside the hospital gown. Her eyes have sunk in but there is an inherent twinkle in them. Like the last flicker of a burning candle.

'Who are you?' the ward boy asks.

'Umm, we are friends of Ritam. You know him?' I ask.

'Yes. He comes here every fifteen days. Nice boy,' the man says without thinking twice. 'Are you cousins?'

'Actually, we don't know him. He died—' I start to tell him but Avantika interrupts me.

'I will tell you. Come with me,' she says and takes the ward boy a little away from Nivedita. She starts to tell him everything that she knows. I wait with Nivedita and watch them from a distance.

I look at Nivedita and she seems to look at me. I smile at her, but she doesn't respond. She looks blankly at me, motionless. I know she isn't expecting me; she is expecting her brother to be near her and to make her smile. There is no way I am telling her that her brother is dead. I look at the ward boy, who looks shaken as Avantika tells him everything. He takes some time to let the news sink in. They come back to where Nivedita and I are.

'She doesn't understand anything,' the ward boy says and looks at me. He looks perturbed.

'What should we do?' Avantika asks.

'I don't know,' the ward boy says helplessly. 'Almost every patient here has been abandoned by their families. Only a few of them get visitors. Nivedita is one of those lucky few. I don't know much about medicine, but human contact and love are what keep these people alive. I have seen many people . . . die when they stop getting visitors. Their bodies get weak and they stop eating. Nivedita needs her brother.'

His voice trails off. Nivedita is not smiling. Her eyes seem even more sunken now. Maybe she sees the horror in our eyes.

'Can she hear us?' Avantika asks.

'Yes, but her brain can't process it,' the ward boy says.

Avantika kneels down near the wheelchair, takes Nivedita's hand in hers, looks at her, smiles and says, 'Your brother, Ritam, loves you a lot, still does and will always do. You are the most precious thing to him. He sent the two of us to tell you that. You're the best sister he could have ever asked for. You are very beautiful, Nivedita.'

She kisses Nivedita's hand and runs her fingers over her face. My eyes well up and the ward boy looks at me. He is moved too. Slowly, Nivedita's lips curve into a smile. The ward boy is wrong. She does understand. There is a moment of silence. Avantika smiles back at her and Nivedita smiles more.

'She reacts to that name,' the ward boy says. 'Ritam.'

'Have Ritam's parents ever come here?' I ask the ward boy.

'No.'

'Have you ever seen a girl come here with Ritam?'

'No, but Ritam often used to say that a friend of his wanted to meet Nivedita. I can't really remember her name. Oh yes, Raaa . . . Ragini. That was her name,' the ward boy recollects.

'Wait,' Avantika says. 'Say that again.'

'What?'

'Ragini,' Avantika says.

'What Ragini?' I say.

'Look,' she says. And we look at Nivedita. She is smiling.

'You know Ragini?' Avantika looks at her, clutches Nivedita's hand tighter and says, 'Do you remember her?'

Nivedita smiles.

'Do you want to meet Ragini?' I say. Nivedita smiles again.

'You like Ragini?' the ward boy says. Nivedita smiles yet again.

'You want to talk to Ragini?' Avantika says. Nivedita smiles.

The ward boy looks at us and says, 'She never reacts like this. She only reacts to Ritam.'

'We need to get Ragini then,' Avantika says. I nod and we smile.

'Do you know Ragini?' he asks.

'We don't know her, but we can find out,' I say. 'Nivedita probably doesn't understand the words people say to her, but she can feel the love of the people close to her. From what just happened, it looks like she considers Ragini as one of her own.

Even though she has never met her in person. Ritam must have told her all about Ragini . . . We can't tell her or make her understand what happened to her brother, but we can make her meet Ragini. If that's possible.'

The ward boy looks concerned. It's sweet of him to care about this crippled girl so much. Things like these make you love the world again. Despite the corruption, the hatred, the animosity that engulfs everything around us, sweet souls like his make the world a better place. The ward boy tells us that it's time for Nivedita's medicines and she needs to be taken away. He tells us that this was not the scheduled day for visitors and Nivedita had to be checked up by doctors, and also that she has been growing weak lately, and not been responding to treatment. We nod worriedly.

'We'll come back to see you again,' Avantika says. She takes Nivedita's hand again in hers and kisses it. I don't know whether anybody else notices it, but Nivedita smiles. *Everyone* loves Avantika.

Avantika tells the ward boy that we would be back with Ragini and asks him to take good care of Nivedita. He smiles and wheels her away. We thank the lady at the reception and leave the asylum. Days like these make me feel so lucky. The girl in that wheelchair has nothing to live for, just the sound of a few names. That's her only happiness in life.

And I? I have everything—a loving family, great friends, the love of my life, a little money to live on . . . I have absolutely no right to complain. But I still do. We all do. It's our tendency. We crib. That's our default state. We always look at people with a better life, a better car, a better girlfriend and wish to have a life like theirs.

Nivedita smiles once every fifteen days when she sees her

brother. A stupid, irrational bomb blast took that away from her. Now she has nothing to live for. So unfair. I have everything.

I clutch Avantika's hand and tell her that I love her, and we head towards our taxi that waits outside the asylum building.

⌣

Avantika is a little disturbed after our meeting, quite understandably. We get back to our hotel and can't find Shrey and Tiya. Their stuff is still there, so we assume they haven't run away again. But this time, we don't even care. We are a bit ruffled from what just happened. Now we desperately need to find Ragini. It's no longer about letting someone know how much she was loved, but a matter of survival for Nivedita. Nivedita needs Ragini and we both know that. Avantika sits in one corner and holds the diary in her hands. Tiny pearls of tears have collected at the corners of her eyes. They trickle down her cheek and wet the page of the diary she has opened.

'This is unfair,' Avantika says.

'Hmmm.'

'She is such a pretty girl. How can life be so cruel to her?'

I shake my head in distress.

'And we do nothing about it,' she says and hides her face in her palms.

I stare at her helplessly. She says nothing and looks away. Avantika clearly doesn't like how this story is turning out. Things have changed. The diary has entrusted us with an even bigger responsibility. It's no longer just a diary of a dead man telling his story. Now we are responsible for the people he has left behind, Nivedita being one of them. We have to find Ragini and we have to do it quick.

'Where do you think we should go next? Mumbai?' I ask.

Piyush had told us that Ritam had completed his college in Mumbai and we knew Ragini was there too, so it made sense. Other than that, we have absolutely no lead to go on. I call up Piyush to check whether he has found anything, but he is as clueless as we are.

'I just hope we find her in Mumbai,' Avantika says, closes her eyes and says a little prayer.

We have no idea where to start with in Mumbai. It's a huge, confusing city. The city that never sleeps. Maybe that's because they never manage to get home in time. I like the city though. It's big, lively and very unforgiving.

Avantika and I are lazing around and discussing how to go about it when there is a knock on the door. It's Shrey and Tiya.

'What's up?' I ask. 'We thought you had run away again.'

'Not this time,' he says. 'Can we talk, Deb? Outside?'

He looks serious. I look at Tiya and she doesn't really look tense. So she's probably not pregnant. *Yet*.

Shrey and I go outside to have the *talk*.

'What's going on?' he asks. He looks a little pissed off.

'As in?' I ask.

'This trip? What's it all about? Not that I care, but I would like to know,' he says.

'It's . . . umm . . . nothing.'

'Just tell me, Deb,' he says.

'It's nothing important.'

'I want to know, Deb! I want to be a part of anything fucked up that you do. And this, by the look of things, is very fucked up.'

'It's a long story,' I reply shortly.

'I know about it. I talked to the ward boy of that fucked-up place this morning. He told me everything. Now I want *you* to tell me.'

'*Ward boy?*'

'We followed you this morning. I thought you'd gone crazy and I wanted to check what you were up to,' he confesses.

'So then, why the drama? You know now, right?' I say.

'I want to see the diary,' he says sternly.

'Fine,' I say.

I get the diary for him and hand it over. His eyes light up. He runs his fingers through the burnt edges of the diary and flips through the pages. He feels the crumbling edges of the pages and looks at me.

'This is freaking awesome,' he says.

I knew he'd say that. This sort of stuff is very Shrey*ish*. He is the one with the passion and the zeal to do things that one would normally stay away from. He is the crazy one.

'You have read it all?' he asks.

'About fifteen times.'

'Do you mind if I read it?' he asks.

'Nope.'

'As if I care . . .'

He starts to read it, and I read with him. Even the zillionth time around, it evokes the same feelings. It brings the same feelings of pity and love like it had brought the first time round. Shrey finishes it in about an hour and then rereads certain portions of it, just like Avantika did.

'So this is why you chose Dehradun? The school?' he asks. I nod. 'And then Bhopal?'

'Piyush, the guy called Pappu, lives there.'

'You bastard. So?' Shrey asks, 'Where do you . . . *we* head to next?'

'Mumbai. That's where everyone is, I guess,' I say. 'Plus, we need to find Ragini. Nivedita needs her.'

'So what's our next lead?'

'No idea.'

Shrey smirks. It's one of those faces that he makes when he's hiding something.

'Why that expression, Shrey?'

'I like what you're doing,' he says. He smirks again. Something's up for sure.

15 December 2010

'The crushing helplessness you feel, when the person you love the most is hurt by someone else and you can't do anything about, is one of the worst pains anyone can ever endure.'

I wouldn't say she was sad, just a little disturbed maybe. Thankfully, she chose to talk to me about it and tell me the reason behind it. Our distances had been on the rise ever since we had reached Bangalore, and today was the first time we got a chance to talk to each other properly. She has been way too busy with Nigel otherwise. So today, I was just glad that she was around.

She told me that she was out somewhere last night with Nigel and a few of his friends. It was the first time she was meeting any of his friends here in Bangalore. Otherwise, it would be just the two of them. Alone. The very thought makes me a little sick.

She told me that she had noticed that every friend of Nigel's was a regular drinker. And even Nigel drinks, for that matter. But that wasn't what bothered her. What really bothered her was that—despite her constant refusal and evident displeasure—they wanted Ragini to drink too.

Despite her pleas and rude refusals, none of Nigel's friends backed down. Irritated, she turned to Nigel for support, but amazingly, even he was in favour of her drinking. But she still said no to even tasting any drink. No matter how much they insisted, she did not cave in. When she told me this, I felt proud. I have not consumed even a drop of alcohol after that accident when I was fifteen and I am strictly against it. It's just a wrong thing to do.

And I really respect her for standing up to them and holding her ground. I remember she had once told me that she wanted to try some drinks. But that was different. She had just wanted to taste it. Being forced to drink is another thing altogether. And caving in is even worse. She asked me if she did the right thing and I told her I was proud of her. She told me that Nigel was probably still mad at her for refusing what he had asked her to do, that too in front of his friends. During our entire conversation, Ragini kept looking at her cell phone. She told me Nigel had not called her since. She was scared that he was really angry about last night.

Though a few minutes later, her phone beeped and her lips curved into a smile. It was a text from Nigel. Sometimes, all I can do is look at her. It feels so good to see her smile. It suits her. It makes her face light up and her eyes twinkle . . . a little colour rises up her cheeks and her lips look lovely in that upward curve. I can stare at her smile for an eternity. But I am not too happy about her smile today. Behind that smile is a mistake. I can see it clearly now. Nigel is not the guy for her. I am.

I wish I could see her tomorrow.

19 December 2010

'Between seeing her cry and not seeing her at all, I would choose seeing her cry because of the simple reason that I can't live without her.'

Ragini had been looking a little subdued for the last few days. I had sensed something was wrong between them after that drinking incident. I feel like breaking Nigel's nose. Why can't he just let it go? If she does not want to drink, what is his problem? Let her be. Isn't she perfect the way she is?

I was concerned about her, so I went over to check on her tonight, and found her in her room. She had not come to office because she did not feel well. Though tonight she looked better and happier than she had in the last few days. It was evident that she had reconciled her differences with Nigel. Before I spoke to her, I had hoped that he was the one who gave in and not her. But I was wrong. I was disappointed and crushed. I could not believe it at first, when she told me. I still do not want to believe it. But living in denial would not change anything. She told me that yes, she had agreed to drink with Nigel a little. But just a little.

It angered me. I was not angry at Ragini. I can never be. I love her. But I was angry at Nigel. What kind of guy does that? When he knows that she does not like to drink, why would he force her to do so? To socialize? That enraged me even further. Nigel lost the little respect I had for him. I wanted to go back home that very instant and take Ragini with me, but I knew that wasn't happening.

There is no such thing as a few drinks. It inevitably goes out of hand and then, you do things you regret later. But you cannot do anything about it. You just have to live with it for a lifetime. Just like I am living with it. And the guilt . . . it never goes. It is always there . . . haunting you. I do not want Ragini to change into something she is not and do something she would later regret. I wish I could tell her what I had gone through. But I won't. What if she judges me? What if she thinks I am a murderer and never forgives me? I must keep that secret within me.

I cannot let her leave me. I need her in my life. It will be so empty without her. I have already lost most of her to Nigel. She hardly has time for me nowadays. I cannot afford to lose her completely. But the very fact that she is changing herself to fit in with someone else infuriates me. Where does she find the need? Does she not know she is perfect? Does she not see it is Nigel who is wrong? Does she not see he would never love her the way I do?

For the first time since I have known about him, today, I feel like asking Ragini to leave Nigel. Love is about accepting the person as he or she is, not changing them. Nigel is in love with what he can make of her, in love with what he can change her into. True love means not having to pretend ever. I wish she understands that. Better sooner than later. Before she loses herself in the process of being in love with him.

I wish I could see her tomorrow.

The Next Trip

None of us is interested in going on a twelve-hour drive again. We've had enough of fighting with the gear box and the brakes of Shrey's car. It doesn't look like it can take any more. We check on the Internet and the drive from Gandhinagar to Mumbai is not a pleasant one. So it's finally time to dump the car—something that I have wanted to do ever since the trip began. Shrey and I decide that we'll leave the car in Gandhinagar and take the night train to Mumbai. It's an overnight train so it will not be too uncomfortable either.

'Which is cheaper?' Tiya asks while we discuss the pros and cons of the train over car.

'The car,' Shrey answers.

'So let's take the car, no?'

Tiya is slowly running out of money and the train tickets booked in Tatkal will be an even bigger expense for her. Renting that exotic bike in Haridwar seems to have cost them a lot. Meanwhile, I have hardly spent anything out of the ten thousand bucks I started with—just CNG, food at local dhabas and two-hundred-rupees-a-night hotels.

Moreover, our budget for the trip was a lot higher than hers.

She is just a kid. And we had never planned to go as far as Mumbai. Anyway, Shrey handles her and tells her that eventually the whole deal with the train will be cheaper because we'll end up taking more time to reach Mumbai if we take the car and might have to stay at a hotel midway. It's amazing how she doesn't let Shrey pay for even the smallest of her expenses.

We go out for an early dinner, overeat and come back to the hotel with fat, bursting tummies. There are still four hours to go for the train and everyone is tired and drowsy, except Tiya of course. Avantika promptly goes to bed and falls asleep. For some reason, I don't feel that tired. I am blank. Too many things have been happening in the last few days. So for a few moments, my mind decides to shut out everything. I leave the room and walk the corridors of the hotel. I stand at a window and stare outside. Suddenly, I hear footsteps coming towards me, and a familiar song.

I turn around. It's Tiya, in her trademark hot pants and loose T-shirt. It's Shrey's T-shirt.

'Not sleeping?' she smiles and asks.

'Nope,' I say. She takes out the earphones from her ears and shuts the music down.

'Isn't it bedtime for you?' she mocks.

'If you are implying we're very old, it's not funny.'

'Aww! Don't mind. I was just playing around,' she says. 'I really don't get the grown-up stuff that you guys do.'

Suddenly, she is like a young kid caught in a boring web of old relatives in a family engagement function.

'You're not supposed to, Tiya,' I say. 'We've had our stupid days too.'

'Oh, please. Just because I don't get what you do and why you do it doesn't mean that I'm stupid,' she says with disdain.

'Well, whatever,' I say and we don't exchange words for a while.

'Best of luck with this whole dead guy thing,' she says. 'I hope that some day I get why you're doing this.'

She smiles and I smile back. I walk back to my room and close my eyes for a power nap.

The alarm rings a little later. We call a taxi and hope we reach the railway station in time to catch the Garib Rath, which runs from Delhi to Mumbai, Gandhinagar being an intermediate stop. We huddle inside the taxi and start discussing the diary again, much to the irritation of Tiya.

'I don't know what the big deal is,' Tiya says.

'*What?*' we echo.

'What *what*? What will happen even if she fucking comes to know that the diary guy was a stalker and loved her. It's bullshit,' she says and goes back to filing her nails.

All three of us look at her with a what-the-fuck expression on our faces and she responds with a fuck-you expression. Maybe it doesn't make sense to her, but it does to us. Shrey takes the diary out and starts reading a note to make her understand. It's amazing how Tiya is not moved by anything around her. While Avantika and I listen to him with abnormally high concentration, Tiya puts her shades on (even when it's dark), plugs in her iPod and leans back into her seat. Her apathy towards the whole situation is astonishing.

'Do you guys even know whom to meet in Mumbai? It's not a small village, you know,' says Tiya.

We look at each other, a little embarrassed. We know it's a long shot, but we still have to go to Mumbai.

'We do,' Shrey says and smirks.

'We do?' Avantika and I look at him, surprised.

'Ah. You guys didn't notice it, did you? Well, I did,' he says with a very condescending expression on his face. I just knew he was hiding something.

'Tell us, please?' Avantika begs.

He laughs wickedly and says, 'Didn't you check the contact person sheet back at the asylum?'

'What contact person sheet?' I ask.

'The one with the details about the person concerned. It had the details of Ritam—his phone number, his parents' address and the emergency contact number.'

'Emergency contact number?' says Avantika. I kick myself for not noticing it.

'He had listed the emergency contact person as Sumi. I didn't know who she was, but now I do,' he says and waves the diary at us.

'You noted the number down?' I ask, sweating in anticipation.

'Yes, Tiya did.'

Tiya looks at him and takes out her cell phone. As Avantika, Shrey and I get into a discussion about who will call Sumi, Tiya dials the number.

'Hey!' she says. 'Is that Sumi? Hi, I'm Tiya.'

We look at Tiya in horror. How can she call her? *Just like that?*

'Yeah, we got your number from where your friend's sister, Nivedita, lives. Umm, yes, yes, Ritam, right. So we wanted to talk to you about Ritam. We are coming to Mumbai in a day or so, and wondering if we could meet. We have something that he might have wanted to give you ... Yeah, yeah ... we will tell you when we meet. Right. Bye. Will call you. Thank you so much,' she disconnects the call and looks at us. 'See! So easy!'

She plugs the earphones of her iPod back into her ears, leans back and starts to hum the lyrics of the song playing. We are stunned. Shrey smiles at us and we smile back. This girl is shockingly crazy. Soon, the taxi drives into the parking lot of the railway station. We are just in time.

'Forty-one, forty-two, forty-three, forty-four,' Avantika reads out from the railway ticket once we get into our coach. Luckily, we got all four seats in a single compartment. The remaining two are unoccupied. It means no creepy men, crying babies or loud aunties around us. It's already late and we are sleepy. Avantika and I bump into each other quite a few times while unfolding the white bed sheets and the blankets provided. There is something incredibly romantic about train journeys, especially the nights. Soon, the lights of the compartment are put out. Avantika and I have chosen the lower-berth seats and we look at each other. Suddenly, I am not sleepy. She stretches her hand and meets mine midway. Even though the train wheels make an overwhelming clanging sound, I can still hear my heart beat louder than that.

'I love you,' she whispers.

'Come here,' I say.

Minutes later, she is on my berth, lying right next to me, sharing my blanket. The railway seats are really not that wide, so we cling to each other to accommodate ourselves. Not that we wouldn't have done it anyway. We start to say every sweet thing we have said to each other over the last so many years, all over again. We stay up a while longer, just talking to each other, listening to our favourite songs on our iPods and looking deep into each other's eyes. I don't know when I fell asleep, but when I wake up early morning, I find Avantika still safely tucked in my embrace. I hug her a little tighter and look at the watch. It's just five. There are still a couple of hours I can spend hugging her. I kiss her on her neck and close my eyes. Life's good.

It takes us around eight hours to reach Mumbai. We reach in the morning and I don't feel sleepy at all. Avantika just got a call from her office and she is not in the best of moods. They are missing her at work and it is affecting their project. I think it's a ploy to get her back in the office. She is so attractive, after all. And her colleagues, well . . . they all are goddamn tharkis.

'Should we call her yet?' Avantika asks us.

Shrey and I shake our heads. It's not yet ten and that's too early to call anyone.

'Should we go to Mulund?' Shrey asks.

From Ritam's contact details which Tiya had noted down at the asylum the number did not work but the address was there. *Mulund, Mumbai.* Avantika and I nod our heads at Shrey's suggestion. It's better than lying sleeplessly in our beds in the hotel. Anyway, I have deep hatred for the hotel where we've checked in. The per-night charges of the hotel go through the roof. Road trip rule no. 2: Never pick Mumbai, it's too expensive.

Tiya stays back at the hotel, while we take the morning local to Mulund. I have been to Mumbai before and the Mumbai local trains never cease to amaze me. I mean, there are just so many people. Osama could have hidden on the Bandra platform for decades and no one would have noticed him. Anyway, Mumbaiites are too busy to notice anyone. I have met some really pretty girls from Delhi who complain that they weren't even given a second look by anyone in Mumbai. The city either has no eye for beauty or it has had too much of it.

One thing is for sure, though. If you can live with travelling by Mumbai locals, you will *love* the city for its sheer energy and honesty. But if you're a spoilt one from Delhi and love your spacious houses—with gardens and balconies, probably a couple of dogs— and long drives, you won't find Mumbai exciting.

Being brought up in Delhi, where shrewdness runs through the veins, you might see Mumbaiites as naive and innocent. No wonder models from Delhi, Punjab and Haryana do so well in Mumbai. We are one set of very wily, foxy people. My ideal city would have the roads, infrastructure, houses and girls of Delhi, the mindset and attitude of Mumbaiites and the weather of Bangalore. Oh, the Delhi Metro too, how can I miss that? And well, girls from Bangalore are pretty cute too, aren't they? They're usually a little too smart for my taste, but I only have myself to blame for being dumb.

We get down at the station and take an auto towards his parents' house. Somehow, we can't find the place. We let the auto driver go and ask around. Nobody recognizes the address. We assume that the name might have changed. A little later, Shrey asks directions from a watchman of a nearby building. He points out to a broken-down building. It's nothing but big stones and rubble. Shrey barks at him, and the watchman says that it's been a year since the building was taken down because it was an illegal construction.

We look at each other, exasperated. It could've been a sure-shot way of getting to Ragini. But it's not written in the diary whether Ritam's parents knew about Ragini. Our shot in the dark gets us nowhere. It's like those notes are taunting us. They bring us that close and then throw us off. It's irritating and it's bugging. Somewhere in the back of the mind, we also know that there is a life at stake—Nivedita's. Time is running out for her.

Our shoulders droop. We don't know what to do. Hungry and tired from the train journey, we enter a food joint nearby. We still have Sumi's number, but we are too disheartened to call her right now. Plus, there is no Tiya around and we feel depressed.

Usually, with her perky and effervescent nature, she keeps us occupied. Irritated but busy.

'Who's calling her?' Shrey asks. 'You,' he answers his own question, pointing at Avantika. I do the same.

Avantika has to call. Guys calling up and telling girls about their ex-boyfriends might be creepy. *Dead* ex-boyfriends—nightmare. Shrey and I really don't want to get into conversations like that. We look at Avantika with eager eyes as she dials the number. She gets self-conscious, gets up and walks away. At a distance, she starts to talk. We get restless. The call lasts barely a minute. She walks back to us with a bewildered expression on her face.

'What?' I ask.

'She's at our hotel!' she exclaims.

'What? How? Oh.'

Tiya. That girl is crazy!

'Tiya asked us to reach the hotel. Sumi is there,' Avantika says. Shrey smiles wickedly. His girlfriend or *whatever* is turning out to be quite a girl. But why would Tiya call her? She was least bothered.

Anyway, my heart starts to pump like a fucking generator as we squeeze into an auto to rush back to our hotel. Mumbai seems to have more autos and taxis than there are people on the streets. And one can hardly tell if those millions of cars and autos are parked for eternity or stuck in traffic.

No one says a word through the entire train journey back. We are not even tired any more. We grab the first auto the moment we're out of the platform and jump out of the auto as soon as we get to our hotel. For a moment, we forget to pay the auto driver. Unlike auto drivers from Delhi or Bangalore (goons!), these guys are sweet. We rush to the lift and reach our room in a flash.

Words will again materialize into a face, into a person, the written word will be spoken, and our dead guy will be alive again through the words of someone close to him. The door creaks open and she is sitting there—Sumi—on the bed, with a tissue box in hand. Tiya is sitting at the television table, chewing her gum and is saying something. She notices us and stops speaking, points to her and introduces her to us. 'Sumi.'

Sumi looks up; the three of us smile and introduce ourselves. There is an awkward silence and I wait for Avantika or Tiya to break it.

'He found the diary,' Tiya points to me.

'Are you sure he is—?' Sumi asks and bursts out crying. I can't think of anything to say. We sit around her and wait for her to stop crying. One tissue box after another, she uses up three. She sniffs, sobs and says something which we don't understand and starts crying again.

'Are you okay?' Avantika asks her as soon as Sumi stops crying. Her eyes are red by now and there are streaks of dried tears on her face. She is okay-looking, but is dressed sharply and looks smart.

'I am fine.'

'Do you want something to eat?' Shrey asks.

'No, thank you. Can I see the diary, please?'

She looks at me, teary-eyed. I take the diary out of the backpack and give it to her. She does what everyone does. She holds it, runs her fingers over it, looks at the burnt edges, probably imagines what might have happened and then sheds a tear.

'Where am I?' she asks, pointing to the diary. I flip the pages and take her to the page where Ritam had first written about her. She is no position to read, so I read it out to her. She clutches my arm and grips it tighter every time Ritam writes anything nice about her. I finish and hand over the diary to her. She goes over those portions again and cries some more.

'Tiya told me that you guys met Piyush too?'

'Yes, we talked to Piyush,' Avantika says. 'He too had no idea that Ritam . . .'

'How is he?'

'He's good. He's working in Bhopal. He still talks very fondly of you,' Avantika says. 'He really loved you back then.'

'I know he did,' she says, and looks sad. 'I was the one who came between them. They were the best of friends.'

'It's not really your fault,' I say.

'Piyush was always very jealous of what I used to feel for Ritam. He had stopped talking to him. That's what I think, at least. Though I never told Ritam why Piyush had stopped talking to him. I didn't want to lose him . . . I was too fond of him. I couldn't have afforded to lose him, so I let the misunderstanding remain.'

She looks guilty. She wipes off her tears that keep trickling down her cheeks intermittently. I look at her closely and find that she is cuter than Ritam's words describe her to be. As she wipes her tears with her hand, I spot a ring on her ring finger. She clearly doesn't look married to me. She is too young.

'When was the last time you talked to him?' Shrey asks.

'I had just shifted to Mumbai in October 2010. I had called him up the minute I landed. He took three days to call me back. He had never taken that long to call me back,' she says.

'Have you met Ragini?' Shrey asks and it looks like he has been dying to ask that.

'No, I haven't and I didn't want to,' she says. 'I was very excited about shifting to Mumbai. I had called him up that day to say that I loved him. When we had broken up, I'd never thought I would miss him so much. It was puppy love, after all. We were still in touch after school but I didn't think we had a chance together until we were in the same city. When I got a job here in Mumbai, I thought things would change. But when he called back, before I could say anything, he told me that he was in love with Ragini. I couldn't say anything I had planned to. After that day, I deleted his number from my phone and never called him again. It was very upsetting for me. He kept calling and texting me for a few days but I didn't respond. I was trying hard to move on.'

'I am sorry,' Avantika says and holds her hand.

'Never mind. Although he did call from an unknown number once and I picked up. It was about two or three months after I had first called.'

'What did he say during that call?' Shrey asks.

'He said he was in Bangalore. He sounded really tense and sad. I had never really seen him like that. But I was busy, so I really couldn't talk to him.'

'You have that number? You called him back?' I ask.

'I called him back a few days later. But it wasn't his number. I wanted to tell him that I was getting engaged and wanted to invite him for the occasion.'

'You got engaged?' Avantika asks. Sumi waves the ring. Sumi tells us that she got over Ritam only recently. All this while, she had been waiting for him to come back to her. She tells us that she is in love again and we congratulate her. We wish her the best of luck for her wedding and her life after that.

'Can you give us that number?' Shrey asks.

She nods, scrolls through her phonebook and fetches the number. Shrey notes it down on a piece of paper. I notice that it's a landline number with a Bangalore area code. Shrey notices that too. He looks at me and we exchange a look. We both have guessed which number it could be.

She looks at us and asks, 'Why are you doing this?'

None of us has an answer.

'We just want Ragini to know,' Avantika says.

'If you find her, tell her that she is really lucky.'

Ironical that she would say that, now that he's dead and gone. If anything, Ragini has to be one of the unluckiest girls ever. But yes, she will know that someone loved her like crazy. That means a lot.

'Sumi, do you know anybody who might know Ritam's whereabouts? Or Ragini's?' I ask her out of desperation.

She checks her social networking profiles to find if Ritam is in anybody's friend list. He isn't. Another dead end.

'I wish I could help you guys,' she says, disappointed.

'Never mind, Sumi,' I say and smile at her.

She doesn't respond.

'I will let you know if I get to know something,' she says.

We talk to her for a little while more and then get her a taxi. She still hadn't stopped crying. It was a shock for her. It would be for anyone. The first love of her life was dead, blown to bits.

26 December 2010

'I can live with the fact that she doesn't love me, but the indifference in her eyes is something I can't bear.'

This morning, I could see her lying unconscious on my bed, right in front of me. I had been looking at her for an hour, trying to comprehend why a girl like her would need to change herself for anyone. She is as perfect as they come. And yet, because of a guy . . .

And as I was reminded of him again, I could feel only one emotion—fury. Nigel is even worse than I had expected.

I wonder why I did not see this before. How did it fail to register in my brain when I first met Nigel that he was a detestable man? Maybe it had. But I must have disregarded it as a feeling of envy. But no, it was not just envy that made him look like such a loathsome creature. It was the fact that he actually was a loathsome creature. It is strange that I had come to Bangalore so that Ragini could spend more time with him. Such a blunder.

Ragini had called me last night after quite a few days, and asked me to take her home, since Nigel and she could not locate Nigel's car and Nigel was on the verge of passing out. Thank God. Had they found it, I shudder to think where they would have ended up. By the time I reached there, she was unconscious—yes, she had passed out owing to too much drinking—but safe. Nigel was barely holding on. I dropped Nigel to his flat and brought Ragini to my room.

I waited for her to get up. I had some questions to ask of her. But when she got up, she had no answers for me. In fact, she was ruder to me than she had ever been, in all the time I have known her. When I asked her why she got so sloshed, she refused to answer in clear words. She said it was none of my business and that she was not a baby. She added that if even she took drugs or smoked weed, I shouldn't be concerned. It was her life, her decisions and she could take care of herself. It felt funny coming from her, because a little while back, she did not seem capable of taking care of herself. And now, suddenly . . .

This is all because of Nigel. I do not have much experience with relationships but I know this one thing—girls go blind in love. THEY SIMPLY CANNOT SEE. Just like Ragini seems unable to see things clearly now. I should not have let this happen. It was my duty to try and help her. I had to make her understand. So I tried to, but she did not listen. She asked me to mind my own business and stop interfering in hers. She asked me to go away. She said she did not want to see me. But no matter what she says . . .

I wish I could see her tomorrow.

3 January 2011

'As long as she talks to me, even if it is to reprimand me and curse me, I don't have a problem. But I will have one if I don't see her being a part of my life.'

It had been a few days that Ragini and I were in that argument at my flat. I tried talking to her the day before yesterday and we again ended up in a fight. Not really a fight, actually. Considering that I did not say a single word after starting the conversation. It was more like—she was shouting at me and I was listening.

I was obliged to tell her the truth when it stared at me straight in the face—Nigel was not a good person. After that one episode in which the two of them had gotten sloshed and I had brought an unconscious Ragini home, it has become a routine. Just that, now she does not call me to take her home. She does not come home. She passes out before making the call and ends up in someone else's house.

That day, I told her in very clear words that I did not think Nigel was right for her. And this is all I said. She got mad at me. She shouted at me and accused me of being boring and forcing her to be the same. She said that I act like someone from a different century, that it was conservative of me to object to something as small as drinking and smoking. And then, she said the most hurtful things she could have—that I am a sadist and that I simply cannot bear to see her happy. That I always try to sabotage her happiness. When all I have wanted, all this while, is to see her smile . . .

Yes, I saw her today. I was sitting in my cubicle, trying to concentrate on the computer screen when I heard her chirp. I looked around to see her enter the office and take a seat in her cubicle. Our eyes met for a fraction of a second, before she looked away. I guess she still does not want to see me. But I did. I kept looking at her for a few more seconds. She looked prettier than usual. Although a little tired. And careless. Her now-straight hair was all over the place, her shirt was not properly tucked in and she was not wearing her stilettos. It seemed like she had not taken a shower.

It scared me a little to see her like that. But what scared me the most was her attitude. It seemed like she did not care about anything in the world. It was as if she could not be least bothered with such mundane things like looking presentable in office, and for someone like Ragini, always very neat and proper, this was new. A little later, I saw her rubbing her eyes and yawning. After dropping her bag at her desk, she made her way, staggering a little, to the washroom. I followed her.

I was a little worried about her first, but then I realized that I might just be getting paranoid. Maybe she had been out late last night and had not gotten proper sleep. As simple as that. And then, when I passed her in the corridor, our eyes met for a brief moment. Her eyes were vacant. Oh. She was stoned, high on something, weed or worse. When I saw her from up-close, I noticed her eyes again and the stagger in her step was evident. I was concerned. But I knew saying anything to her would only result in another earful from her. So I restrained. I wonder if this is going to become routine. I wonder if whatever she is smoking, inhaling or injecting would become a regular thing. Would she be just the way she was today, tomorrow?

I wish to see her okay tomorrow.

The Phone Number

Things just get worse. First, it was a broken-down building, then a name and a number that led us nowhere and now just a number without a name. Shrey and I are pretty sure whose number it is, if we go by what's written in the diary. In one of the notes, Ritam had written that he had called Sumi from Nigel's flat because he was disturbed. Nigel and Ragini had been missing for a few days and he had gone to his flat to find out. Nigel's maid had opened the door and Ritam had waited for Nigel's parents to return from the market. Since he was so restless, he had called Sumi from there to distract himself. Sumi had not picked up calls from his own number so he had called from Nigel's landline.

'Doesn't it fucking look like someone is playing with us?' Shrey says, irritated at the whole situation.

'It's been three weeks for me. Just six days for you,' I say.

'And I don't know why we are doing this,' Avantika says.

'You're lovesick people, that's why,' Tiya butts in.

'Whatever,' we echo.

Shrey flashes the piece of paper in the air on which Sumi had written down the number.

'Could it be Nigel?' Avantika asks. She has realized it too.

166

'Let's find out,' Shrey says and dials the number. The phone is engaged. It's a working number. He calls again. It's still engaged. We wait for a little while and call again. Same result. Our faces droop.

'Is the phone still in service?' Tiya asks.

'Maybe,' Shrey says. 'But I can do something. I can find out the address. We can go to his place, right?'

He logs on to a government website that has the entire database of the Bangalore landlines and the addresses against which they are registered. Bang on! The number is registered in the name of Nigel Abraham. It says M.G. Road. Avantika says she has been in the area.

'Call again,' Avantika tells Shrey and he does. We still can't connect to the other side.

'To Bangalore, then?' Avantika asks. Shrey and I nod.

We start to discuss how and when we should leave for Bangalore, when Tiya says, 'I am not going.' We look at her and she shakes her head.

'But why not?' Shrey asks.

'The trip is getting too long. Today, my mom asked me where I was and when I was coming back home. She checked my bank statement and scolded me for spending so much. I can't go to Bangalore.'

'But, we have to—' Shrey says.

'I can't, Shrey. I have no money left. Seriously, I will have to go back to Delhi. My parents will kill me. I am just lucky that they haven't called my friends yet.'

I can understand. She is a student, after all. We had totally forgotten about that.

'But you don't have to pay for this trip, Tiya.'

'I don't want you to pay for me, Shrey. I will not allow it,' she says.

Suddenly, Tiya has started to sound a little grown-up and sensible. It's almost shocking.

'You don't have to pay for it,' Shrey says and smiles, 'because Chrome Ink Press will.'

'What the fuck? Why should *we*?' I protest.

'What? You wanted a story, Deb? This is your story. So this should go into the company account, right?'

'Such an asshole,' I say.

'I'm not sure,' Tiya says, 'My mom won't allow me to stay out any longer. It's been so many days now.'

'Do you want to?' Avantika asks Tiya and she nods. 'Let me talk to your mother.'

Tiya hands over her phone to Avantika who talks to Tiya's mom posing as Tiya's Department Head. Tiya's mom totally buys whatever Avantika says and extends her trip by another few days. There is a huge smile on Tiya's face.

'So we leave for Bangalore today?' Tiya asks.

'Yes,' we echo.

'I mean, we just reached here. Can't we at least party for one night? It's getting so boring, guys,' Tiya asks, almost innocently.

'We don't have time,' Shrey explains.

'You guys are so stupid, man. Why can't you just let it be? If grown-ups get this screwed-up, I want to remain stupid and childish for the rest of my life.'

'We can't help it,' I say.

'One night wouldn't kill you guys! Please?' she says again, with a puppy face.

I don't know how we fall for it. All of us look at each other and we know we want to leave for Bangalore as soon as possible. Only that our bodies are now a crumbled heap of tissue. We can do with a little bit of rest too, we think.

'Fine,' I say. 'We leave tomorrow? Happy?'

'Yay!' she says in mock excitement. I know what she's thinking inside her head. *'Bloody assholes. Finally, they've got some sense.'*

'Can we sleep for a bit now?' Avantika says.

Minutes later, we have all dozed off wherever we find place to rest our broken, weathered bodies.

~

'GET UP!' Tiya has been shouting for quite some time now.

I was thinking it was a part of the dream but it isn't. I get up to see Shrey asleep on the sofa and Avantika on the floor. Slowly, we all get up, groggy-eyed.

'WE NEED TO GO. IT'S EIGHT ALREADY,' she shouts repeatedly.

I guess we slept throughout the day.

'You guys go, I'm going to sleep for a little while,' I say and place the pillow over my head.

I was in the middle of an interesting dream where Ragini was in tears after we told her about Ritam. Pretty moving it was. It's a great story in my head. I've already decided that I'll write a book about it. It sounds like an amazing idea, but I don't think I'll be able to do justice to it.

'I will stay here with Deb. Anyway, I don't have any clothes to wear,' Avantika says and closes her eyes again.

Shrey ignores everything around him and rolls over.

'You guys have got to be shitting me,' Tiya says. 'Don't be so boring. We had to go clubbing.'

'Not we. YOU!' I say.

'You're such assholes. I come along with you on your crazy chase across cities and you can't do this much for me?'

'Now that's blackmail,' Avantika says.

'Whatever it is,' Tiya says and shrugs. She spends another half an hour telling us how insensitive we are and eventually we give in. We get up slowly. Shrey and I realize that it's a little too late for train tickets, so we call up a travel agent and get ourselves four tickets on a flight leaving the next day at six in the morning.

Shrey goes and get the printouts for our tickets and flashes them once he's in the room, 'So, no back-breaking car drives or train journeys.'

'Losers,' Tiya mutters under her breath. 'It's supposed to be a road trip, not a train and flight trip.'

'What do you mean *losers*? It's tiring,' I protest as Avantika smiles.

'That's what. I can take it, you can't. You are old and boring,' she says.

'Fuck you,' I say.

'Fuck you? You wish. It's such torture fucking one old man,' she laughs and points at Shrey, 'I don't want to add another one to the list.'

'Whatever.'

'Do we have to go? There is still time to decide,' Tiya asks as she unmindfully packs her small bag. 'You'll anyway have to come back to Mumbai. I am telling you, that freakish girl lives in Mumbai,' she insists.

'Shut up,' Avantika says like a mom.

'Anyway, I don't care. I am not paying for this, you guys are,' says Tiya. She is still pretty repulsed by the idea of us taking a flight.

We pack our bags and decide that we'll return to the hotel by three in the night to reach the airport on time. Tiya cribs about the early flight. We ignore whatever she says.

Slowly and reluctantly, we get dressed and move out of the hotel. She had decided on a club in Bandra she had heard a lot about—Hawaiin Shack—probably for its cheap alcohol. Tiya will be a good girlfriend if she ever finds herself in a relationship. She has a formidable grip on how to limit expenses. She makes us stop at the beer shop nearby and we pick up a bottle of vodka and some beers. By the time we reach the club, we're pretty drunk but not enough.

'This is why you're OLD!' shouts Tiya as we get off the taxi. 'No one gets drunk inside. That's just a waste of money.'

No one is really interested in listening to her any more. Hawaiin Shack—the place is nothing much to write home about. We stagger and stumble inside. Before we know it, we exhaust our cover charges and are piss drunk. The people around us become blobs and everything becomes hazy. I don't remember how long I danced for, but it seemed like ten minutes. It'd been long since Avantika and I had done that. I'm thankful to Tiya for this.

'*LET'S GO!*' a familiar voice shouts in my ear.

Avantika and I are almost glued to each other. Man, she can grind! And well, I can't really dance. But yeah, I can do the drunk-guy-out-of-his-senses thing pretty well. We ignore the voice near us. It shouts in our ear again, but the music drowns it out.

'*FUCK YOU. IT'S TIME,*' the voice says in our heads again.

We look around. It's Tiya shouting her head off.

'What?' Avantika shouts back.

'It's *TIME,*' she shouts. 'It's already four-thirty.'

Suddenly, we are not drunk. We look at our watches and get a little freaked out. Though nowhere close to how freaked out Tiya looks. She is almost panicking and it's funny to see her like that. Lately, she has been the definition of the word 'cool' to us.

'Oh, crap,' I say and stare at the watch, mentally calculating the time required to reach the airport.

'We should rush,' Avantika exclaims.

Immediately, we finish the last of our drinks and head out of the door. We find Shrey outside the club, talking to a few stray dogs. He has not changed since his college days. We take an auto, huddle in and get back to our hotel. We are still struggling to find our way to our room's door when we spot Tiya standing there with all our bags.

'What?' she exclaims as Shrey pushes her aside, and we make our way to the beds and couches in the room.

'We need to sleep,' Avantika says and flops on a couch.

'Me too,' I say and take the bed. Shrey has already found a place on the floor and his eyes are closed.

'We have a *fucking flight* in an hour!' Tiya shouts.

'No, we don't,' Avantika says.

'What? The flight's at six, right?' Tiya reminds us.

'It was at six,' I say. 'Oh? No one told you? The flight was delayed moments after we booked it. It's at ten now.'

Avantika chuckles. So do I. And though it looks like Shrey is fast asleep, he's not. His lips curve into a smile.

'But why the fuck didn't you guys tell me?'

'You're not the only one here who can be a pain in the ass,' Avantika says and we all chuckle.

'All of you are *assholes*.'

~

'You guys are crazy. I am not getting up,' Tiya shouts as we wake her up at eight.

All three of us share a quiet smile among ourselves. She had panicked big time a couple of hours back.

'We know you're coming along,' Shrey says. 'You want to find out what happens next too, don't you?'

'Fuck you! I don't. I'm not crazy like you.'

'Oh, is it so? Is that why you acted so hyper? Is that why you so desperately want to go to Bangalore?' Avantika says.

'I do *not* want to go. I just didn't want the money to go waste.' She sits up in the bed and rubs her eyes.

'You weren't paying for it anyway,' Shrey says.

'Whatever,' she says and her lips curve into a smile. We laugh. 'But I'm still telling you guys that it's a waste. By the way, did anyone call that number again?' she says and we laugh again. 'You guys better stop laughing or I will cut your heads off.'

It becomes apparent that despite her outward posturing of being disconnected, she is glued to our little adventure.

'I called,' Avantika says.

'And?'

'Nigel's parents picked up. Nigel has been in a rehabilitation facility in Bangalore for the last few months. He's not doing too well.'

Tiya is dumbfounded. She's not read the diary so she doesn't know as much about Nigel as we do. Tiya looks at Avantika, and then us, and has nothing to say. It's not because she's taken aback at what Avantika has just said, it's because no matter how much Tiya has tried to distance herself from the story, she's a part of it too. We are all a part of it now. There is no escaping it. Our lives, their lives—it's all intertwined now. Tiya doesn't say anything and packs her stuff.

We reach the airport in under an hour. No one sleeps in the taxi. Tiya, tense and nervous, asks us again if Nigel was seriously in rehab and we nod.

'Who's going to talk to Ragini?' Shrey asks and everyone looks at me.

'I would have nothing to say,' I reply.

'But you found the diary,' Avantika says.

'What would I say to her? You're a girl; you'll be able to handle it better.'

My palms sweat even as I imagine the scenario. We are still a fair distance from reaching Ragini, but I'm already nervous.

'We'll just give her the diary,' Tiya says.

'It's going to be so awkward,' Shrey adds.

I had realized that long back. But I didn't give it much thought back then. And now, it is staring right at me. I am just thankful that I have three more people with me in my awkwardness. We get on the flight and I close my eyes. The air hostesses are hot, but they can't hold my attention for long. I wait for Bangalore.

'Don't worry too much,' Avantika looks at me and says.

'I am not worrying. I just feel sorry for Ragini.'

'Hmmm. I am sure she's going to be okay. One just cannot beat fate, right? At least she'll get to know that she was loved by Ritam till his dying breath. That's got to mean something.'

'Let's hope so,' I say.

'You're cute, Deb.'

'Where did that come from?'

'You look cute when you're nervous. And what you're doing is commendable. I mean, no one would have done what you are doing. I'm sure Ritam is watching you from above and patting your back,' she says.

'What crap. You would've done the same. And you're doing the same, aren't you?'

'Whatever.'

'And it was anyway a selfish pursuit. I thought this would make an interesting story,' I say.

'You want me to believe that?'

'Not really.'

She puts her hand on mine and smiles. I smile back. I owe everything to Avantika. She kind of puts my life into perspective. I really don't care what anyone thinks or says about me. All I truly care about is her. My true aim in life is not to be happy or world peace or the Kashmir issue but to see Avantika every day and to keep her happy.

'I love you,' I say after a pause.

'I know you do,' she runs her fingers over my face.

'Those creepy *Twilight* movies . . . ?'

'What about them?' she asks.

'Sometimes, like that vampire in those movies, I stay up nights to watch you sleep.'

'Liar,' she says and smiles shyly.

'I mean I try to. But they are vampires, they don't sleep. I do. But I do watch you. And all I do is . . .'

'What?'

'. . . wonder if you dream about me,' I say.

'Do I look happy when I'm asleep?'

'Yes, you do.'

'Then I'm sure I'm dreaming about you,' she says and puts her head on my shoulder.

These little things are what make my life worth living.

13 January 2011

'No matter how much she insults me and berates me, one smile—just one smile—and she makes it all right.'

For the first time in days, I looked at Ragini and didn't think that she was high on anything. She seemed perfectly sane and in control of her senses. But something about her still seemed a little off. She did not seem like the cute girl-next-door that she used to be. The careless attitude was still there. I felt like going to her to talk. But something stopped me. Something told me that she was still not willing to listen. I was actually nervous to talk to her.

Over the last few days, she has started to look a little strange. She applies something on her eyes that make them look all dark and evil. How can someone change so drastically, over a period of a few weeks? Ragini has and there is no use denying it. It is right in front of me. I am insanely worried about her. And by the end of the day, I decided that I would not keep shut any longer. It was time for an intervention. I could not see her destroy herself right in front of my eyes. I decided I would tell her that Nigel was wrong and she should leave him. But I did not get a chance. Before I could gather up my courage to approach her, she left. I saw Nigel enter the office and I saw her leave with him. They were on a bike. There weren't any helmets in sight. I hoped they did not get into any kind of trouble.

I had not seen her since that day—which was three days ago—and I had been worried out of my mind. If something had happened to her, I would never have been able to forgive myself. I could have stopped her from leaving with Nigel that evening, but I was too much of a coward to take a stand against what Ragini wanted. I did not want her to be bothered with my stupid concerns again. I had been restless the entire day. Both their phones were switched off. I could not help but think of what all could have happened. All kinds of gruesome images were popping up in my head. I was going out of my mind.

Finally, I gave up and went to Nigel's flat. Nigel's parents had gone out so I waited there. I just wanted Ragini to be all right. I wanted to make her understand what's right and what's not. I didn't know how to go about it. I called Sumi a few times, but she didn't pick up. She has been avoiding me lately. Then I called her from Nigel's landline and she picked up. She said she was busy and would call me back later. A little later, Nigel's parents returned and told me he had gone to Coorg for a few days. I left their place. I didn't know whether to be happy or sad about it.

Last night, as I passed her room, I heard her voice. I am sure it was her. It could be no one else. No one else can chirp like her. I wanted to knock on her door, but resisted. It wasn't just her chirp I heard. Nigel was there too.

I went to the office today, though I did not want to. But I needed something to do, so I could distract myself. And then, I saw her. I was amazed at first. She looked clean, almost like herself, like she did before we made the biggest mistake and came to Bangalore. Except that there were dark shadows beneath her eyes and her eyes were a little swollen due to lack of sleep. How was I to know that those circles were an indication of darker times to come?

And then, I decided to go talk to her. Luckily, I was at the water cooler, when I heard her meek 'Hi' from behind me. I turned and smiled, after the initial shock of being face-to-face with such prettiness faded. We stood silently for a short while, after which she asked me how I was doing. We made small talk for a few more minutes before going back to our desks. And when I got there, I found a tissue paper lying on top of my keyboard. It had one word—Sorry.

I smiled and met her eye over the computer screen. She smiled back. Things are getting back to normal. I am glad. I am happy today. After a very long time, Ragini let me come close to her. Though she still did not really talk to me, I saw her eyes twinkle again, the voice chirp again. I saw her lips curve upwards and a little colour flood her cheeks. She looked adorable.

I wish I could see her again tomorrow.

28 January 2011

'Sometimes you have to undergo a lot of pain to realize what's right and what's wrong. As she endures that pain and fights for every breath, I hope she realizes. I have had my share of pain and I don't mind taking away hers.'

It was three hours past midnight when the policeman called me. When he told me Ragini was in hospital, I thought it was just one of my bad dreams. I had been having similar nightmares for the last few weeks. But then, after a while, it registered—it was really happening. Over the past few weeks, Nigel and Ragini had been missing office regularly. On other days, when they did come to office, they used to be in a dishevelled state. A few days back, Ragini had even asked me for money. I knew what she wanted it for so I politely refused.

I rushed to the hospital to find both Ragini and Nigel admitted there. Drug overdose. Cocaine with dangerous levels of alcohol in their bloodstreams. While Nigel was shifted to the general ward just a little while later, Ragini stayed in the ICU for more than six hours. The flashing red light had been sucking the life out of me and killing me slowly. I could not hold it back any longer. I had to call and inform her parents about it and so I did. They freaked out and left from the UK within two hours. They had no idea about all this happening behind their backs. And that was when I had told them nothing about it. I had told them it was a one-time thing. An accident. She had never had drinks or done drugs before. I hoped they would not lose their daughter. I hoped I would not lose my reason to live. But outside the ICU, I was alone. It was a sixteen-hour flight from London to Bangalore. All I did was pace around the waiting area and curse myself for letting it happen. I had been a coward. I hated myself.

Finally, the next morning, twenty-eight hours after she had been admitted, we got the news that she was out of danger. It had been some hours since Ragini's parents had reached. All those hours, her mom had cried, while I had tried desperately to hold back my tears. We had been up all night. She had been talking to me about her. She told me all about Ragini, right from when she was a fat little girl. Some of it I already knew. A lot of it was news to me. I had kept listening.

The doctors said that Ragini had suffered kidney and liver damage, which was irreversible, but she would live. When her mom stopped crying, I took her slowly towards where Ragini lay. She looked at her and cried some more. It was a depressing sight—the white bed, Ragini in a hospital gown, needles sticking out of her, her uncombed hair and the strange, sickening hospital smell. Ragini's dad stood in front of the ICU, looking at Ragini's still form. And then he looked at me, as I tried to console his wife. His eyes told me he was grateful. I couldn't take my eyes off Ragini. She looked weak. Frail. Her complexion was chalky. I could not bear to see her like that, but I kept looking. She was alive. It was enough for me.

Today, it has been three days since the drug overdose incident. She is still in the ICU. The recovery of her kidney would take a lot of time. Full recovery is impossible. I have been watching her from a distance for the last few days. But I went to see her today. There was a police case filed and they were both recommended to a rehabilitation centre. Her parents wanted me to tell her that. I slowly entered her ward and stood at the foot of her bed. She looked up and saw me. Then she looked away. She kept staring blankly at the wall for all the time that I was there. I sat next to her bed and told her about what was supposed to happen. She is to be shifted to the rehab in a few days and so is Nigel. As I described the details, she kept staring at that favourite wall of hers and crying. I did not like the tears that were flowing from her eyes on to the pillow. But I could not do anything to stop them. She did not look at me even once. When I left the room, I felt her eyes follow me.

I wish things are better tomorrow. I wish I could see her tomorrow.

Bangalore

It seems like the flight is taking forever to reach Bangalore. I have a certain respect for that city. It's probably the only city where Rock 'n' Roll, metal signs and sticking your tongue out in public and shouting 'Metallicaaaaa!' are not frowned upon. I'm not really a fan of the congested traffic and that the city closes down at ten in the night. It has way too many cute women to keep them hidden behind closed doors. Bangalore desperately needs a night life, because it certainly has the people needed to sustain one—rich, good-looking people.

When I wake up, I find Avantika running her fingers through my hair. I feel like sleeping some more so that she keeps doing it. But soon the fasten-your-seat-belt sign comes up and I get up. I look at my right to see Shrey and Tiya holding hands. They seem to be in love. I have begun to accept Tiya as a part of our little world. Despite all her unnecessary bravado, Tiya seems like a sweet girl. We already know that she is super sharp. So it's not all that bad having her around.

The airplane stutters and shudders to a stop. That's really the best part of flying. A certain part of me always wants the plane to crash, just to know how it feels to be seconds away from a catastrophe and feel that thrill and the rush. Yes, I'm a little creepy. The airplane stops and everyone rushes to take their bags out, like they are the busiest people around. We sit and wait. Avantika points to Shrey and Tiya, who are holding hands and talking to each other. They look cute, even though Shrey distinctly looks about ten years older than her.

'What do you think of them?' Avantika asks.

'Them? She's too young, isn't she?'

'Yes, but she's smart.'

'I thought you didn't like her,' I say.

'I didn't. She was a little too brash. I thought she would go down the same terrible path I went on. Or *her* way,' she points to the diary meaning Ragini. 'But she seems a little too smart for it.'

'And how can you say that?'

'Remember when we mentioned that Nigel went to rehabilitation? She was shocked. When I was told such things, I always thought that it could not happen to me. That's cockiness. But she was shocked. She is scared of what happened to Ragini and Nigel. She isn't stupid. I was,' Avantika says.

'You're not stupid! You're lovely!'

We see Shrey and Tiya get up, with their hands wrapped around each other's. We follow suit. Finally, we get off the plane and enter the Bangalore airport. The weather, as expected, is awesome.

'I'll go and find out where the rehabilitation facility is located,' Avantika says and walks towards the tourist information counter. She comes back with a map that has a circle marked around where we have to go.

'Should we leave?' she asks.

'Is it really necessary?' Tiya asks nervously. We look at her strangely.

'Yes, we have to go,' Shrey says. 'Maybe after seeing the rehabilitation facility you'll understand why Avantika is so concerned about you and why she asks you to behave sensibly. She has been through all that and knows what it's like to be in there.'

'Huh?' we echo. We don't get the point behind what Shrey just said. Usually, he just encourages Tiya's stupid behaviour. This was strange and totally out of the blue.

'You mean I don't act sensibly?' Tiya asks, surprised. 'Why would you say that? All of a sudden?'

'It's because—'

'Because?'

'Nothing,' he says. 'I just don't want anything to happen to you. It's for your own good.'

Yeah, right! We all know what Shrey had almost said out aloud. He was about to say that he is in *love* with her. He had just *almost* said it. It's been years since Shrey has told anybody that he loves her. Avantika and I look at each other and smile. Tiya doesn't react. I think she missed the point and is just offended by what he said.

The rehabilitation facility is located fifty kilometres outside the city. We take a taxi and the driver tells us that it's a long drive. We don't really mind. We are not driving any more. A part of me doesn't even want to get there. The thought of Ragini's dead guy is freaking me out.

'Why does your trip always have to include scary places?' Tiya remarks as we stand outside the rehabilitation facility. It's eerily similar to the place where we'd gone to meet Nivedita. It looks like a British structure, really old and imposing. In fact, this place is a little worse than the mental asylum where we went. We go through the same exercise of asking the receptionist whether we could meet the patient. She asks us to wait in the visiting room.

It's a little strange to think that Ragini has been here too. Avantika tries to ask the receptionist if she can give us the details of Ragini and she refuses. She states that every patient signs a confidentiality clause when he or she is admitted that bars the hospital from revealing any information to anyone.

'I don't really like Nigel,' Tiya whispers in Avantika's ear.

'What? You don't even know him.'

'Had he not been there, all of this wouldn't have happened. Asshole,' Tiya says.

'And Deb wouldn't have had his story,' Shrey taunts.

'Whatever,' I answer.

A little later, we see a man walk towards us. I had prepared myself for the worst, but he is far more pitiable. He is much worse than I had imagined him to be. Nigel looks nowhere near the *stud* Ritam had described him as. He looks like a corpse. He must be a little older than me and is thin, scrawny, with barely any skin left on his face. He walks towards us with a limp. He has a little stubble and his skin is red with rashes. But I don't feel sorry for him.

'Do I know you?' he asks in his throaty voice.

It's scary. He is a living example of why one shouldn't get into drugs. His eyes look at us. They look dead and are sunken deep within their sockets. He looks dead already. It freaks us out. We just sit there and stare at him. We were angry at him for being the reason behind Ritam and Ragini not being together, but now he evokes sympathy and pity.

'We are Ritam's friends,' Avantika says.

She puts her hands on both Shrey and me to stop us from telling him the story. I know why she does that. Avantika too had been admitted to a rehabilitation facility in Delhi about seven years ago for her addiction to meth. She knows how to deal with these things. Avantika told us while we were in the taxi today that when in rehab, you need reasons to continue your life. Often, the patients who are admitted are suicidal. She had been one of them.

'Ritam . . . ? Oh.' He remembers and smiles. He has a few teeth missing. He might have stumbled down the stairs when stoned. It happens frequently, Avantika had once told me. I wonder how she had managed to stay so spotlessly beautiful even after going through everything that Nigel has.

'Do you know him?' Tiya asks. We are surprised to see her piqued interest.

'Yes, I know him. Ragini's friend,' he coughs. 'Sweet guy.'

His voice is very strange. And he makes a strange face every time he says something. It looks like it hurts his throat each time he tries to talk.

Shrey asks what's really important, 'Are you in touch with Ragini?'

He pauses. Our heartbeats stop, our breaths wait in our lungs while he looks at us with pitiable eyes. We try to read his eyes, but all we can see are hollow, sunken eyeballs.

'No, not really. I haven't seen her in a long time,' he says with a sigh.

'How long?' Shrey asks, exasperated.

Nigel looks at Shrey strangely. Yes, we are all angry. How can he not know where Ragini has gone? He took Ragini away from Ritam and now he doesn't know where the heck she is. This is just unfair. He had been an unreasonable boyfriend and maybe he deserves what he's going through. I have only hatred for him.

'It's been long. I have run away from this place thrice to look for Ragini. I have never been able to find her . . .' His voice trails off. 'I will never forgive myself for what I made her go through.'

Even though his face constantly tells me he is a person who is sad, morose and regretful of what he has done, I am still not moved. I was and will always be in Team Ritam. Not the guy who destroyed not one but two lives.

'What happened when you ran away the last time?' Avantika looks at him and asks. Avantika's kind eyes make anyone open up his or her heart.

'I ran away from here and reached my house. I had been off medication for three weeks and was tired and sick. I called Ragini and she told me she never wanted to see me again. She was angry at herself and angrier at me. She wanted to be alone and she didn't let me say anything . . .' he says.

'What would you have said?' Avantika asks.

'I would have apologized and . . . and I would have told her that . . .' he pauses and adds in his barely audible voice, '. . . that Ritam loves her and she should be with him.'

'*You knew?*' Shrey asks.

'It was obvious. One look at Ritam's face when he used to see Ragini and me together, and anyone could see the pain in his eyes,' he says.

The conversation just continues to make me hate Nigel more and feel sorrier for Ritam. Nigel is and was such a bastard.

'You think Ragini knew about what Ritam felt for her?' Avantika asks.

'I had told Ragini a few times, but she said I was wrong and that Ritam could get a much better girl. She didn't take me seriously. But she was ashamed about what happened. She said she had disappointed and let everyone down—Ritam, her parents, her aunt in Mumbai, everyone. She was very disturbed. She said—'

'Yes? What did she say?'

'She said that Ritam was right about everything . . . that she should have stayed away from me. She was full of regret that she had spoilt her bond with Ritam and fought with him for my sake. She told me she would never be able to face Ritam again. Not after all that Ritam had done for her and she repaid him only in pain.'

Nigel has tears in his eyes. They still don't move me. He destroyed lives. He deserves no pity.

'I have called her a million times after that, but I think she has changed her number,' he adds.

'So you have absolutely no idea about where she can be now? Which city? Anything?' Shrey asks.

'After that phone call, she had sent me a Get Well Soon card. There might be some address on it,' he says and his voice gets worse. He can barely talk now.

'Can you get it for us?' Avantika says.

'Sure,' he says as more tears trickle down his hollow cheeks.

He gets up, staggers a little and then leaves the waiting room. I feel a little sorry for Nigel now, but he himself is responsible for his condition. It is such a contrast. On one side, there is Nivedita, the beautiful girl confined to a wheelchair, robbed of all her happiness due to her cruel fate and here is Nigel, who did this to himself. Sometimes, life makes no sense at all.

A little later, he staggers back inside the visitors' room with an envelope in hand. He sits before us and hands over the envelope.

'Here,' he says, showing us the card too. There is nothing written on the card. We give it back. We have no use for the card. But our eyes widen as we see the address on the envelope. Finally. *Ragini*. There is a Mumbai address on the envelope. We smile. Tiya sighs and mutters under her breath, 'Mumbai again.'

'Huh?' Nigel says.

Shrey fetches his cell phone to save the address.

'You can keep it,' Nigel says. 'I have no use for it now. I have lost her forever.'

'Hmmm,' Shrey says, folds the envelope carefully and keep it in his pocket.

'What else do you know about Ritam and Ragini?' Avantika asks.

'They could have made a really good couple,' Nigel says. He looks guilty as he says that.

'You know you screwed up, right?' Tiya almost scolds him. Shrey asks Tiya to shut up.

'She's right,' Nigel says. 'I screwed up. And I am sorry for that.'

'You're *sorry*? He is *dead* now! And he couldn't even tell Ragini that he loved her. *All because of you*. And you say you're *sorry*?' Tiya, with tears in her eyes, almost shouts at him. We look at her, shocked.

He looks back at us and shouts, '*WHAT*?'

Before we can say anything, she runs out of the room. *Is she crying?* It's freaking weird. What happened to her? We look at Nigel, who looks back at us. His eyes have many questions and his face is blank. We don't know where to start. And in this story, if there is a villain, it is him. And, obviously, some guy across the Indian border, who planted the bomb.

'Is . . . is it . . . true?' he asks, choked. We nod. '. . . H . . . how did it . . . ?'

As Avantika starts to narrate the story, he holds his head in his palms and breaks down. Avantika tells him everything that has happened till now. He takes time to compose himself. Finally, he says in his croaky, broken-down voice, 'It's my fault.' And breaks down again.

'It's *not*,' Avantika says.

'I should just die.'

Maybe he should. He is detestable. Avantika looks at us and asks us to go and take care of Tiya. It's another way to say *get lost*. We get up and walk away from them. Shrey starts to look around for Tiya. I look through the glass to see Nigel break down time and again, as Avantika consoles him. She has that magic touch and those enchanting eyes that make everything seem better.

I don't know how she is so kind-hearted and empathetic. I still don't feel a thing for the guy. Guys like Nigel are pests and should be treated like that. A little later, Avantika walks out of that door and smiles at me.

'What did you say?' I ask.

'Nothing. He will be okay in a while,' she says. 'Did you find Tiya?'

'Shrey is looking for her.'

We leave the building and spot Shrey and Tiya sitting in the car. Shrey is hugging her as she lies in his arms.

'Tiya really psyched out in there,' I say.

'She is a love-struck kid, after all,' Avantika says.

I chuckle.

⌒

'Such a bastard,' Tiya mutters as we sit in the car.

'Yeah,' I say. 'You gave quite a performance in there.'

'I was just so angry. How can he throw away his life like that? And he even dragged down Ragini with himself!' she says.

Avantika nudges me and says, 'What did I tell you?'

I smile back. Tiya knows better than we'd assumed she does. She knows what's right and what's not. She is not stupid.

'What did she tell you?' Tiya asks me.

'Nothing,' I say.

'*Tell me!*' she exclaims. 'You guys bitch about me behind my back?'

We chuckle.

'Whatever.'

The conversation ends and Avantika asks the taxi driver to take us to the airport. Another flight. Like last time, the flight tickets are paid for by the company. This trip is proving to be quite an expense.

'Please tell me that this will be the last stop,' Tiya pleads.

We know it's fake. She's equally interested in it now. Not once during the whole exercise from entering the facility and coming out of it, did she make a face or plug in her iPod and appear disinterested. She was listening intently, had shouted at Nigel and almost snatched the envelope from Shrey's hand to read the address.

'I think we have established that Avantika is going to handle all our conversations from now on?' Shrey says.

'That's a stupid question. Obviously it's going to be her,' I say.

'Fine,' Avantika says.

The taxis whizzes through the streets of Bangalore as we head towards the airport again within the space of five hours. There is nervousness writ large on our faces. It's going to be our last spot and it's going to bring to an end our wild chase. I wish I had more time in Bangalore. It's a wonderful city. Anyway, I can't even begin to anticipate how Ragini would react. I'm glad Avantika will handle all of it. But I'm super curious to meet this mystery girl from the diary. I wonder what she's like. And, as the dead guy says, 'I wish I could see her tomorrow.'

3 February 2011

'How long can she be ignorant of my love? It seems like it's been forever.'

I was just in time to see her being transferred from the hospital to the rehabilitation centre. When I got to the hospital, I saw her dad complete the formalities at the reception and her mom was in her ward, packing up all her stuff. I understood that she had decided to go to the rehab. After everything was done, I went to help her get up from the bed. She did not accept my support.

Two male nurses helped her out of bed, on to a wheelchair and into the van that waited outside. We waited for Nigel to come, but he never did. I was a bit shocked at first. How could he go against this so carelessly? But we did not wait for long. We knew he would not be coming.

When she was brought to the rehab, I saw a strange look in her eyes. She looked defeated and detached, as if anything that happened around her had ceased to matter. She did not protest to any number of needles piercing her body and any number of medications pushed down her throat. The only thing she did refuse to do was to talk to anyone. She did not talk at all. Her parents kept trying to make her speak, but she did not utter a single word. I had decided to not give up that easily. I would keep trying and keep hoping she would reciprocate. Maybe she was just weak.

I went to see her again today. She was in a much better condition. She was talking properly to everyone and looked at peace. Seeing her like that gave me some kind of relief. In the week that she had spent there, there was considerable progress. No one who would look at her from a distance would ever be able to guess that she was a patient and there was anything wrong with her. She looked normal. It made me happy.

She seemed kind of happy too, until she saw me. After that, her attitude changed. It was as if she would have run away from me physically had she been capable of doing so. She looked disturbed on seeing me. I took the doctor's permission to see her. But as soon as I got close, the nurses came and stopped me from getting in. The patient did not want to see me, they said. They had been given clear instructions. I have no idea why she did that, but all I know is that it hurt. Still, I did not force her. I honoured her wishes and stayed out of her range. I just saw her from a distance, like before, and made sure she had everything she needed. She seemed okay. She looked way better than she had looked some time back. I was happy with her progressing health. I did not ask for too much.

I just wish I could see her tomorrow.

⌣

7 February 2011
'Did I lose her forever? Just the thought is enough to stop my heart from beating. But I won't let that happen. I have to be there. She might need me.'

This time, when no one could find her, a part of me said that we would not find her alive. She had been recovering beautifully ever since she got shifted to the rehab, but suddenly, one day she refuses to see me, and the next day she disappears? Where did she go? This is a high-security rehabilitation centre. The security is almost as strict as that of a jail. It is impossible to even think of the possibility of an escape. And why would she go anyway? What was she not getting here? Wasn't everything happening just the way she wanted? And she had seemed happy with the progress . . .

I didn't know where she was. And I didn't know what to make of it. Had she given into the craving? I didn't know where to search for her, but somehow, I just knew that I did not need to worry too much. I knew it in my heart that she would come back. Or else we would find her dead, somewhere in the campus. There was nothing I could do. I was helpless and powerless. But she came back. Within twenty-four hours of disappearing. When asked, she told them she was with Nigel. He had come to take her away from the rehab. And she ran away with him. But she did not have eloping with him on her mind. She went because she had thought she would be able to change Nigel's mind and convince him to come to rehab too. He did not agree and she had to come back. Alone.

When I heard about this, I smiled in relief. I knew that the bad times were over. She is okay now. Sane, sweet and caring, like she had always been. I was touched by the way she still wanted to try and get Nigel's life back on track, even after what he did to her. I had almost lost her. Twice. Once to Nigel. Once to drugs and alcohol. But now, I am sure I have her back.

But while I had started seeing us together again, she had different plans. Ragini's mom gave me a letter today that

Ragini wanted me to have. As I read it, I knew it was the end of the road for us. Ragini has decided my fate and it's on that piece of paper. It's a small message and it has wrecked my life. I don't know what to do now. I am defeated. I am lost. I look at the paper in one hand and my ticket back to my city in the other. The internship ends tomorrow and with it ends us—Ragini and I.

I know it won't happen . . .

. . . but I wish I could see her tomorrow.

Where's Ragini?

We are back inside a flight. This time we're flying back to Mumbai. Things have changed a lot since our last flight. Even though we were always just a phone number away from Ragini, somehow we had never imagined that we would come so close. We are now just a few hours away from meeting her and I am shitting in my pants.

There is palpable excitement as we leave the Mumbai domestic airport and look for a taxi. But with it, there is nervousness. Thank God I didn't take this journey alone. It would have been difficult to talk to all these people and especially Ragini. There was no way I could have done it alone. We leave the airport and are blankly looking at each other. We have no idea what to expect.

'We should go, right?' Shrey says.

Avantika has the envelope in her hand. It's a Sunday so it's probably the best day to catch her at home.

'Yes,' we echo.

Finally, after a little while, Avantika calls out to a taxi and it stops in front of us. She is the only one who shows a semblance of courage. The rest of us are pissing in our pants, and it shows on our faces. Even Tiya—our enfant terrible, give-no-shit-take-no-shit kid—looks nervous as hell.

'Bhaiya,' Avantika says and shows the paper to a taxi driver. 'Can you take us here?'

He nods and we board the taxi. We hope that we find Ragini home. Nobody says anything as the taxi leaves behind the Mumbai airport and crawls through the Mumbai traffic slowly. I don't know how we're going to approach this conversation. Everyone who has ever met Ritam likes him as a person and has reacted very strongly to the news of him passing away. I wonder how she will react. After all, she was the closest to him. And she had pushed him away. The guilt could be a little too much to bear for anyone in her place.

We hope Ragini finds reason enough to go and meet Nivedita. I wonder how Nivedita is doing. It's probably the day when her brother should have met her . . . but he won't be there. Will she ever smile again when she finds her brother missing from her life? How would she come to know? Who will tell her? As I battle these questions, the taxi driver informs us that we are about to reach. The taxi drops us outside a modest-looking apartment building. We all look at each other—clueless, fighting questions—and wonder how this would end.

'This is it,' Shrey says.

We enter the apartment building and recheck the address. It's the right address. Seventh floor. We step out of the elevator and find ourselves standing right outside the door of Ragini's house. Stupid Mumbai cramped apartments. We look at each other with blank faces. I take a deep deliberate breath and tell myself, *This is it*. Shrey knocks on the door. There is no answer. He knocks again. A voice, probably a maid's, asks from the other side to wait. The door opens and I brace myself for the worst.

'Where are you from? What do you want?' The maid looks at us inquiringly.

'Umm . . . we are Ritam's friends,' I say.

'Come in,' she says and points to the couch. 'Wait here. *Main batati hoon.*'

We are a little surprised that the maid knows who Ritam is. She didn't react even a bit when we said we are Ritam's friends. For a moment I think what if Ragini knows about Ritam? But that can't be. The last note, dated ten days before the blast, said that it had been forever since he had had any contact with Ragini.

The house is very boringly furnished. It looks good but is devoid of colour. It also looks expensive, but there isn't much around. I had expected Ragini to live in a flat with pink curtains, blue sofas and aromatic candles. This was nothing like it. No flower vases, no photo frames, no nothing. Very strange indeed.

I try not to think too much about it and wait for Ragini to come out. I breathe heavily and my eyes are stuck on the door of the bedroom behind which is the girl about whom I've been reading for the last so many days. The moment is finally there. And my heart is pumping like it did the first time I had seen Avantika. That was quite a day and this belongs right up there in terms of tension and anticipation.

At a corner of the room, I spot a small photo frame with a picture of a guy—smart, wheatish complexion, decent build, probably in his mid-twenties—who stares back at me with kind eyes. *Oh shit*. Did she get married? That will be such an anti-climax. I nudge Avantika to show her the photo. As soon as she looks at it, we hear the door creaking open. Shrey and Tiya see the photo too and Tiya almost mutters, 'What the . . .' We all get up to receive Ragini. Our pupils are dilated and our heartbeats hit the roof as we look at the person. '. . . fuck!' Tiya completes her sentence.

'Hey,' the voice says.

We look at where the voice comes from and our mind draws a blank. We look at the face and we are dumbfounded. We exchange glances and look in the direction of the person again. It's like all four of us are in severe shock-induced trauma. Ragini? Wasn't she supposed to be a *girl*? We are bloody shocked. And it strikes me, then Avantika and then the other two. Our eyes move to the picture in the photo frame on the corner table. The person standing in front of us right now is the nice-looking guy from the photo. Darn. *She got married*? Is this Ragini's husband? This simply can't be. How can Ragini do this to Ritam? This can't be the end of the diary.

'Hi,' we echo, a little confused. Well, not a *little*. We are mindfucked.

'I am Ritam,' he says and shakes my outstretched hand.

28 August 2011

'I have realized that I am nothing without her. She gives me meaning. Life's worthless without her and I want my life back.'

I read the note again today. It's been too long that I have read it and abided by it. But it's time I went against it. Some things need to go my way. She needs to know what I feel for her. Things have to change, for the better, and they have to go in the direction in which I want them to go. Ragini will have to listen this time. I will not let her be stupid any more. I read the note for the last time today and tore it off. Not that it helps because I know it by heart.

I have been a coward for too long. It's got to change. I have to disregard the note. It means nothing to me. I can't let my love die like this. But the note . . .

Hi,

I am sure you will be angry when you read this and I agree that it is justified. There are a lot of mistakes I have done in my life, but I have never hurt people who cared about me. My parents, my friends, my sisters, brothers and you. I have managed to do that this time. I know what I have been doing over the last few days is unpardonable and I hope you find it in your heart to forgive me some day. I am ashamed that I dragged you with me to Bangalore, because I wanted to be with Nigel and promptly forgot all about you. I have made mistakes but none as big as this. I have failed you, and I am sorry. There is not much love left in my heart, but if there was, I would have given it all to you. It's been only a few months that I have known you, but you have meant more to me than anyone else. While you were always there to guide me, scold me and tell me right from wrong, all I did was to give you pain. I don't deserve you.

Ever since I have been shifted to rehabilitation, I can't help but think of all the pain I have brought to you and my parents. Mom and Dad have no choice but to live with their degenerate daughter, but spare yourself the trauma. You need to leave me. I can't bear to see you any more. I won't be able to. Yesterday, when you came to see me, something inside me wanted to die. I wanted to slit my wrists and end my worthless life. If you stay, you will be a constant reminder of my mistakes in life and I can't take any more of it. If you ever considered me a friend, and I know you did, I need just one favour from you. Save me. Please go away and never come back. It's my last wish from you. Please don't make it more difficult for me than it already is.

Please know that you hold a very special place in my heart and it will always be that way. Try to forgive me. I won't blame you if you don't. Best of luck for your life.

Ragini.

I wish and I will see her some day. And she will be mine. I will make it happen.

Ritam?

itam? Did he actually say that? Is this even real? Someone is playing around with us. He doesn't look burnt. And he seriously doesn't look like a girl! He is definitely *not* Ragini. What on earth is happening here? We look at each other, and look at him, clueless at what just happened. *What the hell?*

'Umm . . .' Avantika says. 'You're *Ritam*? Isn't this Ragi . . . I mean—this is *your* house?'

'Yes,' he says, a little taken aback. 'This is *my* house. Who are you guys?'

'But how can you be Ritam?' Shrey says.

'*Excuse me?*'

'Ritam Dey? Who studied at Imperial Academy, Dehradun?' Shrey tries to confirm.

'Yes, I am. What do you mean? I am really not getting you guys.'

'But you're *dead*! You're dead, right?' I say.

'*What are you talking about?*' he says. He is freaking out and so are we. He should be burnt and dead, and definitely not be in Ragini's house.

'Yes, you are dead!' Tiya shrieks. 'And this is *not* your house!

This is Ragini's house! What are you doing here? Why aren't you dead?'

'*What*? Ragini? How do you know her?'

'We just know and this is her house, *not yours*,' Tiya shouts again.

'I am really *not* getting you. How do you know her?' he asks again. We can see that he is now a little angry and very confused. We are no better.

Avantika says, 'We have your diary. You were in that blast in Delhi sometime ago, and you are dead!'

She takes out the diary from my backpack and hands it to him. His eyes look like they would pop out of his head. He is stunned.

'Here it is. It's all burnt. How can you be alive? We found it at the blast site. You should be dead. But you're not! How?' Avantika exclaims.

'Yes,' he says and takes the diary. 'I should be . . . I . . . I . . . should be dead.'

Suddenly, he is lost. His eyes go blank and vacant. He looks at the diary like he has never seen it. The same ritual unfolds for the umpteenth time in front of our eyes. A few tears, the running of hands over the burnt pages, the pause, the flipping through the pages. He looks at it, teary-eyed for quite some time and looks at us, his eyes flooded with questions he needs answers to. We look at him with the same expression. We have no answers for him.

'Where did you get it?' he asks. His feet are staggering.

'Near the Chandni Chowk blast site. I was there when the blast happened. The diary was all burnt. Are you sure it's yours?' I ask.

'Wait,' he says and opens the drawer next to the sofa. 'Look, I have copies of it. This is mine. But how is it with you? I sent it to Ragini a few weeks back . . . and . . .'

His voice trails off. He asked a terrible question and he answered the question himself. Tiya staggers and leans on the sofa. Avantika clutches my hand. Shrey and I look at each other in sheer horror. Our hearts beat out of our mouths. *Fuck.* This can't be. It was *Ragini.* We look at him. The copies of his diary drop to the ground and his tears begin to flow in abundance. He stumbles and leans on the sofa. He sits there, puts the diary on the table in front of him and looks at it. He looks lost. It looks like he would faint. My head's in a mess. I have no idea what he must be going through.

Ritam looks at us, his eyes filled with tears, and he asks, 'Are you sure?'

'I don't know,' I say. 'I thought it was you.'

'Oh God,' he says, now looking very close to fainting.

'But . . . let's not assume that she is . . . she is . . . *gone*. I mean, when I got this diary, we assumed that you were dead. We assumed that the owner of the diary did not survive. When we did not even know if the diary was with its owner at that time. Maybe . . . maybe it was with someone else? Maybe it wasn't . . . her?' I suggest.

'But I sent it to *her*. Why would she give it to someone else?' Ritam asks, trying to make sense of the whole situation.

'Did you courier it?' Shrey asks.

'Yes . . .'

'Then maybe it did not reach her? Maybe it was with the courier guy?'

'Was it in an envelope when you found it?' Ritam turns to me and asks.

I shake my head. We don't say anything else. We are all expecting the worst.

He frantically gets his laptop and searches for helpline

numbers for the Chandni Chowk victims. He finds them and starts calling those hospitals like I had. I tell him that I have done that and the hospitals can't tell him anything. He doesn't listen to me and still calls all the numbers. We still don't know what's going on. Or we do, but we don't want to accept it. Tiya looks at me. She has tears in her eyes too. She passes on the envelope that Nigel had given us. She asks me to check the writing on it. And it strikes me. It's not Ragini's handwriting. It's the handwriting from *the diary*. That's why it has Ritam's address. The card with Nigel wasn't from Ragini, it was from Ritam.

Meanwhile, he keeps calling these hospitals up and asking whether there is a patient by the name of Ragini in their list, dead or survived. There is no trace of her. He has written down the list of the people who had been killed and Ragini is not one of them. I tell him again that it will not help. But I don't argue. He looks frantic and is all over the place. Soon he starts to look like a maniac.

An hour passes by and he is still trying to trace Ragini through news articles, hospitals and YouTube clips of the news channels reporting the blast. We just sit there and watch him cry and frantically do everything to get to Ragini. Though slowly, he starts to accept defeat and his face droops, his movements become more restricted and the flow of tears increases. Nothing comes through. He holds his head and sits in the corner. He looks devastated. It's not easy to know that one's love is dead in such an unfortunate incident. It's probably a feeling that we can't understand unless it happens to us.

It's just unfair. I am sure he is thinking, 'How can *she* die? How can it happen to *me*?'

It feels like someone has ripped my heart out. So, for him, it is bound to be even more painful. Ragini might have just come to know that Ritam loved her. She might have read the entire diary and then died. It is just so unfortunate.

Suddenly, something strikes him. He flips open a telephone diary and goes to the page where Ragini's home phone number is listed. It's a London number.

'Hi,' he says. 'Can I talk to Ragini's mother? No longer live there? Why? What happened? India? Why? *Death*? Whose? What? Ragini? Fine.'

Our eyes widen and our hearts sink as we hear the word *death*. It is final. It is no courier guy who died. We look at Ritam and he is disturbed as hell. He has reasons to be. It's worse. Ragini knowing that Ritam was dead was much better than this. Ragini can't be dead. This is not happening. And we just told Ritam that? Oh God. This is a worse nightmare than we had ever imagined it would be.

He hangs up and flops on the sofa. He covers his face with his palms. I can't imagine what he's going through. We are devastated too. I can barely sit still, my head spins as I look at him. I can feel his pain. It's even more real now. It's like imagining Avantika blown to bits and someone telling me that. I would want to die that very instant. It would kill me. And it seems like it is killing Ritam too. It has to. After reading everything that he feels for the pretty girl from the diary, the pain would be unbearable. It shows on his face, which is red and looks like it would burst.

After a little while, Ritam is not crying. He sits still, looks down and breathes heavily. Ragini is dead, blown to bits. Not Ritam. He looks at us and again a few tears trickle down his cheek. He almost faints as Shrey holds him up. He holds back and cries softly. He leans back on the sofa and looks at the ceiling. He doesn't say a thing. A few moments later, he tries to stand up and does so. He walks up to me and hugs me.

'Thank you.' The words barely escape his throat. His eyes look vacant.

I don't know what to say other than 'I am sorry'.

'How did you get here?' he asks. 'You want something to eat?'

He instructs the maid to get something for us. He is still crying. We feel sorry for him. All of us are close to tears. Tiya and Avantika have tears in the corners of their eyes. It feels like we have known Ragini forever—and now, suddenly, without any warning—she's left us.

We show him the envelope Nigel gave us.

'We met your sister too. We read about her in the diary,' Avantika says. 'Very sweet girl.'

'Did she look happy?'

We nod.

'She liked Ragini. I had promised her that I would make her meet her some day . . .'

He doesn't say anything for a while. Obviously, there are other things on his mind. He tries to talk a few times but his voice gives way. Words refuse to come out of his mouth.

'I was leaving today to meet Nivedita. You met everybody?'

'Piyush, Sumi, Nigel. We met them all. We thought you had . . . They all had good things to say about you. We wanted to meet Ragini. Nigel showed us the Get Well Soon card and said it was from Ragini. We didn't know it was you who sent it to him . . .'

Since he isn't talking, we decide that we would. Avantika tells him everything that has transpired since I found the diary. How we got to Piyush, then Nivedita, Sumi and Nigel. She tells him everything—the kind words and love everyone had for him—and we wait for him to smile. It doesn't work. I look at Ritam and feel terribly sorry for him. He is a good-looking guy. We already know he is a sweet guy. Ragini would have been really lucky to be with such a genuine person.

'Ragini had started to hate him,' he says and looks out of the window. The tears don't stop. 'Nigel.'

'Nigel told us,' Avantika says.

'Nothing should have happened the way it did,' he says and holds his head again.

I can imagine the feeling. Of loving someone and not letting that person know. And the only time that Ritam had tried to tell her about her feelings, it didn't end well. Ragini died with that diary in her hands.

'It took a lot of courage to send her the diary,' he says, with regret in his voice. 'I should have done it long before, but I wanted to give her time. I ne . . . never knew that . . . I just wanted her back.'

We don't want to say anything that would make him regret it more. Shrey and I look at Avantika, who is our expert at handling such situations.

'I'm sure she knows that you love her . . . wherever she is,' she says and pats his hand.

He starts to sob again but stops immediately. He sees us looking at him and maybe realizes that it must be awkward for us. I really don't mind. He should get his time to cry it out.

'But why did you go out looking for Ragini in the first place?' Ritam asks.

I say, 'I read the diary first. I just thought that Ragini deserved to know. And it was your intention too—as you mentioned in the last note—that you will disregard what Ragini had said and will tell her everything. I just wanted your story to have an end.'

'Thank you,' he says and we nod. 'I would never have known . . . had you not . . .'

None of us says anything. The air around us is still one of shock, we are still grappling with the stark reality—that Ragini, the girl we had been looking forward to meet, is dead—and none of us is getting used to it. The feeling of denial hangs unceremoniously in the air. Everything changed in a matter of a few seconds. Neither he nor we know what to do. There is an awkward silence. It's a consolation that Ragini probably knew that Ritam loved him.

'Why didn't you drop in your number in the diary?' I ask, just out of curiosity.

'The last few pages of the diary are burnt,' he says. 'I had . . .'

He tells us that he had poured his heart out on the last few pages, which were now burnt. He tells us that he had even written his number and had been waiting for her call ever since he had couriered the diary. He tells us that he was beginning to think Ragini wouldn't ever reply and that he had lost her forever.

He was right in a very twisted, unfortunate manner. Indeed, he had lost her. Instead of the call from Ragini, we landed up at his place. If only those pages hadn't gotten burnt, it would have been so easy to trace Ragini/Ritam down. But I am glad they got burnt. The chase and the search for Ragini made me realize how important it is to keep your loved ones close and let them know what you feel. Who knows what tomorrow has in store for you? Or worse still, for them?

Once again, silence hangs around the room.

'Umm . . .' he tries to say something.

'Yes?' Avantika asks.

'I have to leave . . . to meet Nivedita . . .' he says, still a little disoriented.

'Are you okay?' Tiya asks.

'I am fine,' he says and looks at his feet. 'I need to go now . . . I have a flight in an hour . . .'

'Do you want us to stay? Or come with you?' Avantika asks.

'I am okay,' he says and looks at his watch. He gets up from the couch and we follow suit. He looks at us and smiles. 'Thank you,' he says.

We just look back at him, not knowing what to say.

'How long are you in Mumbai?' he asks, his voice quivering.

'Not for long,' Avantika says.

'Maybe we will meet in Delhi some day.' He hands over his card to us. Avantika and I give him our cards. There is silence again.

'I think we'll go now,' Avantika says. He nods.

He comes to the door with us, hugs all of us, and bids us goodbye. He closes the door behind us. We stand there and wait. We don't hear any sounds from inside. Tiya asks us to move. We get into the elevator. My face is flushed red. What just happened was so surreal and incredibly saddening. No one says a word. The atmosphere is tense and we don't know how to react.

As soon as we leave the building, Shrey says, 'He won't kill himself, will he?'

His tone is serious and solemn. We all look at each other and suddenly, we are concerned.

'Let's just wait here,' Tiya says. 'If he has a flight, he needs to go soon, no?'

We nod. It's silly, but we are concerned about him. He looked so broken when he got to know about Ragini. And if we were as shocked as we were, it must've killed him. So, we walk a little distance from the building, find a pavement to sit on and wait. No one talks much. We have our eyes stuck on the main gate of the apartment building.

'Should we check?' Tiya asks, scared.

I nod. Shrey says no. Avantika nods.

With every minute that passes by, the situation becomes scarier. What if he decides to end his life? I guess I would have. I am just not that strong to endure what Ritam has to right now.

'Now?' Tiya says five minutes later. This time, all of us nod. We are scared now. Just as we get up from the pavement, we see Ritam walk towards the gate with a trolley bag trailing behind him. A sigh of relief. We see him call out to a taxi and leave. We look at each other. I feel strange. After all that we've been through over the last few days, this can't be a suitable end, can it? But then again, life doesn't play according to your rules, does it?

'This is it?' Tiya asks.

'Seems like,' I say.

'This is like the worst love story ever,' Shrey says and looks at me. 'And you're to blame.'

'Who knew it would end like this,' Avantika says.

'It feels so strange now,' I say. 'All this time we had been telling people that Ritam was dead.'

We look at Avantika and she knows what she has to do. Call up everyone and tell them that it was a mistake. It would be pretty embarrassing. First, we intrude into everyone's lives, tell them a gruesome story, then call them and say it's a mistake and tell them another gruesome story instead.

'Taxi then?' Shrey asks.

I nod. It's time for us to leave. It's a strange feeling. It's odd not to clutch at that diary and think about what's coming next. It's feels out of place not to think about which place we will now head to. Suddenly, we are out of a life which was exciting and exhilarating and our everyday life stares at us. No more tears. Or old stories. No more nostalgia. No more feeling sorry for *the dead guy*.

There is no dead guy now. I had gotten used to all that. We sit in the taxi and my mind rewinds to the first day when everything started. And whatever followed—Dehradun, Piyush, Nivedita, Sumi, Nigel and finally Ritam. I am lost in my thoughts and no one talks much. Maybe everyone is thinking what I am.

'Stop thinking so much,' Avantika finally says as we board the plane.

'Can't help it,' I say. 'I feel so sorry for Ritam.'

'So do I,' Avantika says sympathetically.

'It couldn't have been more unfortunate,' I say and clutch Avantika's hand as we sit in our seats.

Fear grips me—a fear of losing Avantika—just like Ritam lost Ragini. I try to tell Avantika that I love her but I can hardly say anything. She senses it and kisses my forehead.

'I am not going anywhere,' she whispers.

'You'd better not,' I meet her eye and say. She clutches my hand tighter.

We both smile, and tell each other that we will always be around. The plane lifts off the ground and we leave Mumbai behind. I look outside the window and think about Ritam. I say a little prayer in my heart for Ragini. No one should suffer the fate that Ritam has. It's unfortunate and unfair. I close my eyes and wish the best for Ritam . . . and Ragini, wherever she is.

May her soul rest in peace.

Soon, our plane lands in Delhi. I don't have the diary in my hands any more, but I know every word of it by heart. The story of Ritam and his last attempt to get back the girl he loved the most, cruelly cut short by the bomb blast. As we take our bags out, my mind wanders to the last note that Ritam wrote in the diary—the one where he said he would fight back, the one that never materialized, the one written ten days before that fateful blast which took Ragini away—and my eyes are clouded with tears.

Everyday Life

Slowly and steadily, life has crawled back to normal. No more long drives on dusty roads without a destination in mind. No chasing around clues and asking people about dead people. No sleeping in cheap motels and living on dhaba food. No more spending every moment with Avantika—in her aviators, hot pants and vests—and no more getting irritated by Shrey and Tiya's insanity. I miss all that. So does Shrey. It's been three months. And the exhilarating feeling of the road trip still hasn't gone.

'We should plan something,' Shrey says as he looks away from his desktop screen. He has been pretending to work, but I'm sure he is reading or watching porn. It's been days since I've heard anything about Tiya. Ever since we landed in Delhi, I haven't seen him talk about her. Shrey and Tiya had briefly posted an album with all the beautiful pictures that Tiya had clicked on the trip, but both of them had removed it soon after.

I have tried asking Shrey about what's going on between him and Tiya, but he never really gives a straight answer. He hints that he is back to his old ways but he has not had a meeting with anyone 'from the *Times*' in about three months. There is something really wrong, but I don't want to intrude.

'Avantika is a little busy these days. We'll plan as soon as she's free,' I say.

'How's the book coming along?' he asks.

Yes, I have been writing that book. The story of Ritam and Ragini. Ever since I got back to Delhi, I've been struggling with it. It's not coming out too well. It's very hard to capture death in a book. The emotions are just too hard to understand for anybody.

'Umm . . . it's going pretty slow,' I say.

'Did you talk to Ritam?'

'Yes, I did. He doesn't want to read it. It's understandable. But I have his full support.'

'That's nice,' Shrey says.

'Fuck nice. It's just extra pressure. I just can't do justice to their story. It's so moving and whatever I'm writing is pure crap. I feel so screwed,' I say.

'Then I guess some things are just meant to be left like that. Maybe that story should only be confined to that diary,' he says.

Maybe he has a point. But I haven't really taken Shrey's advice. It has never done me any good. I look at my screen and get back to my book. Ritam and Ragini's story. A lot of things have changed since that road trip. Not that I didn't love Avantika before, but now I make an effort to make her feel what I do. Life's rude and it does things that are uncalled for and beyond our control. Ragini was a young, pretty girl with many years ahead of her. Why did she die? Why did she have to go? I am sure Ritam must have asked these questions a zillion times. I can't even begin to think what Ritam must be going through. There are a lot of days when I stare into the void and try to imagine his state of mind. The pain is almost unbearable.

'You're leaving?' Shrey asks.

'Yes, Avantika and I sort of have a plan today. She is cooking after a really long time. I think she just got tired of what I give her to eat every day.'

'Nice,' he says.

'It's been long since I have seen you with Tiya. What happened?'

'Nothing, really. We just grew apart.'

'Just grew apart? I thought she was special, wasn't she? I hadn't seen you so close to anybody.'

'She was special and she will be. But, you know, she's a little strange.'

'Strange? Coming from you, that's odd.'

'I don't know,' he says, wistfully. Something is wrong.

'What's wrong, Shrey?'

'I have no idea. Ever since we came back to Delhi, she started saying that she didn't want it to go on, there was no future and that what we had shared was meaningless. She stopped picking up my calls and started avoiding me. So, I just let it be. If she doesn't want me around, why should I be bothered?'

'Okay. And, when was the last time you went out on a date?' I ask matter-of-factly.

'Not been out since we came back.'

'That's three months, Shrey. And you say you're not bothered? Obviously, she is still special to you. You've got to tell her that.'

'But she doesn't want to talk. She doesn't even pick up my calls. So just leave it,' he says, exasperated.

'I don't know how you do it, but you have to go and tell her that it's bothering you that she doesn't talk to you any more.'

'That's so gay.'

'Either you do it or I will,' I threaten.

'Fine, I will tell her.'

⌒

I can't wait to see Avantika. Lately, she has been busy with her office projects and I haven't seen much of her. Ever since we came to know what happened to Ragini, I am constantly scared. I want her to be around. We spend a lot of time just talking to each other. Sometimes, we go out and have very cheesy, romantic dinners—as if it's an anniversary or a birthday—and celebrate our love. After all, who knows what tomorrow has in store? I knock on my house's door and put on my best smile like I always do. Avantika takes more than the usual time to open the door.

'Hey,' I say and hug her. She is cold.

'Hey,' she says.

'What happened?' I hold her close and ask her. Her eyes are vacant and they aren't encouraging. I wonder what's wrong.

'Something came in the mail today.'

'Mail? What?'

'Ritam sent you something,' she says and hands over a torn envelope to me.

'What is it?'

'Read it yourself,' she says and sits on the sofa.

She has tears in her eyes. *Oh shit. What now?* I stop thinking and frantically open the envelope and hold the paper inside it before me. I prepare myself for the worst. It's a crumpled piece of paper. It's a familiar handwriting—almost like a girl's, but it degenerates as the note reaches its end—and it brings images flashing back to my head. I have read a whole diary in that handwriting. It's Ritam's.

I read the title of the note and my blood curdles. It's titled 'The Last Note'.

3 January 2012
'Life doesn't make sense any more.'

Nivedita died exactly sixteen nights ago. Multiple organ failure, the doctors say. I spent three hours with the lifeless, pale body of Nivedita. She didn't smile even once. Not even when I told her stories about Ragini and me. Maybe she knows Ragini is dead. I can't take Nivedita's silence any more. I want her to talk and she will talk to me. I know a place where that will happen. Not only will she smile, but she will talk and laugh with me.

If there is one thing that Nigel did right, it was to demonstrate how to nearly kill yourself. I am not taking any chances. Ragini and Nigel had been taken to the hospital for they had overdosed on heroin. It didn't kill them, but I had overheard the doctors talking about 'speedball': an injection of both cocaine and heroin, if taken in more than mild quantities means certain death. A certain death—that is all that separates me from Nivedita . . . and Ragini. Just a few moments more of my pitiable existence. I have pierced the sharp needle of the first injection through the vein on my upper arm. I already feel a little light-headed. I am already on my way. I can feel her around. Ragini.

I have a habit of taking this name before I do anything. People must think I am crazy, but people don't matter to me. She was all that mattered to me. I woke up this morning and the path was clear to me. I stood in front of the mirror and saw a soul devoid of meaning. The alcohol from last night was ruining my mind but I was thinking clearly. I took a few sips of the bitter-tasting whisky and it became even clearer. I had to die. I had to put to an end to my life. I stare at the other injection as it invites me into a different world.

Ever since the day Deb and Avantika came to my doorstep with the news of her death, days have become unbearably long. Her name no longer brings fond memories. Her violent death haunts me every day. The thought of her skin burning to charcoal, the images of her being torn apart and bruised by metal shrapnel . . . it kills me. I am dying a slow death—every moment, every day—and I can't take it any more. For the last three months, all I have done is taken medicines and visited therapists and doctors, just to stop myself from imagining and reconstructing images of Ragini's body being carried in a bloodied stretcher to the hospital. The doctor pronouncing her dead. Images of the funeral of her mortal remains, her charred body, the hand I held, the face I loved to look at, mangled and burnt.

That's all I think about. The doctors, the hospitals, the funeral setting, the clothes her parents wear, everything changes in those scenes in my head but the end is always the same—Ragini dies. She leaves everyone behind. I can feel the pain that she went through and I feel it every day. The medicines don't help. I sit locked in my bedroom for days on end, and sedate myself with pills and alcohol. I wake up after days, only to find myself in pools of my own blood and bile. Nothing disgusts me more than my life itself. Every day, I drown myself further into alcohol and multiple doses of anti-depressant pills. I wait to pass out and go to a world where there is no sorrow, where I can live a new life. One in which Ragini doesn't die an ungracious, painful death and Nivedita gets to walk, smile and talk like there is no tomorrow. I wish to be there. Forever. And the injection in my hand will take me there. Far from here. Far from this diary which she held before dying, far from the heart-wrenching memories. I want to run away from all of it. Shut them out myself before they consume me. I have no reason to live now. Nivedita was the only person that kept me together all these years. She knew she was my only family. Couldn't she have waited till I weathered this storm . . . ?

It's the only option I have. I don't want to be embarrassed about my existence. If I don't kill myself now, the alcohol will, or I would go crazy. It would be a lonely and painful death. I don't want to curse Ragini's or Nivedita's death for my woeful existence. I will do everyone a favour if I kill myself. Soon, I will be asleep and never wake up. I am already a little drowsy. I already feel I am closer to her. The pain is dying out. It's time for the second injection.

I don't know what lies on the other side of death, but if there is a chance that I would meet her, then I am ready to take it. I know it's stupid but this is the only way out. My life has no meaning left. I should be dead.

I wish I could see her now.

The Shock

I put the piece of paper down and look at it, scared. I look at Avantika . . . my mind throws up nothing. There is darkness in front of my eyes. This didn't just happen, did it?

'But . . .'

Avantika says, 'This came in the courier minutes before you came. I have been calling on his number. It's switched off. I have tried his landline too. No one's answering that phone either.'

I'm not crying, but I'm close. Did I lead a man to his death? He wouldn't have known had I not been stupid and followed the clues from the diary. He would've lived. At least for a few days more.

'But who sent you this?' I say. 'If he committed . . . ?'

I frantically grab the envelope from the table and see the person it's from.

Ritam Dey
56/A, Karkol Apartments
Santa Cruz, Mumbai
+91-9826784334

It's his name, address and number. How did he send the letter then, if he was dying when he wrote the last note? Horrifying images of Ritam lying dead in his own vomit and blood engulf my head. Questions flood my brain and I find no answers to them. There has to be a reason behind this. I hope this is not a prank by Ritam. But Ritam is not a person who would do such a thing. Why would he say that his sister died? But . . .

'Who couriered us then?' I ask, still horrified at what I just read.

'I have no idea,' she says.

'But even the handwriting is his!' I exclaim as I try his number on the side. My head is spinning.

Avantika looks at me and says nothing. I keep trying his phone but the phone is switched off. I have started to panic now. Finally, I call up Shrey.

'Shrey? Where are you?'

'Office. Why?' he asks.

'Can you come home? It's urgent.'

'Now? What happened?' he asks.

'Can you just be here? And call Tiya too.'

'I called her. She didn't pick up my call.'

'Fine, I will call her. Just fucking reach as fast as possible.'

'But what happened? Tell me,' he asks.

'Ritam is dead,' I say and disconnect the call.

He sends me a text saying he will be there in twenty. Avantika is equally scared. I ask her to call Tiya and she does so.

'What should we do?' she asks.

'Let's wait for Shrey to come,' I say and try the number again. I am hoping against hope that someone picks up. I pace around the room in anxiety, and Avantika sits nervously on the couch. Her legs are shaking and her hands have gone cold.

The bell rings.

'I will get that,' I say and open the door. It's Shrey. And Tiya.

'What the fuck is going on?' Shrey comes in with Tiya and stares at us.

Avantika hands over the envelope to them, 'This reached us just a while ago.'

They take the crumpled piece of paper out from the envelope and start reading it. They read it and momentarily look at us with horror in their eyes. They read it again.

'Who sent this?' Shrey asks, shocked. Tiya's eyes are still stuck on the envelope.

'The handwriting on the envelope is his,' I say.

We all sit down. We have nothing to say. Tiya is still reading it over and over again. She is teary-eyed.

'Deb and I should go and check it out?' Shrey says.

'Mumbai?' Tiya asks.

'This is so fucked up,' Shrey says. 'What will change even if we go there?'

'Maybe he is not dead,' Tiya says, with forced optimism in her voice.

'Maybe,' Avantika adds. 'I never imagined that he would do such a thing.'

'No, you did. We all did. Didn't you look at his face that day? Maybe Nivedita was the only reason for which he was still living?' Shrey argues.

It looks like a curse. Ragini. Nivedita. Ritam. All dead. We are speechless and distraught. I had never seen life being so unfair to someone. It's horrible. I understand Ritam's pain. It must have been unbearable. But killing himself? It's easy to say it's unjustified, but it's hard to understand how difficult it must be for that person.

Ritam had become much more than *the dead guy from the diary*. At least to me, he had grown to be a very good friend. I didn't talk to him every day, but I have been writing his story for months now. I literally spend hours with him every day. I might not have been close to him, but he was close to me. I had started living his life, seeing things like he did, reading and rereading his diary over and over again; I had started to even think like him.

I don't know how the others feel about Ritam's death, but his loss is an irreparable blow to me. Even as Avantika and Tiya talk in whispers that he might be dead and the police or whoever found the envelope must have couriered it, I still don't believe that he's dead. For me, Ritam's had one of the strongest hearts I have ever seen. Yes, death changes a lot, but I had just not foreseen this. I am angrier than I am sad. How can he do this to himself? Our lives were connected with his. Couldn't he have lived for all the lives he touched every day? Was it that difficult for him? At certain levels, we are responsible too . . . especially me. I could have saved him. I should have saved him. Why didn't I fully understand what he was going through? As I sit in denial staring at everyone's face, my phone rings repeatedly. I ignore the call.

The phone rings again. It's an unknown number. I reject the call. The phone rings again. I reject it again. And again.

'You should take that!' Shrey says, irritated at my ringtone.

'Fine,' I say.

I wait for the phone to ring again. It rings again and I pick it up.

'Hi Deb,' the voice says. It's a familiar voice. *What? No! Is it? Fuck!*

'Umm . . . huh? Who's this?'

'Ritam. You forgot me?'

'Ohh. NO. Are you crazy? No. Hi . . . Ritam . . .'

I cover the phone with my hand and shout to the others, 'IT'S RITAM!'

I put the phone on loudspeaker and we all huddle up near it.

'Yes, I am Ritam. I know why you're surprised. But don't worry, I am Ritam. I am in Delhi,' he says.

'Delhi? We received your note by courier. What was that . . . ?' I ask him.

It's a strange feeling to know that he's alive. One part of me feels highly relieved. The other part is angry and wants to fucking punch him through the phone. Though most of all, I am intrigued. What's wrong with this diary? First he sends us across the country to find his girlfriend? And now this?

'It's a long story,' he says.

After reading what he had been through in the note we just read, he sounds surprisingly cheerful.

'What does that mean? *You fucking killed us here!* Why are you in Delhi?' I ask. 'How long are you here?'

'I don't know. I don't plan on going back to Mumbai,' he says.

'As in? Got transferred?' I ask.

'I am at Ragini's place,' he says.

All of us look at each other, bewildered.

'Ragini's place?'

'Yes . . .'

I don't know how to react. A part of me tells me he has gone crazy. He was on medication as that note said. I think he is losing it.

'Ragini . . . she's alive,' Ritam says.

'*What?*' Now I'm sure of it. I start to feel sorry for him. He has lost it.

'Yes, she's alive! You should meet her. She really wants to meet you. All of you,' he says.

'Ritam . . . you're joking, right?' I ask.

He's going crazy, we all think. I don't say anything. We look at each other and are speechless at Ritam's nonsense.

'I am serious, Deb. I will text you the address,' he says. 'Please come. I need to go now. I am leaving Delhi tonight for a few days. Please be here soon. And please get Avantika, Shrey and Tiya too.'

'Ritam . . . ?'

'I really have to go. I will text you the address,' he says and before I can say anything, he disconnects the call.

We wait for the text. We have no clue what's going on. Supposedly, he was dead. Suddenly, not only is he alive, but he says Ragini is alive too? Something is grossly wrong. And my guess is that it's his head.

'He has lost his mind,' Shrey says.

'I guess,' I say.

The phone buzzes. It's an East Delhi address, a two-hour drive from my place in peak traffic.

'Are you guys coming too?' Shrey looks at Avantika and Tiya.

'Obviously,' they echo.

⌒

We get into Shrey's car and he drives as fast as he can, but the traffic slows him down. I am still not sure what's going on, so I call on the number Ritam called me from. He picks up, talks normally and asks us to reach as soon as possible. He sounds normal . . . and it's strange. The pieces don't fit at all. I want to ask him if Ragini is really alive but I don't. I am totally confused. We tell each other that everything is going to be just fine, though we are really scared.

No one is talking in the car, but Avantika notices the distance between Tiya and Shrey.

'This car brings some strange memories back, doesn't it?' Avantika says. We all nod. 'Is there something wrong between the two of you?'

'Who? *Us?*' Tiya asks. 'No! Nothing.'

'They haven't been talking for the last three months. Shrey has been calling her but she doesn't pick up his calls. So, Shrey thinks why bother? He doesn't call her at all now,' I blurt out.

'Thank you,' Shrey says.

'Why don't you pick up his calls?' Avantika asks Tiya.

'We have nothing to talk about,' Tiya says.

'He doesn't call you to talk to you, Tiya. Shrey calls you to tell you that you're the only thing he ever thinks about. He has wanted to tell you that for the last three months. He has not been able to concentrate on anything because you're not there in his life and he misses you like crazy. Basically, he loves you and he can't do without you,' I say.

'Deb!' Shrey says, shocked.

'I warned you. Either you tell her or I will.'

'B . . . but Shrey never said that to me . . .' Tiya says, her voice faltering.

'Because she never gave me a chance,' Shrey says.

'A chance? The moment we reached Delhi, I told him that we don't have a future together and he had nothing to say. He said he liked me and the decision was mine to make. How could it be my decision? It was about *us*. And he never said anything. He was least interested,' Tiya says.

'You guys can talk to each other, right?' Avantika says.

'I thought you didn't want to be with me?' Shrey says.

'Why would I not? I love you. I always have.'

'I love you too, Tiya. But why did you say that we shouldn't be together?'

'You weren't serious about me. Any time I said something like *I love you*, you never noticed it. You would just shrug and talk about something else. I thought I was one of those many girls that Deb told me whom you date and forget. I didn't want to be one of them.'

'You were special. You *are* special,' Shrey says.

And I have to tell you that this is a day of shocks. As if Ritam and Ragini supposedly being alive wasn't enough, Shrey has tears in his eyes. For a girl. So does Tiya. They tell each other how much they love each other and how painful the last three months have been. It never ceases to amaze me how easy it is to destroy your chance at true love, and how getting it to last forever is even easier. People just don't see it.

Avantika holds my hand and says, 'You're the best thing.'

I smile at her and say, 'I love you.'

With that out of the way, and an hour still to go to reach the place where Ritam has asked us to come, the mystery just keeps building up. No one has anything to say. Finally, we reach the address.

'Seems like this is it?' I say.

We get down from the car outside a one-storey house, decent-looking and well maintained. Tiya rings the bell and we wait. Shrey and Tiya are holding hands.

'This is so screwed up,' Shrey says.

I am kind of scared about what we will have to see now. A little later, we see a door opening. *Ritam!* We see him walking towards us. He looks good. And really not dead. He is smiling as he walks up to us. We are almost shocked to see him all right. It even scares me a little. Has he gone completely mad? Is that why he is smiling so much? The note said he was a living corpse. But he looks better than how he had looked when we had met in Mumbai. Somehow, seeing him in person feels like someone just lifted a boulder off my chest. He doesn't look crazy. He looks just fine . . . *Normal*.

'Hey!' he says and smiles at us.

'Hey, long time,' I say. I can't believe we're making small talk.

'Yeah, how's the book going?' he asks.

'Good,' I say.

'Ritam, are you okay?' Avantika asks.

'Never better,' he says and flashes a charming smile. 'Why don't you guys come in?'

We nod and he makes us sit in the drawing room. It's a well-decorated house with pink curtains, blue sofas, aromatic candles, and is lined with photo frames and flower vases. Just like I had imagined . . .

'Coffee?' he asks.

We shake our heads but he orders the maid to get coffee for all of us.

'Then what the fuck was the note all about?' Tiya asks, exasperated.

He starts to grin a little.

'You better stop fucking around, Ritam. You had us scared,' Avantika says.

'I am sorry for that.'

'We are still waiting for an explanation,' Shrey says.

'Okay. When Nivedita passed away, I did try to kill myself. So what you read in the note did happen,' he says. His eyes look sad when he takes his sister's name. But there is a kind of happiness on his face too.

'You did? So the note is real?' Avantika asks.

'Yes,' he says. 'I took the first injection.'

'And?'

'I passed out before I could take the second,' he says, embarrassed and relieved at the same time.

'Then?' we echo.

'So, I didn't die. I woke up many hours later, coughing and bleeding. It was horrible. A few neighbours got me admitted in a nearby hospital. I was there for a week before I was discharged,' he says.

I am glad he is alive, though somewhere I had wished that the Nivedita part was a lie too, but it is not.

'Then why did you send me the note?' I ask.

'Since you were writing about me, I thought I should send you that. I didn't want to scare you guys. I called you up to say that I had couriered something and explain what had happened. I called you a few times and couldn't reach you. So I thought, since I was anyway coming to Delhi, I would personally tell you guys. There was already so much on my mind,' he says.

'Don't ever do that again!' Avantika says. 'It was stupid.'

'I know.'

'And Ragini? She is dead, right?' Tiya asks. She is growing impatient by the minute.

'She is not,' he says and smiles.

'*She is not?*' Avantika asks.

Ritam shakes his head. 'When I woke up in the hospital bed and the doctors told me that I was very lucky to be alive, I started thinking. Maybe there was someone who wanted me to live. Maybe it was Nivedita. Maybe Ragini. They wanted me to live a fulfilling life which they couldn't. Or that's what I thought. Anyway, from that moment on, I banished all thoughts of killing myself. I resolved that I would sort out my issues and emerge stronger. I was sure Nivedita and Ragini both would have wanted me to live.'

'And us,' Tiya says and smiles. He smiles back. 'How could you fucking forget us?'

'And yes, you guys. So, I called up Ragini's home in London. The people I had called when you were in Mumbai? The ones who told me that her parents had to go back to India because of the death of their daughter?'

'Yes, I remember,' Shrey says and we nod.

'I took Ragini's parents' number from them. It took me three days to muster up the courage to call them. But when I did, I was in for a shock,' he says with a smile.

'What? Ragini is alive!' Avantika exclaims.

'Exactly,' he says and smiles at us. 'She is sleeping in the other room right now or I would have introduced you guys to her. But later maybe.'

'You're not kidding, right?' Avantika asks.

'No! Why would I?' he says.

Needless to say, I am stunned. I am too confused and too happy to say anything.

'Umm . . . if you don't mind . . . can we see her?' Avantika says. Yes, a part of us still says that Ritam has gone crazy.

'Sure,' he says, 'Come with me.'

We all get up. My heart starts to pump furiously. Whatever has happened since day one flashes before my eyes. It's so strange. *Ragini is not dead?* I walk right beside Ritam and he takes us to the adjacent room. I am sweating and I feel I'll pass out from the anticipation. He creaks open the door. My eyes dart around the room to spot Ragini. The girl from the diary. The girl we searched for across the country. The girl we thought was alive when she was dead. And alive when we thought she was dead.

We finally see her. There is she, lying on the bed. I have seen her pictures by now. Ritam had sent me some a month back, but she looks nothing like that. She is barely recognizable. Her skin is not the pale colour that I saw in the pictures. Her hands are not smooth like a small kid's. Her hair is not the black cascading waves that Ritam had described them to be and I had seen in the pictures. I wonder if it's even her. I look at her intently as we go close to her. Yes, it is her. Her eyes are exactly like what I had seen. It is Ragini, in front of us, finally.

Ragini is in a single, long, white robe that covers most of her. The skin on her body is a strange tinge of pink and black. It's the same, on her hands, her face, her toes, everywhere. Her hair, where there is any left, is a crumpled mess, but she has lost most of it. She is making some sounds like she is in pain. I am aghast. Avantika, who has been holding my hand, clutches it tighter and her nails dig in. I look at Shrey and Tiya and they have the same expression on their faces. Of terror and bewilderment. Just looking at her is so painful.

Ragini is burnt beyond recognition.

It looks like the blast and the fire had totally consumed her body. She isn't missing any of her limbs, but her skin is totally charred. It's terrifying. Ritam goes and sits on the bed and asks us to sit. He looks lovingly at her, holds her hand and kisses her forehead. She purrs between the moans of pain.

The expression on his face—when he looks at her and says, 'Isn't she beautiful?'—is unbelievable. Had it not been for Ritam, the question would have been a cruel joke. But we know that he means it and he says it because he still sees her like that. She is still the most beautiful thing to him.

'Is she in pain?' Avantika asks Ritam softly.

Ragini slowly opens her eyes and looks at us.

'I am,' she says and smiles at us. Her voice is a little throaty. 'But I'm getting better.'

I guess that's from the blast too. I feel so sorry for her. She looks very bad. With the kind of burns on her body, I think she is really lucky to be alive.

'We have heard so much about you,' Avantika says and smiles.

'I have heard about you too,' she says. Her voice gives way a few times. She can barely talk. 'Had you not tried to find me, I would never have gotten him back. Thank you.'

'It's the least we could do,' I say.

'You should rest,' Ritam says and looks at Ragini. She smiles at him and closes her eyes.

'We'll wait outside,' Avantika says and we leave the room.

The door is still ajar and we look inside the room. Ritam whispers something in her ears and Ragini smiles, almost laughs a little. He hugs her and it seems like they would never leave each other. It looks like they attempt to say 'bye' a million times before Ritam can finally leave her side. He kisses her hand about a zillion times before he lets it go.

'Sorry,' he says as he comes out of the room. He is smiling his widest.

We go back to the living room and take our places on the sofa.

'Isn't she perfect?' he asks and smiles. 'Can you believe that she says she loves me? It's amazing.' He adds, 'She might not be beautiful to you, I understand that, but she is still very pretty to me. She will always be.'

Avantika holds Ritam's hand and tells him, 'Ritam, you're the nicest guy I have ever met. Please don't do anything stupid like you did a few days back.' She starts crying and Tiya joins in.

'Oh,' Ritam says as both of them hug him. 'I won't. And now that I have Ragini, I have all the will to live again. I am the happiest I could ever have been.'

'Where are her parents?' Tiya asks between her sobs. She is now crying like a baby, almost howling.

'They are out to see her doctor,' he says. 'But why are you crying, Tiya?'

'I am just so happy for you,' she says and hugs him again.

'That's sweet.'

'But why did the folks in London tell you that there was a death in the family?' she asks.

'They must have assumed it. Ragini's parents had rushed to Delhi as soon as they got to know that Ragini was in the blast and was critically hurt. When the people in London did not hear from her parents, they assumed that she must have died . . . Her parents were supposed to go back to London in a month or two, but . . .'

'Supposed to? Now they are not?' I ask.

'Nope,' he says. 'They have plans in Delhi now.'

'What plans?' Avantika asks.

Ritam smirks and says, 'They have to get their daughter married off.'

'What?' Tiya almost blurts out.

'I already have the ring,' he says. 'Her parents have agreed to it. I just need to ask her now.'

He gets up and fishes something out from a drawer nearby. It's ring case. He hands it over to Tiya and Avantika, who open it and their eyes pop out as they see the ring. I don't know much about rings, but the diamond in that one is fucking huge.

'You're going to ask her to marry you?' Tiya says.

He nods.

Avantika and Tiya look at Ritam as if to say, 'Awww.'

'She might say no, though,' he says, the enthusiasm in his voice dipping.

'Why would she do that?' Avantika asks, almost offended.

'I don't know. She has hinted that she would.'

'But why would she do that? You're the best guy anyone could ever have. I will talk to her,' Tiya says, almost like a little kid, and looks at Ritam.

'Doctors don't give her more than four months to live.'

What? Suddenly, the atmosphere turns gloomy again.

'Don't make faces yet,' he says and tries to smile. 'I will make her live. Now that I have her back, she is not going anywhere.'

We try to smile too, but our eyes have only sadness and horror.

Ritam adds, 'Ragini has to live. For me. And she will. I will make her live.'

A lone tear trickles down his cheek.

Epilogue

Three months have passed by and Ragini's health is progressing. She still hasn't accepted Ritam's proposal, but it seems that she might do that soon. They look like the happiest couple I have ever seen. Only last week, Ragini started walking on her own, without a stick. She also saw the mirror for the first time since the blast. Ragini now wants to have an extensive reconstructive surgery if she manages to live. Ritam opposes it. He says that it's a waste of money and she is still beautiful to him. And also, 'Now I will have to fall in love with a different face all over again!' And Ragini replies, 'At least I will have a face!'

Sweet couple.

Talking about sweet couples, there is, as always, Avantika and I. The only thing that has stuck in her mind out of the whole ordeal is *the ring* that Ritam had bought. Now, she wants it. Girls, everywhere, are the same. Vanity and materialism rules them. One wants a face, the other wants a ring. Where does it leave us? I have been looking for a ring that could show how much I love her. No headway yet. If only we had not spent that much on the road trip, maybe . . .

Perfect boyfriends like Ritam are such a pain in the ass.

Talking about *pain in the ass*, I think Shrey has finally gone down the love lane. Tiya and Shrey are still dating and they are still very much in love. After dating strippers and a lot of underage women, the time has finally come for Shrey to slow down. Tiya and Shrey are going strong and it seems like this would last. They break up once every fifteen days, but with Avantika's and my intervention, they patch up soon enough. I like them.

And lastly, I finished the book. It's in your hands. I couldn't do justice to what Ragini and Ritam share, but at least I finished it. They are pretty happy about it though. I had struggled with different titles for this one for quite some time until Ritam called me up one day and said, 'Ragini and I were meant to be together. After all, *if it's not forever . . . it's not love.*'

True, that.

ALSO IN PENGUIN METRO READS

Till the Last Breath . . .

Durjoy Datta

When death is that close, will your heart skip a beat?

Two patients are admitted to room no. 509. One is a brilliant nineteen-year-old medical student, suffering from an incurable, fatal disease. She counts every extra breath as a blessing. The other is a twenty-five-year-old drug addict whose organs are slowly giving up. He can't wait to get rid of his body. To him, the sooner the better.

Two reputed doctors, fighting their own demons from the past, are trying everything to keep these two patients alive, even putting their medical licences at risk.

These last days in the hospital change the two patients, their doctors and all the other people around them in ways they had never imagined.

Till the Last Breath . . . is a deeply sensitive story which reminds us what it means to be alive.

You Were My Crush
Till You Said You Love Me!

Durjoy Datta • Orvana Ghai

Would you change yourself for the love of your life?

Benoy zips around in a Bentley, lives alone in a palatial house and is every girl's dream. To everyone in college he is a stud and a heartbreaker. But is he, really? What no one sees is his struggle to come to terms with his mother's untimely death and his very strained relationship with his father.

Then once again his world turns upside down when he sees the gorgeous Shaina. He instantly falls in love but she keeps pushing him away. What is stopping them from having their fairy-tale romance? What is Shaina hiding?

It's time Benoy learned his lesson about love and relationships . . .